I0530672

Grits to Granola

By

M. A. Moone

This is a work of fiction. Names, characters, places and incidents either are the product of the author's imagination or are used factiously. Any resemblance to actual persons, living or dead, events, or locales is entirely coincidental.

Published in the United States by M. A. Moone

Printed by CreateSpace.Com--an Amazon.com Company

Available from Amazon.com, CreateSpace.com and other retail outlets.

Copyright © M.A. Moone, 2014
All rights reserved

To Rebecca Brown, whose tough and dedicated instruction at the University of Washington has helped many gain a strong foundation in literary writing.

CHAPTER ONE
JANUARY

I've got strong feelins on how a family should be fed, so meal time is special at our house. Always has been. I figure home cooked an' a happy table, with a prayer aforehand, is the glue thet hol's a family together. Even with three youngens, two bein teenage boys an' the third bein a girl headin fast towards puberty, thangs generally go smooth as silk at suppertime in the Perkins house; all five of us takin our turn talkin 'bout this'n thet between bites.

George an' I got good young'ns, even if I'd say it so by my own. They're good lookin too, what with the boys both bein brown-haired an' sparkly, blue-eyed like their daddy an' the girl lookin more like me with her purple eyes an' blonde hair. She didn't get my curl though. She ended up with hair thet's string straight, jest like her daddy's.

Lately, George Junior, our first born, is talkin a lot 'bout college. He's got a good scholarship at the University of Tennessee over in Knoxville. But on this particular night I'm tellin 'bout, I knowed somethin different was up with him. He was thet shined up, actin real polite. Said, "Please pass this," an' "Would you like some of thet?"' as the food went 'round. I got to wonderin what he was up to with a clean shirt tucked in an' his brown hair all slicked down an' parted jest right.

Outside, the temperature was jest at freezin, which is 'round normal for January in East Tennessee. We'd fixed up our ol' house some in the fall with new blue shag carpet, paint an'

1

such. Got it done by Christmas time so it seemed like the holidays clean through the new year an' on into 1980 were tickin right along with us all fit as fiddles an' me startin to look forward to gettin my seed catalogs.

So, what with the col'ness outside an' the spiffed up look on the inside, thangs were feelin cozy. I'd even cooked a little extra special since Junior had invited his girl, Bonnie, to join us. She's a purty red-headed, brown-eyed thang. Moved in down the block 'bout six months ago an' our son fell head over heels. Even spends money on her, which is how we know he's in love. Generally, he's tighter'n a tick.

Vikki Ann, thet's what we call our girl, is near as crazy 'bout Bonnie as her oldest brother is; always copyin her ways, her clothes, her hair--you know--stuff thet a twelve-year-ol' girl will do. Makes a real pest of hersef to hear Junior tell it. My husband an' I figure she's a free chaperone.

The only thang I could come up with was thet our son was bein on his best behavior 'cause he wanted to borrow his daddy's pickup to take Bonnie for a Royal Crown Cola at the Shoney's Drive-in. I knew he was bound to be disappointed. No way was George Senior goin to let his 1938, fully-restored, straight-pipe, half-ton, Ford pickup truck with its new candy-apple red paint job, out on a slick Saturday night, jest so George Junior could buy two RC Colas an' show off his girl at the drive-in.

Too bad, I thought, recollectin back on how much fun his daddy an' I used to have drivin 'round, glued at the hip, me doin the shiftin, in thet very same truck. Course the truck wasn't near so fancy back then.

Found out plumb quick I was wrong 'bout where Junior's mind was. We'd jest gotten everthang passed an' I'd got the first tender bite of chicken-fried steak in my mouth, when he gulped like a fish out of water an' asked, his blue eyes real serious, "Whatda ya'll think 'bout me and Bonnie gettin hitched?"

Praise the Lord thet I am a careful eater so I didn't do myself in chokin on a piece of chicken-fried steak! Them youngens were only seniors in high school, for Lord's sake, an' here he was, askin what we thought 'bout 'em gettin married? Well, what I thought was in no way fit to be speakin, so I kept

2

right on chewin, givin the eyebrow signal to my husband for him to say somethin instead. But he didn't.

Lucky for us, our daughter didn't have food in her mouth or a brain in her head at thet moment. She gave a squeal thet could call a hog from a mess of slops, closed her eyes an' said with a sigh, "Well, if that isn't the most romantic thing! I just can't believe it! Bonnie, if you marry Junior, we'll be sisters!" Like it was her fondest dream come true.

Bonnie, who generally doesn't talk much, jest blushed an' smiled. I kept on pretendin to chew on thet steak bite, hopin it would last long enough for me to thank of somethin to say thet I wouldn't regret for the rest of my borned days. But, once Vikki Ann got done talkin, it felt like everbody at the table was starin at my mouth, watchin an' waitin.

My son put his arm 'round his bride-to-be. His eyes were lookin real worried. She jest sat there, mouse quiet. I quick ran some practice sentences through my head.

> "What 'bout the University of Tennessee?"
> "Haven't we brought you up to be smarter than this?
> "How can you do this to your daddy an me?"
> "Son, are you tryin to ruin your life?"

Soon as I thought any of them words, I knew they weren't right. So I kept right on chewin, knowin they were all gettin suspicious thet I was stallin. Inside my head I tried the words, *"My, this is a big surprise!"* They sounded purty good! I swallowed thet little mess of pulverized meat, looked at the youngens, smiled as best I could an' said, "You aren't pregnant, are you, dear?"

Now, I do admit thet thought had snuck into my mind afore, but I swear, I did NOT mean it to pass my lips! Well, them little slipped-out words caused quite a commotion! First of all, the youngens all looked at me like I'd grown horns an' a forked tail. Then Billy, our fifteen-year-old, started to snicker like he sometimes does when he gets too tense. Thet gave cause to Bonnie, who doesn't know his habit, to bust into tears. She jumped up an' ran from the room with Junior an' Vikki Ann right behind her. Chairs tipped over like there was an earthquake

3

goin on. Vikki Ann turned at the doorway, tossed her Bonnie-look-alike, straight, blonde hair back over her shoulders, stomped her foot an' said, real disgusted like, "I never thought a momma of mine could be so hateful!"

Well, thet did it for Billy. He started laughin so hard he slid right off his chair an' under the table, he was thet unnerved. I knew he was bound to be plumb embarrassed 'bout it later.

Some folks may wonder why I am so foolish 'bout my husband. But it isn't thet hard to figure. Besides bein real smart, he is, bar none, the kindest man I have ever known. He looked at me real sad an' said, tryin to take the blame, "I knew I was supposed to say somethin, Marilue, but the words you said were the only ones I could bring to mind." He got up an' come 'round the table. "You just said the exact words I was thinkin, honey."

Billy's laughin had turned to gurgles like it always did when thangs started to settle. "Them aren't the words I thought were comin out, George," I said, feelin real lumpy-throated. "I swear it!"

George slid back my chair an' pulled me up by my hands. "Well, maybe they weren't the right words, but since they were asked, I can't help but wish one of 'em had answered."

He put his arms 'round me an' patted me real gentle on the back. I nodded into his shoulder, wishin thet very same thang.

Our supper was gettin colder by the minute. I sighed an' said, "I'll go find 'em an' apologize. Tell 'em it wasn't right to be suspicious, ask 'em to come back an' eat. You an' Billy go ahead an' keep eatin."

I found the three youngens all cuddled together on the den couch, Bonnie in the middle with Junior's arm 'round her. "I ain't pregnant, Mrs. Perkins," she said, lookin up at me with tears in her big brown eyes. "We ain't even done it yet."

The word 'yet' branded itself on my brain an' all of a sudden the reason them youngens was so quick to want to get hitched come clear.

"Sweetheart," I said, "I'm glad to hear it an' I do apologize. I always said, 'If you thank the worst of your children, you're bound to get it.' I know you two are good youngens an' I'm sure sorry for sayin what I did."

4

I looked at Junior an' Vikki Ann. "Did you explain 'bout Billy's laughin?" They nodded, lookin at me with eyes hound dog sad.

"Well then, get yourselves together an' come on back to the dinin room so we can finish supper an' talk some more 'bout this notion of yours."

When I got to the dinin room, George was still standin by my chair. "She says she isn't P.G.," I whispered in his ear.

He smiled an' then leaned over as he heped me with my chair. He said, real quick an' low, "Let me do the talkin for awhile, honey. I think I'm gettin an idea."

I can't tell you how them words cheered me. Somethin George is good at is thankin up thangs. Mostly, what he thanks up are inventions, but he's a real good thanker on other thangs too. I promised myself then an' there to keep my trap shut an' listen.

The youngens come in an' we ate our lukewarm supper. It was real quiet with everbody bein extra polite an' pretendin they liked coldish mashed potatoes an' gooey gravy, but nobody askin for seconds. I could tell Billy was concentratin on his food, one careful forkful after another, so he wouldn't start laughin. There was a sadness 'bout him thet touched my heart.

George finally ran a biscuit 'round his plate to sop up the last of the gravy. I got up an' got a plate of fresh-made moon pies from the kitchen an' poured more milk for the youngens. Felt like I was one of them robots my husband is so taken with.

George put his "pie" on the edge of his plate, looked at it an' raised his eyes to mine. He said, "Marilue, I believe I like your moon pies even better than the ones from the bakery." He seemed real calm an' in charge. He smiled at me an' then looked at Billy an' said kindly, "Son, if this talkin we're goin to be doin is goin to make you nervous, you'd best leave the table."

Billy's ears turned real pink but he shook his head an' stayed put. "I gotta try and lick this thing, Daddy," he said, lookin George in the eye, real determination in his voice.

George nodded, givin him permission to stay, an' turned to Bonnie an' Junior. "All right then, youngens, we're all ready to listen."

5

George Junior grabbed onto Bonnie's hand like it was a life raft. I noticed then thet there wasn't an engagement ring on her finger.

"Bonnie and I love each other more'n anythin and we want to get married soon as we graduate." Junior said, his voice wobblin jest a touch.

Bonnie added real soft, but plenty steady, "I just can't live without him any longer." They looked deep into each other's eyes.

I heard Vikki Ann give a big, happy sigh. I come near to losin my supper. George cleared throat again. "Well then," he said, his voice was real respectful, as if what the youngens were talkin 'bout was the most reasonable thang he had ever heard, "gettin married is the easy part, only takes a little money. Bein married and stayin married is the hard part."

He looked at Junior an' said, real firm, "If this is what y'all are set on, son, you'd best let me help you work up some figures." He smiled at Bonnie. "We Perkins men take uncommon pride in carin for our women. We always have."

It sounded a little old-fashioned, but somehow it was real comfortin to hear.

"Sure, Daddy," Junior said. He looked a little confused. "Just what do you mean by figures, exactly?"

"Well, a budget," said George. "You should look over the family checkbook so you can see what a month of bills comes to. You know, rent, groceries, heat, light, insurance and such."

I put my hand under my chin to keep my jaw from droppin. I was thankin, *George Everett Perkins, have you lost your mind?* Sounded like he was all for this deal. The youngens started lookin real perked up, seein as how they were bein taken serious.

"Why, sure," Junior said, squeezin Bonnie's hand afore lettin it go. "That would be real nice, wouldn't it, honey?"

"Of course, son, there are other things for y'all to think on, too." George went on in the same serious voice. "I noticed your gal isn't wearin a ring yet. It's real important to let folks know your intentions. The diamond in a ring says how proud you are that this woman has given you the honor of agreein to be your wife."

6

Bonnie's little face turned redder than her hair, but her eyes got real bright at her future father-in-law's words. It was plain to see she liked the idea of a ring jest fine.

"Why, Daddy, that's right," Junior said. "We do want to declare. We just thought y'all and Bonnie's folks should know first-off."

"Well, thank you for that, Junior. Your mother and I sure appreciate your thoughtfulness." George caught my eye when he said them words. He didn't wink, but the wink was there. I could see it. Made me half-mad, to tell the truth. Seemed like he was havin a real good time where ever he was goin with all the talk. It was soundin to me like he was pushin 'em to get a ring. I figured next he would be pushin for the weddin date. I was workin real hard to keep my faith in him when he paused, like he was thankin somethin through.

"Course, son, none of this would be possible, except that you've always been such a good saver."

Bingo! Them words did it. I finally got his drift. I may only have a high school education, but I'm not stupid. I must have been thet upset not to have caught on sooner. I sat up straighter an' tried not to smile.

Then, my husband started in on his longest speech yet. "Now, I know a man's savins account is private. So, what we'll do tonight is put the numbers together. You two can do the rest. Why don't you and Bonnie sit down at the kitchen table, put together a list of the things you'll need to set up house? Vikki Ann, you go find the Sears Roebuck catalog. And, Billy, why don't you go and collect last Sunday's paper from beside the stove so your brother can see what rents are goin for?"

Then he turned to me, easy as you please. "Marilue, honey, what do you say we clean up the dishes so the youngens can concentrate on what they have to do?"

"Why thet sounds like a right tolerable idea, George, honey," I said in a mountain twang thet would have done my mammaw proud, relief makin me want to get up an' do a jig. 'Stead, I waved my hand at the youngens. "You scoot along now."

When they were gone, George an' I looked at each other. "My, but you are somethin!" I said real low. "Had me convinced

7

for a minute thet you'd gone plumb crazy. Then I finally caught on. Reckon puttin my foot so far in my mouth addled my brain."

As we were clearin the table, George brushed by me an' whispered, "How much do you think Mr. Tightwad has squirreled away?"

"I don't have to thank," I whispered back. "I know. He showed me his pass book." Well, thet stopped him. He come back an' I put my mouth close to his ear. "Two thousand one hundred dollars an' forty-seven cents is what he's got."

George looked surprised but plumb satisfied. "My, my, he sure is a thrifty one, isn't he?"

I nodded an' smiled. "Once it's in there, he sure is partial to it stayin put."

My husband smiled right back at me. "I'm hopin takin out most of a thousand dollars for a little ring that looks like a chunk of glass might just be what the doctor ordered to cure him from wantin to get hitched."

I held up two crossed fingers an' whispered, "Maybe. I did notice Bonnie thought your idea 'bout gettin engaged proper was a fine one."

We stopped whisperin, finished pickin up a load of dishes an' headed for the kitchen. Purty soon the youngens come in. Junior carried a tablet an' a couple of pencils. Vikki Ann was carryin the Sears catalog an' Bonnie had the Montgomery Ward's catalog. Both of those girls looked tickled to death.

Billy spread out *The Daily Times* on the oilcloth. He'd already circled four or five ads. "Rent for a little place isn't more than a hundred fifty a month," Billy said, proud to be able to hep.

"There's weddin rings in both catalogs," Bonnie said, real excited. "It's hard to tell what the rings are like from the pictures, but they sure do look pretty, don't they, George?"

She looked at him an' he nodded, but his eyes had already started to glaze over.

Vikki Ann added, "Bonnie and I liked the one with the two little diamonds on each side of the big diamond and it wasn't near as expensive as some."

She was huggin thet Sears catalog like the diamonds were really inside. I got the checkbook out of my purse for Junior an' Bonnie to study.

8

"Maybe you'd best be makin two lists; put the thangs you reckon you gotta have on one list an' the thangs you want for later on the other," I said over my shoulder.

It had become a family project. George an' I listened while we finished loadin our new dishwasher. Bonnie made the two lists. RING was first on the "must have" list. Junior thumbed through our checkbook register. Billy circled more "places to rent" ads. Vikki Ann opened the catalog to the section on rings again. I stopped wipin the counter an' looked over her shoulder.

"Aren't they pretty, Momma? I like the one Bonnie picked better than some that cost almost twice as much."

She laid the catalog flat on the table an' pointed. "Look here."

I looked. It was a real purty ring. I read the price out loud, sayin each word real slow, "Six hundred ninety-eight dollars an' ninety-nine cents. You youngens have got good taste," I said, tryin hard not to sound cheerful.

Junior wasn't lookin so good. He'd started thumbin through our check register. His blue eyes had the look of an animal with its paw in a trap. Ever once in awhile he'd read somethin thet would cause him to shake his head an' frown. His daddy looked over my shoulder at the ring picture an' nodded.

"Yep," he said, "it looks just like somethin a Perkins man would be proud to give his intended. Course, I agree with Bonnie. You can't really tell much from a picture. Why don't you borrow the pickup, Junior? Take a spin down to J.C. Penney's in the mall, look over the real McCoys. This stuff with the monthly bills can wait." He jingled the keys.

"My, isn't this excitin," I said. "You youngens be careful now, it's likely to be slick out."

I could barely get the words out, bein all choked up an' near to tears thet my husband was puttin his son's future ahead of thet little truck he an' his brothers had worked so hard on.

Junior's face lit up at the thought an' he closed the checkbook real quick, stood up an' reached out his hand for the keys. Then, quicker than an eye blink, he put thet same hand in his pocket afore he took em. I figured he'd been doin some quick arithmetic in his head an' realized his nest egg was fixin to disappear, what with rent, monthly bills an' an engagement ring.

9

He looked so pale I figured the numbers weren't sittin so good on top of the chicken-fried steak in his stomach.

"Naw," he said. "No sense in takin the truck out on such a bad night just for that."

Right away, I could see his words didn't set at all well with Bonnie. "Why then, George, honey, maybe we could borrow your folk's station wagon instead," she said jest a touch sharp.

Junior shook his head. "Naw, what with all the other bills, we probably can't afford a ring with a diamond right now anyway."

Well, I was right. Them wise words didn't sit well with a gal who was prolly imaginin hersef sashayin into school flashin a ring with one real nice diamond in the center an' two little diamonds on either side. She flipped her hair back over her shoulders.

"What are you sayin, George, honey?" she asked, her voice purrin velvet, but her big brown eyes narrowed to a squint.

"I mean," Junior said, "we don't have all the facts yet. We gotta sit down with Momma and Daddy's checkbook and see what else we gotta figure on payin for before we go off half-cocked to buy a ring."

Bonnie slammed shut the catalog, stood up, crossed her arms an' said, "You gotta have a ring to get engaged, George." She forgot to say 'honey.'

Billy started to snicker. He clapped both hands over his mouth. My husband leaned back against the sink counter an' crossed his arms like he planned to enjoy the ruckus he'd created. Junior tried to ignore his brother an' sweet talk his girl.

"I know that, honey. Course I know that. But there's no sense gettin engaged if you don't have the money to get married on."

I decided not to correct his grammar. Bonnie's foot started tappin. Her fists were jammed on her little hips. The word "spitfire" come to mind. I reckoned she didn't have thet purty red hair for nothin.

"I can't believe this!" she said, glarin at the boy she couldn't live without jest minutes afore.

10

Behind Billy's hands, a snortin sound could be heard. Vikki Ann's face turned blotchy, a sure sign thet waterworks were 'bout to start.

Then Junior made a terrible mistake. "Now, Bonnie, honey," he said, "be reasonable."

Billy gave it up an' busted out laughin. Vikki Ann put her head down on the Sears catalog an' started to bawl. Little Bonnie went off like she'd been shot from a rocket launcher.

"I ain't feelin reasonable, you jackass!" she hollered over the din. "A body don't feel like bein reasonable when she's jest been jilted!"

With thet, she jumped up, clopped Billy a good one alongside the head an' whammed out the kitchen door yellin, "Ain't no way I'd marry somebody with such a crazy brother anyhow!"

After the door slammed, 'cept for Vikki Ann's cryin, it got real quiet in the kitchen. The "idea man" was lookin a little amazed at his own success. Junior was lookin gutshot. I thank he had jest figured out he wasn't savin all them years to buy a weddin ring for Bonnie so he could do more than kiss her. In a way, it made me real sad. He looked at me.

"You think I should go after her, Momma?" he asked.

"Not afore you can thank of somethin to say besides, 'Honey be reasonable.' Else you'll get the next clop on the head," I said, noddin towards Billy. "Maybe you should go thank her. I do believe she cured your brother."

Billy was rubbin the side of his head, lookin real puzzled. "Maybe my laughin spells are like the hiccups," he said, soundin hopeful. "Surprise me good enough and I'll stop."

Junior looked at the four of us, but he was thankin 'bout somethin else. "Maybe I don't want you cured, Billy Boy," he finally said. "Momma's probably right. If Bonnie hadn't clobbered you, she might have clobbered me." He grinned an' got his coat from the coat rack then reached for Bonnie's. "Yessiree," he said, sorta to hisself as he headed out the door with her coat over his arm, "that laughin came in mighty handy this time." Then he stopped an' looked back at George. "I liked what you said 'bout how Perkins men take good care of their

11

women, Daddy," he said. "But you sure spent too much money doin up this house last year."

CHAPTER TWO
FEBRUARY

Lately, it seemed like my life was losin its pep. I expect part of it was realizin thet here it was, 1980. George an' I had been married for exactly one half of my lifetime. Then there was the fact thet I didn't much like lookin in the mirror anymore. Course, my hair bein blonde, the gray didn't really show less I looked close. Thet's when I could see it--right along with the crow's feet 'round my eyes. I had passed my prime an' I knew it.

I kept tryin to toss my feelins off as the winter, dreary-day, after-holiday blues. But it seemed like the articles in my *Ladies Home Journal, Redbook* an' *Good House Keeping* magazines thet talked on how to improve yourself or your marriage started catchin my eye more than the movie star stories, fashion tips or the recipes.

Then one day I read an article thet talked on how men an' women don't understand each other's way of thankin. It made me sit right straight up in my easy chair. Seemed thet they were sure talkin 'bout George. It said, "When a man gives you some gadget for your birthday, anniversary or Valentine's Day, it doesn't mean he doesn't love you, or thet he isn't sensitive. It means HE likes gettin gadgets, so he figures YOU like gettin gadgets." I figured the woman who wrote thet article knew what she was talkin 'bout.

George an' his buddies truly were partial to gettin such thangs. I mean, if it was miniaturized, transistorized, computerized; if it had bells, beeps, whistles; or did thangs faster, slicker, neater, they couldn't wait to show out to each other. They'd play with it 'til they broke it, most times.

Now, I didn't feel a bit thet way 'bout a new mixer, toaster oven or the like an' I didn't reckon I had any girlfriends thet did either. Mostly, when they squealed 'bout gettin thet new Mix Master, they were jest bein polite, wantin to make their husbands feel good.

This article said if you feel thet way, you gotta tell your spouse. You can't expect 'em to read your mind. So, awhile after last Christmas, I did. Kindly, gently, lovingly, jest like the article said.

It floored George. "But Marilue, what would you want instead?" he asked, sorta scratchin his head an' puttin down his *Popular Science Magazine.*

Well, I put it to him straight. "George," I said, "you aren't goin to find it in thet gadget magazine."

I sat down in his lap an' started fiddlin with his hair the way he likes. "Honey, a woman is partial to flowers, perfume, lingerie, candy, them sorts of thangs. They don't like gettin veg-o-matics, George!"

I could see he looked a tad confused an' I worried if I had said it right. But later, I come to find out he was jest thankin.

"Dang," he said, "reckon I do see what you mean. It's like fellas gettin shorts or socks under the tree. They're nice to have, but they don't feel much like a present."

Well, thet was news to me. Made me duck my head a little since I'd gotten all my men new underwear for Christmas. "Yep," I said, "you caught my drift."

I kissed him on his forehead. "An' I caught yours. No more boxers for Christmas, George," I said. "I promise."

Come Valentine's Day, I'd plumb forgotten our conversation, but I knew somethin was up, there was such a smirk on George's face all durin supper. Right between finishin his pot roast an' startin in on his cherry pie, he gave our boys ten bucks an' the keys to the Chevy wagon. He said thet they had been such good youngens he wanted to give 'em a special Valentine's present...an' so finish their pie an' hep emselves to a movie...but they'd have to take their little sister.

14

They looked 'round the table at each other, then at me, wonderin 'bout it bein a school night an' all. I recollected the look on George's face an' decided on the spot to play along. "We'll take care of the dishes, but you be home by 9:30," I said, like I knew 'bout the plan all along. "Remember, it's a school night."

When they'd recovered from their shock, they said, "Thank you!" 'bout a million times, gobbled up their pie an' shot out the door to the garage afore we could change our minds. I looked down the empty table at George an' raised one eyebrow.

"You plannin to tell me what this is 'bout any time soon now, George?"

He grinned, pleased as punch with hisself for some reason. "Maybe later," he said. "But for right now, let's get these dishes cleaned up."

He was a touch nervous the whole time we were puttin the kitchen to rights. I could tell by this mite near silent whistle he has. After we'd finished, he gave me a big hug an' headed out the door thet connects to our garage.

I'll tell you, I couldn't figure heads or tails 'bout the way he was actin. I quick put my ear to the door, an' could hear the "thunk" of him openin an' closin the door to his beer an' bait refrigerator. I jumped back real quick an' started foldin the dish towel when I heard his footsteps, tryin not to look like the nosy Rosie I was. He come back in carryin two thangs. In one hand was a bottle of champagne. "From California," it said. In the other hand was a black box with some fancy gold letterin in one corner. The writin said, "Frederick's of Hollywood."

He showed it to me, grinnin. "Look at this, Marilue."

I reached out my hand, but he put the box behind his back. "Not yet," he said.

He got two of our "special occasion" wine glasses out of the China closet, tucked thet box under his arm, handed me the champagne, an' led me by my free hand, up the stairs towards the bedroom. It wasn't even eight o'clock.

"George Everett Perkins, what have you got on your mind?" I asked. As if I didn't know.

He locked the bedroom door behind us. "Here, Marilue," he said, handin me the box to open while he popped the cork. So,

15

after givin it a heft an' a shake, I did. I recollect thankin thet the box was awful light. *Not much in here,* I thought to myself. There wasn't either...jest this see-through black thang with furry lookin feathers 'round the neck an' on the sleeves, an' this little, bitty, black, wispy pair of silky panties. I can tell you I was plumb speechless then!

George an' I had been married since God was a boy. I thought I knew him back to front an' front to back. Not more than a month ago I had been frettin 'bout thet fact some.

I smiled at him real tender, takin my glass of champagne, lovin thet his face made a beet look pale, thet his hands were sweatin an' thet he chugged his whole glass of champagne like it was beer.

"Thet isn't how you are supposed to drink champagne, George!" I said, sharp as a shrew, while I tried to recover myself.

Now, I'm not a dainty, little thang; haven't been a size twelve since before the boys an' Vikki Ann were born. An' thet was nearly twenty years ago.

I looked at George an' he looked at me. "Put it on," he said, real serious like.

I nodded, took a gulp of my own champagne an' kissed him on the cheek. Tryin to sound real sincere, I said, "These are real nice. Thank you, honey. I do reckon I will." Then I set the champagne on the nightstand an' made a beeline for our new bathroom.

"I want to surprise you," I said over my shoulder, as I shut the door, leavin him standin there lookin after me.

I stood behind thet closed door an' looked at what he had given me. It tied in bows down the front. But you didn't have to untie 'em unless you wanted to; the neck was thet big. The panties were somethin else! I knew dang well there wasn't enough material in 'em to cover my stretch marks an' I couldn't figure out for sure what was front an' what was back. While I was lookin, I noticed what I first thought was a busted seam down the middle of the crotch. But it wasn't. I knew for sure, 'cause it was all trimmed with lace an' finished off real nice.

'Bout then, I began prayin to God the rig wouldn't fit. But it did. Thet fru-fru top slipped like water over my head an' the panties didn't even pause at my thighs; jest went right on.

16

Well, I'll tell you, the whole thang threw me for a minute. I stood there with my eyes squinched shut for awhile, feelin some foolish, wonderin what I'd do if I walked out of thet bathroom door an' George started in to laughin. It was then I recollected my little talk with him. I mean, tellin him how women wanted feminine thangs an' such. I gave a groan an' opened my eyes, one at a time.

After a little, I smiled. For a fact, lookin back from the mirror was no cover girl. But, on the other hand, I noticed the outfit did have a way of showin off a gal's assets. I fluffed my hair. I noticed it looked blonder than usual an' my eyes looked darker, near like purple velvet. I gave myself a quick squirt of White Shoulders perfume an' made up my mind then an' there to go for broke.

I took a deep breath, practiced a sexy smile in front of the mirror, sucked in my stomach, pulled back my shoulders, fluffed my hair again an' opened the door. I caught George in the middle of pullin off a pair of the boxers I'd got him for Christmas.

"Well, Georgie," I said, kinda leanin against the door jamb like I saw Marilyn Monroe do in a movie. "Whatta ya thank?"

"Geez, Marilue," he said kinda weaklike, "Geez Louise!"

He straightened up an' let go of those drawers. He wasn't laughin. In fact, with his boxers all settled 'round his ankles, there wasn't any hidin his attitude towards thangs--if you know what I mean.

I gave a little twirl so he could see the feathers float an' slinked across the room, tryin to look like Marilyn. We held each other real tight for a minute. Then I kissed him. An' it wasn't a little peck on the cheek like afore I went into the bathroom to put the outfit on. It was a movie kiss. Then we leaned back an' laughed, sorta proud-like.

George poured hisself more champagne an' handed me my glass. He was lookin an' his eyes were shinin. We toasted an' drank. Thet time, I didn't say how to drink it. I drank mine fast too. Then we clicked them empty glasses an' hopped under the covers, jest thet quick.

Afterwards, when we were lyin there all soft an' snuggly, George blowin on the feathers, I asked him how he come to get me such a present.

"Marilue," he said, real serious, "when you told me how women like gettin female things, it made me feel foolish not to have figured it out for myself in all these years."

He gave a chuckle. "Knowin what you finally told me, made me see what a good sport you had been. Made me want to do somethin real special for you. But, there was no way in heck I could work up my gumption enough to go to any underwear department, even wantin to get you somethin frilly as bad as I did. But I had to do somethin because it just didn't seem like flowers or candy would do."

I smiled an' snuggled tighter under his arm. "So, how did you come up with this black rig?"

"Well, I was still workin up towards orderin you some stuff out of the Montgomery Ward's catalog, and havin it sent to work, when I went to get my hair cut. I was lookin through the magazines at the barber shop and right under my thumb was this ad for ladies' things from Fredericks of Hollywood. It said you could send for a free catalog."

He blew on the feathers again. "After I looked at the pictures in that ad, I knew there wasn't a thing I wanted to get you from Montgomery Wards OR Sears Roebuck. So I went ahead and sent for the catalog."

He laughed. "Thank the Lord that catalog came to work in a brown paper wrapper or Andy and the boys at work would be teasin me yet."

We smiled at each other an' he looked at me. The bows were all untied. Then, we sighed knowin it was time to get movin afore the youngens come home. But we sure didn't want to.

Finally, George got hisself together an' downstairs in front of the TV. I took off the panties, went into the bathroom an' washed 'em real careful with Woolite. Then I put 'em under my ol' hair dryer hood to dry. It didn't take any time at all.

I took off my feather top an' put on my robe. Put thet top in a shoe box under my good, black patent leather pumps. But, afore I put the panties away, I looked at 'em one last time, recollectin when I thought they were too little to be worth much.

Then, I put 'em flat between our mattress an' box springs. Seemed like a good place to keep the youngens from findin em.

I looked at myself in the mirror one last time afore headin down. Blew myself a Marilyn kiss, feelin inside, jest like she looked on the outside.

CHAPTER THREE
MARCH

George hasn't ever come home from work durin the middle of the day unless he was real sick or the plant closed for one reason or another. So, thet's what I figured was wrong when I looked out the kitchen window an' saw him pullin his pickup into the driveway on two wheels an' hoppin out, makin a bee line for the front walk without even shuttin the door on the truck.

"You rushin for the pot, honey?" I asked as I quick opened the door for him.

He stopped on the bottom step real sudden an' looked up at me, blinked his eyes like he was wakin up an' shook his head. "No. I'm fit as a fiddle, Marilue."

He didn't look right though. Not to me. There was the strangest air 'bout him even though his color was good. Looks crossed over his face quicker'n sticks over a waterfall an' I couldn't figure out a one of em. He didn't say anythin for a minute, jest stood there on the front steps lookin up at me. I reached to put my hand on his forehead.

"No," he said again, "I'm not sick, Marilue." He ran his fingers through his hair like he does. "But I sure am agitated."

He saw he'd left the door on the truck open, sighed, shook his head an' went to shut it. Then, without sayin a word, he walked on up the stairs an' in through the door straight on past me. After I shut the door, he reached out an' took my hand, still

20

without sayin a word an' led me to the couch. We sat so our knees were touchin a little but so thet he could look at me.

He cleared his throat an' reached out to take my closest hand in his. "Marilue, honey, remember thet little gizmo I invented thet saves time and labor in manufacturin the cylinders we make down at the plant? The one thet makes sure there aren't any steel filings left in them?"

I nodded to show I recollected, not thet I understood exactly what it was he had done. George is a tool an' die man, an' when he starts talkin 'bout machines, my brain jest plain shuts down. I mean, how can a body understand a man who uses a computer to design the machines thet makes the machine parts?

Not thet I'm not proud of what he does, I am. But, when he says tool, I thank on a hammer or screwdriver. When he says die, I thank on Ritt or Clairol.

"Well, honey," he said, "out of the blue, I got a call from a man in Seattle, Washington, name of Bill Johnston. He works for a place that makes airplanes. It's called the Boeing Company. He said he'd heard about my invention and figured I might just have the experience he needs, what with the work we've been doin for Huntsville and NASA. He said, 'I might be just the sort of man they were lookin for.' He invited me to fly out to visit him the end of this month and said he'd be payin for my trip. Said if things worked out, he might like to talk 'bout hirin me."

George didn't say his piece like I'm tellin it. His words were all run together an' he didn't hardly stop to take a breath. By the time he was done my head was spinnin, but I did finally catch his drift an' it seemed like all the heat in my body turned straight to ice. I swear, I was near to shiverin 'cause what his words meant sunk in an' I knew, sure as shootin, my husband was fixin be offered a job clean across the country.

Now, this next part I'm not proud of. But since it happened, I'd better tell it straight. Fact is, sittin there knee to knee an' col' as death, I busted into tears an' put my apron to my eyes, jest like my momma an' Mammaw Ada do when they need to hide their sadness.

When I thank back on it, I reckon it was the suddenness of it all thet did me in. Right out of the blue, my husband was seriously talkin of leavin Tennessee, goin to some place I only

21

saw on television when they had the World's Fair there in 1962. Only thang thet stuck in my mind 'bout the place back then was a tall, skinny buildin thet looked like it was from some other planet. They called it a Space Needle, which to me didn't sound friendly at all. Right then though, with my apron still to my eyes, it finally come to me what the look on George's face had been. Excitement, pure, plain an' simple excitement was what it was.

George gets plumb flustered when I turn on the water works, always has. He doesn't know what to do, so he jest kept sayin, "Now, honey, now, honey, don't cry, please don't cry," an' pattin me on the back like you would a baby.

When I finally took down my apron an' looked at him, part of me was already feelin shame at ruinin his big news. I mean, I knew this man. He had to want thet job real bad to even thank 'bout uprootin his family an' movin thet far from the Horseshoe. He loves thet creek like it was a person. He'd fished it with his twin brothers, Harlen an' Karlen, ever since he was a boy. We buried our ol' dog, Pepper, in a nice little grove of spruce an' balsam right above his favorite fishin hole there.

Fact was, other than servin Uncle Sam, an' goin away to Georgia Tech, George had seemed real content livin here in Maryville. An' me, well, I was mountain born. I'm such a homebody, it's plumb disgustin. I can't get a look at my Smokey Mountains ever now an' again, I don't feel right. I mean it. Ever once in awhile I can feel 'em pullin at me. Thet's when I say to George an' the youngens, "Reckon it's time to go up Mount LeConte an' see Mammaw an' Pappaw." An' they know I got to go…with or without em.

But now, sittin all blotchy-faced in our livin room, there was no mistakin the look on George's face after my spree on the pity pot. Misery!

He said, "Geez, Marilue, I'm sure sorry, honey. I figured this would take some digestin for you, but I didn't reckon on you takin the news this bad. Guess I got so excited I didn't stop to think things through."

He kinda croaked out the words, real sad-like. I shook my head an' tried to tell him I was the one who was sorry but my throat was thet closed up I couldn't even pull out a whisper.

22

Lucky for us, we're good at huggin. He tucked me into his shoulder an' we sat snuggled up on thet couch thankin our thoughts for the longest time. When we finally spoke, our words come out at the same time.

George said, "I'll get ahold of Mr. Johnston and let him know I won't be comin," the same time I said, "You are NOT goin out to Seattle by yourself, George Everett Perkins, so you'd best get it arranged."

He pulled back an' looked at me then. "What's that?" he asked, his eyes blinkin like he didn't hear; his forehead so furrowed I could a planted carrots.

I repeated, "You are NOT goin to Seattle without me an' thet's final!"

Well, then the man was plumb confused. He sorta ran his hand through his hair again, pushed his glasses up his nose an' said like he was thankin hard, "I don't know, honey. Like I said, maybe I didn't think this deal through enough. I guess I got the big head when that fella said how interested they were in findin folks like me. He even said, 'The aerospace industry is cryin for new blood' and called me an 'innovative genius.'"

George shook his head, real sad-like. "It got me excited to have somebody think that. I didn't stop to consider what I was askin of you and the kids, especially with Junior's scholarship at the University and all."

"I'd fret myself to death worryin 'bout you alone in such a big city, George," I said like I hadn't heard a word he'd been sayin. "We'll get Daddy an' Momma to look after the youngens."

He'd been kinda mumblin an' lookin at his shoes when he'd been talkin 'bout not goin, but with them words, he lifted his head. He could tell by my tone thet I meant what I said an' a little spark of hopefulness come back into his blue eyes. I saw it.

He looked at me hard then. "Would you really want to get on an airplane, Marilue?"

I'll tell you now, them words 'bout stopped my clock. I hadn't ever been on an airplane. Fact is, I haven't ever been further west than Memphis…an' I only went thet far with my friend, Betty Jean, to hear Elvis sing after he got done servin his country in the Army an' come home. Even back then, I couldn't

23

wait to get back on the bus after the concert an' neither could Betty Jean. Jest one day away an' we were already homesick for them ol' blue-colored mountains, an' thet's a fact. So gettin on an airplane to fly clear across the country jest hadn't occurred to me.

But now, raw feelin as I was, I knew I wasn't goin to take back a thang 'bout goin. In my heart, I knew for a fact thet my husband deserved to have the chance to meet face to face with the man who called him an "innovative genius." It was, after all, a real proud thang.

I also knew if I said the words rollin 'round in my head, which were, *I can't do this, George, I want to, but I can't,* he'd be on the phone in a heartbeat, callin Seattle an' cancelin the whole deal.

After a little, I sighed an' leaned forward to run my hand along his cheek. "It's not somethin I ever thought on afore-- gettin on an airplane an' all, but I reckon I can do it."

At suppertime, when we told the youngens, they didn't know what to thank. Course George told 'em straight out. "We haven't made a decision. We're just goin to go and listen to what the man has to say, maybe look the country over some while we're there," he said.

Our youngens are hardly ever speechless, but this time he got em. After them words come out of their daddy's mouth, they jest sat there for a minute, like they had been listenin to a foreign tongue an' didn't understand a word. Then, like they had swivels on their necks, they turned an' looked my way. Me, bein the one always braggin on our state an' sayin how I didn't understand how anybody could thank of livin anywhere else, they had to hear the truth of the news from me too.

I nodded, my face as bland as tapioca puddin, lookin at George. "Like your daddy said, we're jest lookin thangs over. The final decidin is goin to be done right here at this table, same as usual with everbody gettin a vote after we got all the facts."

"Why, Daddy," Junior finally said with a grin on his face, "it's not every day a fella finds out he was fathered by an 'innovative genius.'"

24

Them words sort of broke the tension an' it didn't surprise any of us when, after a minute, Billy asked could he go get the "W" encyclopedia. He does like to look thangs up. I did notice thet he had followed the family rules 'bout leavin the table an' asked his daddy afore he went.

I got up an' cleared the dishes while he told everbody thet the state bird was a willow goldfinch, the state tree, a western hemlock an' the state flower, the coastal rhododendron. Seemed like I could barely stand to hear it.

"Look here, Momma," he said as I come past his chair, "they got a whole page of colored pictures."

He got up an' brought the book to my end of the table, waitin. I sat back down, tryin to look interested, an' took my turn at turnin the pages. It looked to me like the state was mostly water, trees an' big mountains. "Looks like it's a real purty state," I said while I was thankin to myself, *But it don't look friendly. What with all thet water, be hard not to drown.* Even then, I knew it was jest sour grapes thankin.

I did take some comfort knowin they had rhododendrons. I wondered if the coastal kind looked at all like our Catawabas thet turned the Smokies purple some years, there were thet many blossoms. The little picture made it seem thet it might be so.

Right away, Junior wanted to know 'bout the fishin. I noticed George was listenin hard. Billy read off five kinds of salmon, even more kinds of trout. His daddy tried not to act pleased but he couldn't hep it thet a little happy whistle come out when he looked at the size of the salmon. He knew what I was feelin, but he was so excited, if he'd had a tail, he'd of been waggin it.

Then Junior surprised us. "Seems like even if we moved, it wouldn't be until after graduation. I reckon there's colleges as good as the University of Tennessee out there."

He an' Bonnie had made up, but thangs weren't the same for 'em after the big fight. It looked like leavin her wouldn't break his heart like it would of afore. I tried to see thet as a good thang, but I wasn't feelin much. Like I say, I was purty much froze up. The col' spot inside me was as big as Tellico Lake.

All through Billy's readin an' the passin 'round of the pictures, Vikki Ann kept mind of her own thoughts. Still, she is

25

my daughter an' I figured next to me in our family, she loved them old, foggy, worn-down mountains best. *We're all goin to have to adjust ourselves to this deal,* I thought, an' felt even colder.

I knew I should have been feelin real good watchin my husband in them next days. Purty soon he was whistlin all the time, tellin little jokes an' talkin airplanes to anyone who would listen. All the while, thankin of pullin our roots out of Tennessee soil was 'bout doin me in. I went plumb off my food an' thet's a thang thet I jest never do.

Meals at our house got to be slapped together affairs 'cause it seemed I spent most of my time out in our yard prunin, dividin, paintin our picket fence an' doin any other chore I'd put off doin for years, tears runnin down my cheeks most days, but never when my family could see me.

My big purple iris patches were in full bud. I cried when I thought 'bout not ever seein 'em bloom again. Got so I'd stand under the big walnut tree or in the shelter of our big lilacs thet were jest gettin their leaves back, an' go into a kinda trance. I'd come to myself with a jump, only if a car back-fired, a dog barked, a door slammed or some such thang.

At church on Sundays, got so I didn't know which side to pray on, for us to stay put, or for George to get the job in Seattle. I mostly ended up prayin for God to give me strength. Even then I thank I knew we would be goin.

Course, word spread like wildfire an' it seemed like half the town of Maryville, mostly our friends, stopped by when George was at work to have a cup of coffee or a glass of sweet tea an' tease me 'bout marryin an "innovative genius" or commiserate with me, if thet's what I wanted—which I did not. I was doin my best to keep a happy face on this whole deal.

But I will tell you thet it got harder an' harder to keep a smile on my face when I had to keep tellin the story over an' over of how it was Andy, his boss, who started the whole ball rollin. For some reason he took it upon hisself to call his friend from college, a Mr. Johnston, in Seattle, Washington, an' brag 'bout George's invention. Andy even got carried away an' sent him a prototype. As Andy said, "It was my second big mistake."

26

Seems thet Mr. Johnston turned out to be mighty interested--both in the invention AN' in George. Andy wasn't happy at all 'bout the George part, but since he was the one who started the deal, he said he understood an' sure wouldn't stand in George's way. If thangs worked out, he'd let him out of his contract...but he'd sure like to be considered for the Boeing Company's tool an' die work, should somethin come up. He told George if they had coughed up the money for both of us to come, they were dead serious 'bout wantin him--which they had.

Our neighbor down the street, Mis' Adel, a widow lady whose family has known mine for years, listened to me recite my story without sayin a word, jest lookin at me. Then, after I'd finished, she looked me in the eye.

"Marilue," she said, "I been a talkin to your momma." She let thet sink in for a little an' then she reached out an' touched my hand. "I'm real happy for George. He's a fine man. But, honey, we'ns both know this whole thang is a'goin to be mighty tough on you...mighty tough. I don't know as how I could do it, even were I younger."

I didn't like it at the time, her callin me out like thet, mostly 'cause it caused me to break down some, somethin I had promised myself I would NOT do. But later, it felt good somehow, thankin thet maybe there were some folks out there like Mis' Adel, who had deep feelins for the land like I did an' were commiseratin with me without sayin a thang, knowin thet's how I wanted it.

A week afore George an' I left, he tried on his weddin suit an' then went out to buy another with a more generous cut. What with my home cookin an' his stoppin smokin in 1978, his ol' suit was headed for The First Baptist Church's clothin ministry.

I figured I'd do fine with this nice little rose-colored dress with black trim thet I had bought to wear to special occasions. It had a darker pink jacket with the same trim. I'd paid full price for the outfit an' it wasn't mor'n a couple a years old. But when I tried it on, bein so far off my feed, it hung on me like a sack, an' the hemline jest didn't suit; hemlines had been goin up steady.

27

No way was I goin to get on an airplane lookin like I was wearin hand-me-downs.

The next day, I marched myself into Betty's Apparel in downtown Maryville. (She's the friend I went to see Elvis with.) I said, "Betty Jean, George an' I are flyin out to Seattle, Washington, next week an' I need a new dress."

Betty Jean has this nice little shop for ladies. It has the sort of clothes thet have what she calls "fashion flair." She grew up in Pigeon Forge same as I did. We started first grade together. If one of us skinned our knee roller skatin, the other one put on the iodine an' blew away the hurt afore puttin the band aid on. When we were in the fifth grade she decided goin to break ourselves of sayin the word "ain't and such."

"Marilue," she had said, "No reason two girls who get near straight A's should be usin "ain't," "hain't," "cain't," and such. We gotta break our habit. And no more we'uns and you'ns either. Soundin like hillbillies just won't do in this day and age."

We did, too, startin with the word "ain't. We got a little bucket an' ever time we said thet word, we would have to throw in a penny. No tellin how much progress I would've made if Daddy hadn't moved us to Maryville.

Betty Jean was one of the school friends I missed the most, though we still talked on the phone all through high school. After we got our driver's licenses, we got together from time to time. Still do to this day.

Anyway, Betty Jean always had real good taste. Even her dolls were dressed up like real class when we were little. After high school, she went to New York to study fashion design. She didn't finish her course though. Jest like when we went to Memphis, she finally got to missin our ol' blue mountains so bad she had to come home.

When I come into her shop thet day, she gave me a longish look an' straight away took charge. "Well, I heard that, honey," she said lookin' me over. "And I'll tell you, you're goin to need more than one outfit for that trip, Marilue Grace Perkins, and they aren't all goin to be peasant blouses and jeans," she said real sharp, knowin my inclinations. "You have do George proud!"

28

Well, them words, the fact thet I had gone down a dress size an' thet I always had let Betty Jean boss me 'round, got me some carried away. We were only goin to be gone for four days but I had to make a second trip to the station wagon; I had thet many boxes an' pokes.

The first thang Betty Jean talked me into was a navy blue jersey dress with a vee neck, fit snug at my waist an' then flared over my hips. It was two inches above my knees, though Betty Jean said, beins my legs were one of my best features, I could go higher.

"No mini-skirts, an' thet's final," I said, twirlin 'round to see the skirt flare. I had some blue suede pumps at home thet might look real good. The youngens called 'em my "Elvis shoes."

She had me try on a pair of bell bottom kahki-colored jeans she thought would do for any casual event. So, I bought 'em an' a soft baby-blue, cowl neck tunic an' a macramé belt to go with it. Then Betty Jean showed me a real nice rusty brown A-line polyester dress with a matchin jacket. "This will be perfect on the airplane, Marilue, because it doesn't wrinkle or bind."

Course, I HAD to have thet outfit…an' a black A-line skirt with a real purty white polyester blouse with a bow at the neck. She put a red cinch belt on me an' said, "If you have red shoes, a red purse and a red necklace, it would really tie this all together, Marilue."

The last thang she talked me into was a little black dress with capped sleeves. "Even if you can't wear that rose-colored dress anymore, that jacket should work with this little black dress like a charm," she said. Course, I'd bought the pink dress from her, so she knew what she was talkin 'bout.

Like I say, I got some carried away. As I was makin my second trip out the door, Betty called out, "Marilue, don't forget to accessorize."

"I won't, Betty Jean—an' thanks a heap," I said, both of us knowin if we even said one word more 'bout George maybe gettin that job out west, we'd both break down.

I gotta tell you thet Betty's Apparel was only my first stop. I left her shop an' took myself to J. C. Penney's an' bought

29

red heels, an' a red necklace. Then I went to their lingerie department an' bought new underwear in case the airplane crashed. Then I bought a new robe an' nightie in case the hotel we were goin to be stayin in caught on fire. On a whim I even went to the "outerwear" department an' bought a purty three-quarter length black raincoat with purple cuffs an' linin thet could be said to compliment my eyes an' blonde hair.

I looked at myself in the mirror careful when I was tryin it on, an' made a mental note to call up Perlie, the gal who cuts my hair, an' have her give me the works. It was goin to surprise her some, especially the manicure an' pedicure I was aimin to get, but it couldn't be heped. Like Betty said, I had to be an asset to my husband.

The afternoon afore George an' I left, my momma an' daddy come in from Pigeon Forge where they'd moved back to after Daddy retired from Alcoa Aluminum an' Maryville got too big for their comfort. I had been makin casseroles an' pies for the freezer afore they come. All the time I worked, I kept tellin myself not to be a baby when I saw em.

Daddy always heads straight to George's garage refrigerator for a beer when he comes through the front door. Then he watches the color T.V. in George's recliner in the den an' has a smoke or two while Momma an' I drink sweet tea an' visit.

On thet particular afternoon though, Daddy got his Pabst Blue Ribbon an' stayed in the kitchen with us. He looked real sad as he sat down at the table an' studied on me like he was memorizin my face. I could tell he was takin in the effect of Perlie's House of Beauty. "Honey," he finally said in thet soft way he has, "I didn't recollect how purty you are. You look a heap like your momma—all thet shiny blonde hair an 'em iris-colored eyes."

Well, I can tell you thet did it for me. Up come my apron an' Momma wasn't much better, her grabbin napkins, one after another out of the napkin hol'er on the table. Daddy didn't try to comfort us. He was too busy blowin his own nose.

After a time, we got ourselves settled down an' purty soon Momma said, "I kept thankin on why our kin are such

30

powerful homebodies, Marilue. I took it in my head to go up the mountain an' I asked your Mammaw Ada why our blood kin seems tied tighter'n trees to their land."

She reached out an' took my hand. "It took her a bit to ponder on it, but then she allowed hit was 'cause they had such a terrible, fearsome time gettin to this country in the first place. An', in the second place, makin a livin in these ol' mountains took ever bit of grit they had. 'em thet stayed felt real proud of what they'd done, nary askin for a handout, clearin thet mean ol' land for farmin such as they could grow, an' jest makin do."

Momma smiled at me but I could read the misery she felt for me. Her voice held steady but it was near to bein a whisper when she said, "Myself, I wonder if it thet was true for the menfolk, but thet we womenfolk are jest plumb full of memories. We don't want to be too far from the bones of all them children we lost to illness an' wars over all 'em years. We got bones in the ground here older'n than the United States of America!"

Her voice trailed off an' her eyes were far away, like maybe she was lookin inside her own memories. I figured she was thankin 'bout the babies she had lost afore she had me.

"Yep," she said real soft, "I reckon we'uns are jest plumb full of memories."

I nodded an' sipped my tea, recollectin the glass was one of the nice tall ones Mammaw Ada an' Pappaw Joe gave to us on our weddin day for jest this purpose. I thought, *right now what I'm full of is misery with a little sweet tea tryin to fill up any empty spaces.*

A piece later, what Momma said settled like truth in my heart. Then I sighed real deep, looked at 'em an' said, "You know I got to do this thang. I owe it to George. I thought 'bout tellin him I wasn't goin, but I can't. I got to get on thet airplane tomorrow like I done it ever day of my life. I got to meet people I don't know, sleep in a bed I never slept in afore an' pretend best I can thet everythin is jest fine."

Daddy nodded, took a long swallow of his beer an' thumped the bottle down on the table. "Yes'm. I reckon you do, little girl. Ain't never been a coward in the Cable bloodline. Best not start with you. You married a man who don't have the mountains in his blood, but he's a man worth keepin for all thet."

31

Momma said, "I keep tellin myself not to borrow sorrow. It ain't for sure you'ns'll be movin out there."

I sighed again an' shook my head. "Momma, I've been thankin on this some an' I believe what thet Seattle fella says 'bout George bein real smart in a special way is true."

I looked at 'em sadly. "Wait 'til you see him. He's so tickled to even go an' talk with this man, makes you realize he's been needin somethin like this to happen. So, I figure we'll be goin. It's not likely I'd want to stand in his way."

With my words, tears started slidin down Momma's face again. But I didn't break down this time. Seemed like for me, the time for tears had passed...or maybe I had jest had finally emptied my whole tank.

I reached across the table an' held out my hands for 'em to take, tryin to give comfort. "We got to recollect thet I'm not the first person to leave land they loved. 'Least I don't gotta get in a leaky ol' boat an' cross the Atlantic Ocean like the folks did back then. Goin out to Seattle on an airplane is nothin at all compared to thet."

After awhile Momma said, mite near to hersef, "Well, I expect thet's right, Marilue." She raised her eyes to mine. "An' look at all of us'ns now 'cause they had the gumption an' the grit to git hit done."

CHAPTER FOUR
APRIL

Now, I'm not one to borrow trouble. But then, I'm not one to back down from a fight, either; never have been. Daddy says it's 'cause I got the blood of Tennessee fightin men in my veins. But the only thang it seems like I was fightin the whole entire month of March was bawlin spells.

One good thang happened jest afore we left though. Bill Johnston's wife, Mis' Caroline, had given me a call straight out of the blue.

"Marilue," she said after she got done introducin hersef, "I know from Bill that you've never been to Seattle before. So, since your husband is going to be kept fully engaged during your visit, why don't we have a little fun together? Be sure and bring your tennis shoes, I have a spare set of rain gear for you. If you're game, I'd like to teach you how to sail!"

It come to my mind what I'd thought 'bout Washington bein a place you could likely drown, but there was such welcome in her voice; I managed to say, "Well, since I've never been near a sailboat or any water much bigger than a pond, other than Tellico Lake, you better be a fine teacher."

"Actually, I am, Marilue. I have a little Flying Junior sailboat and have been helping students learn to sail in it for years. I help our school district with their Young Sailors' program. So, we'll have some fun."

I gotta admit, her enthusiasm was catchin. I tried picturin myself on one of them big sleek sailboats I'd seen on TV when

33

George was clickin 'round on the sports channel, but it was a stretch. "Well, I reckon I'm willin to give her a try, if you say so, Mis' Caroline," I said. "I'll brang my tennis shoes." *Nobody'd better say George's wife isn't a good sport,* I was thankin to myself.

Then we talked of other thangs, like the nice hotel we were stayin in an' thet it rained 'bout the same amount out there as it did back here. I told her I'd be sure George packed a rain coat. When I got off the phone, I was some perked up, like maybe the trip could be gotten through after all.

On the day we left, the ride to the McGee Tyson Airport went by way too fast. It was a good thang Daddy was the one takin us. Wasn't any way I was goin to let him down by bein a bawl baby. By the time he pulled up to drop us off, my teeth were achin from the grittin I gave em. But I got out of the wagon purty as you please, leaned in to Daddy's window an' kissed him on the cheek. "You take good care of my babies," I said an' gave his shoulder a squeeze.

He quick grabbed my hand on his shoulder an' held it tight. "I will, baby girl," he said, lookin straight ahead as he let go.

Then, I walked 'round the back of the wagon an' picked up my vanity case while George hefted the other two suitcases to the curb an' then went to say his own goodbyes to Daddy. Thet man of mine was practically dancin he was thet excited.

I stood on the curb waitin for George with my new rain coat over my arm an' our luggage at my feet, prayin for my mind to be real still an' strong. *This is George's big chance an' you are NOT goin to do less than your best for him, Marilue Perkins. You are goin to get on the airplane like you do it ever day! Got thet?*

I did too. With George doin the directin, I got on thet airplane, put my vanity case under the seat in front of me an' fastened my seat belt 'afore bein told. I DID NOT take the window seat even though George offered. No way I wanted to look down an' see the ground thousands of feet below.

34

In truth, the take-off wasn't much at all to my likin an' the landin was worse, what with all the engine noise an' bumpin 'round. But I managed by hol'in tight to my husband's hand an' hearin the proud in his voice when he whispered, "Why, Marilue, you did that like you've been flyin all your life." I jest nodded an' gave a little smile. It wasn't for him to know my throat was so dry I couldn't answer.

After we got to Seattle, turns out what Mis' Caroline said was 'bout right. The Boeing folks had ever minute of George's four days packed, startin with breakfast the first mornin. It didn't take me long to see the days were 'bout more than business. Plain as the nose on your face, they were courtin my husband, wantin him to see how much fun it was to live in Seattle. Ever blessed minute was busy! Wore us both to a frazzle an' it had nothin to do with jet lag.

Thet first mornin, we ate right in the Sorrento Hotel where we were stayin. Mister Bill and Mis' Caroline joined us. It was real nice to finally meet em. They were older than I thought they were goin to be, what with Mis' Caroline's voice soundin so young like over the phone. He was a medium-sized man with a silver crew cut an' eyes the color of a hickory nut. She was real slender, with black hair sprinkled with gray 'round her temples. Her blue eyes an' George's were a close match in the sparkle department. There was a lot of laugh lines 'round her eyes, or maybe squint lines from all thet sailin she talked 'bout doin.

Seemed like we started in talkin like ol' friends, jest like we had over the phone, mostly ignorin the men. It didn't matter a bit though, as Bill was talkin to George 'bout their schedule an' my husband was noddin an' smilin like he was runnin for office.

It was a real nice place to have breakfast, up on a hill, lookin over the city. I thanked Bill for puttin us up in such a nice hotel. "Boeing looks after their people," he said, smilin an' wavin my thanks away. "Besides, we wanted you to see a bit of the old Seattle."

After we ate, George an' Bill went their way an' Mis' Caroline an' I headed for what she called the Seattle Yacht Club. It turned out to be a white, colonial lookin ol' buildin with a fake light house built into it an' lots of green lawn an' tall ol' pine

35

trees with big rhododendrons an' azeleas in full bloom. It was real purty; looked like a movie set what with all the views.

Mis' Caroline said the reason it looked so historic was thet it was built back in 1919. I told her thet didn't seem at all old to me; part of Mammaw an' Pappaw's cabin had cedar logs under it more'n a hundred years older than thet.

Anyway, when we got out of her purty little gold Mercedes, she handed me two canvas pokes. "This is our foul weather gear. You'll be wearing Bill's and they are going to be a little too big; but they should keep you perfectly dry," she said.

I looked at the sky an' didn't see more than a few wispy, wind driven clouds an' wondered how I was supposed to get wet. "It sure doesn't look like rain to me, what with the breeze blowin them clouds away," I said.

Mis' Caroline laughed as she walked 'round to her trunk an' hefted out a wooden paddle. "It won't be the rain, dear," she said. 'It will be the spray. This is a perfectly glorious day for sailing!" Had she been a warbler, I'd say she was jest 'bout at full song. As for me, I jest followed her, tryin to stay calm an' breathe steady as we walked this long dock with sailboats tied up on both sides. We'd gone quite a ways when she stopped, set down the paddle an' spread her arms, "Here we are," she chirped, "and there she is!"

For a heartbeat, I thought she was talkin 'bout a person, but it wasn't. Instead it was this little bitty toy of a boat sittin on the dock next to a whole bunch of other little boats. I judged it to be somewhat short of the length of our station wagon back home. "Mis' Caroline," I said, tryin to keep calm an' hopeful, "are you pullin my leg?"

She turned to smile at me an' must have seen thet I was lookin some spooked. "Why, no, dear, I'm not. We do have a 38-foot Beneteau, called the *Flying Tarpon*, but it's out on Puget Sound at the Shilshole Marina." She pointed towards the horizon as she said them words, hardly a one of 'em I understood. "Besides, it would be way too big for just the two of us to handle."

36

Thet part I got. I looked from where she pointed back to the "toy." There were fancy letters scrolled across its back end thet read:

The Flying Minnow
Seattle, Washington

My heart dropped right down to my tennis shoes. It was clear as the nose on my face thet I was goin to be expected to step right onto thet little boat an' pretend to like it even though it was so skinny if I laid crossways my feet would be danglin off the side. "Well," I finally said, more to myself than to her, "Daddy said there weren't no cowards in the Cable line so I'd best not be the first."

But she heard me. "Really, Marilue, I was serious. This is the sailboat I use to teach the students; some as young as twelve. I'm going to give you the same instructions I give them. By the way, I meant to ask before; do you know how to swim?"

I nodded, lookin 'round. I didn't like one single thang I was seein. It was real hard to believe I was goin out on thet black lookin water in a boat thet didn't have sides more'n 'bout a foot high. "Get me thet life vest you were talkin 'bout, Mis' Caroline Johnston. I'm not settin foot off this walk without somethin to keep me afloat if I manage to sink us by doin somethin stupid."

Mis' Caroline laughed again. "It won't sink, no matter what you do, Marilue. Sometimes sailboats do tip over, but they don't sink," she said as if thet fact was supposed to relieve my mind. "But, before we put her into the water, I need to teach you a few sailing terms and show you how to do several things."

In a way, it heped thet Mis' Caroline threw so many thangs I needed to learn at me. She seemed plumb tickled thet I knew how to tie a knot or two.

"When you got two boys in scoutin, you learn such thangs on table legs," I said when I showed her I knew how to tie a bowline knot an' a square knot usin the long rope tied to the front of thet little boat. A bow line she called thet rope; which was some confusin beins it had nothin to do with the knot I showed her.

37

After thet, she taught me the difference between the bow an' the stern end of a boat an' then once I got thet, she pointed out both the bow line an' the stern line for keepin it tied up. She taught me a real easy knot called a cleat hitch an' told me thet when we came back in, I'd be the one to tie the *Flying Minnow* back to the dock usin jest such a knot.

"Now," she said, "with your help, we will ease her into the water."

I was feelin doubtful, but it wasn't more than we could do. Still, afore we even put on our waterproof gear an' life jackets, my mind was feelin like a bee in a hive. Mis' Caroline said, real cheerful, "Just step to the middle of the boat and keep your weight low, Marilue. I'm going to hold the *Minnow* tight to the edge of the dock while you get settled."

Once I got planted, I watched her operate. She was as sure-footed as a mule, fixin the sail, checkin this, stringin thet, talkin all the while. "I really can do this by myself, Marilue," she said. "But once we're underway and the sail is up, I'm going to be asking you to change sides every now and then. I'll also give you other instructions. For example, when I bring the sail around, I'm going to ask you to duck your head. I'll give you plenty of warning, so please don't worry."

She had us untied an' pushed back in the shake of a lamb's tail. "See," she said, grabbin onto a little handle, "this is the tiller. When I push it left, the *Minnow* turns to starboard, or right. When I pull it right, she turns to port, or left."

Purty soon we were doin what she called "tackin" towards what she called the Montlake Cut. Back home we would have called it a canal. *Marilue Perkins,* I thought to myself, *you jest pay attention an' you'll prolly get out of this alive.* An' jest like a finger snap, we sailed down the little canal an' headed towards the open lake with Mis' Caroline gently pushin an' pullin thet tiller an' the little sailboat followin her lead.

Once we hit the open water in Lake Washington an' the wind filled them sails tighter'n a tick, we started scootin right along. I had my jaw clenched an' was hol'in on so tight I likely left my fingerprints in the wood. Ever once an' awhile Mis' Caroline would tell me to 'hol' on tight an' lean back' like she was doin. Thet little acrobatic act of faith she called "hikin out."

38

I'll tell you, the first time we did thet, I started thankin hard 'bout gettin on airplanes an' drownin in a lake without givin proper thought to leavin my children motherless an' George a widow.

But, I kept on doin what she said an' it didn't take long afore I knew when she was goin to ask me to change sides an' I got real good at dodgin the boom. After a bit, I got the hang of the whole thang an' started to relax a touch. I mean, it was a real different world out there on thet lake with jest the sound of water slappin on the little boat, an' the sound of the seagulls screamin overhead mixin with Mis' Caroline's laughin ever now an' again as we skimmed right along.

Thet night, by the time Bill an' Mis' Caroline had dropped us off at our hotel, we fell into bed without so much as a goodnight kiss, knowin the next day, we would be up an' goin again. Finally, on day three, George put his foot down with Bill at breakfast. He was plumb done in from all the brain work durin the day an' all the fun stuff we were doin at night.

George was callin Mr. Johnston "Bill" by then. They were gettin along real good; too good, if you know what I mean.

"Look here, Bill," he said, "Marilue and I are planin to bow out of this evenin's festivities after we have our drink with you at the Space Needle."

Bill started in protestin, but George was real firm. "It's not that we aren't havin a real good time, Bill, but we want to spend our last evenin here gettin to know the city on our own. So we're goin to opt out of supper and the play to do some explorin."

Mr. Johnston seemed real pleased at thet, thankin it was good we were showin such interest. I had to put my hand over my smile. I knew exactly what was in George's mind, an' it wasn't only explorin a city.

Thet mornin, while we were waitin for the phone to ring-- Bill sayin it was time to come down for breakfast--I saw George sittin on the edge of the big Jacuzzi tub. He had picked up this little packet of bath crystals thet had been on the top of a pile of fluffy white bath towels. "Sure would be nice if we had time to use this stuff," he said, hol'in the packet of "Herbal Essence with

39

moisturizin essential oils and pure sweet almond protein with fig extract" under his nose.

I nodded an' arched an eyebrow the way I do. We looked at each other an' grinned. "You women really goin sailin in this weather?" he asked as the phone rang.

I looked out the window. It was rainin purty hard right then, more like it did in Tennessee than I'd seen so far in Seattle. He sighed, looked at me, the tub, then out at the grayness. Made the room with its soft caramel colored carpet an' puffy peach pillows seem real comfy. I brushed close to him, an' then past, sorta wigglin my rear on my way to answer the phone. "Maybe not, I don't rightly know. I might jest spend the day tucked up in bed."

"Dang!" I heard him mutter real soft, like there was maybe somethin on his mind stead of airplanes.

'Cause, there we were, three days in a fancy hotel room with a movie star-sized, round bathtub, a bed big enough for a family of five an' two dogs with not one minute, night or day, to enjoy it--together I mean. An' we were leavin in the mornin! We were on a 6:00 AM flight an' so planned on takin a taxi straight to Sea-Tac. I had called the youngens ever night, but I was still so danged homesick for 'em it seemed like we hadn't seen each other for months.

Mis' Caroline an' I did go sailin. "What's foul weather gear for if you don't use it for more than stayin dry when you get a little splash on you?" I'd said grinnin at her over the breakfast table.

Turned out, I was startin to get jest as foolish 'bout it as she was. After I got over the part of bein scared peeless an' feelin all thumbs an' fumble-footed, I could see thet there was somethin 'bout cuttin across thet big lake with thet ol' snow-covered Mount Rainier standin like a giant sentinel up on the horizon an' the wind in my face thet had a lightenin effect on my spirit. Mis' Caroline was as fine a teacher as she claimed an' she said I was 'a natural.' I guess I was.

If ever anyone would of told me I be reared over backwards alongside a woman who was at least fifty, a woman who was laughin with pure joy 'cause we had managed to tip thet

40

little boat practically on its side an' were slicin through thet lake at eye-waterin speed, I would NOT have believed it. But thet jest goes to show how much we really don't know ourselves.

"Marilue, I don't know how I could maneuver in the corporate world as well as I do without this outlet," she said then. An', after jest three days, I thought I could see jest what she meant.

By the time we were done with our sail thet last day, the weather had cleared enough for some sun breaks. Afterwards, Mis' Caroline drove me through an arboretum near her house in Madison Park to look at the flowers. It was real purty what with all the different trees an' the spring flowers all in full bloom. I started to wonder what my iris buds were doin back home an it made me so homesick I could hardly act interested when she started to pointin out some of the real nice homes for sale. I looked out, noddin real polite, knowin there was no way on God's green earth we'ns could afford what she was showin me.

After a little, it was like she read my mind. Of a sudden, she said, "Marilue, why don't I take you back to the Sorrento right now? That way you can get a rest before we go to the Space Needle."

I looked at her and sighed real deep. "You are a fine tour guide, Mis' Caroline. I mean thet real sincere. These three days, goin sailin with you, has 'bout saved me. But I reckon I will admit thet at least puttin my feet up fer a spell sounds real good 'bout now."

We said no more, but I was sure she caught my drift. If it come to it, I'd look at houses, but thet was down the road a spell. So thet's what she did, took me back to the hotel. I went through thet purty lobby with all its potted plants an' breath takin views, up the elevator to our suite an' had a nice nap. Then afore Mis' Caroline picked me up, I had a nice shower an' put on my navy blue dress with the "swirly" skirt. I accessorized it with a real purty set of cultured pearl earrings an' a necklace Momma had given me one Christmas, jest like Betty had told me to do.

When we drove up to the Space Needle thet evenin, I still thought it looked unfriendly, but I gotta say thet I was taken by

41

the way you could ride the elevator to the top, lookin out clear glass at the view all the way. Mis' Caroline smiled some at my excitement, but not in a mean way. She liked me, I could tell. Said I was her good luck talisman, thet she hardly ever got such good sailin weather three days in a row in April.

Seemed like I liked her too…a lot. If I'd had a livin sister, I'd have wanted one like her. "The next time you come, we'll nab Bill an' George and we'll take the Beneteau out on the Puget Sound," she said. Like our comin back was a fact of life.

We saw the men an' walked towards where they were sittin. Turns out we were lookin out at the Puget Sound. Mis'Caroline pointed to where the *Flyin Tarpon*, their other boat, was moored. Even though I couldn't see it, the view was somethin else! But I could feel the floor movin under my feet, or at least I thought I could an' it spooked me jest a little. Course I didn't say a thang.

One look at George's face an' I could see he was figurin out the mechanics an' engineerin of the whole deal. I mean, the way the innards of the buildin were makin the restaurant give us a 360° view of the city an' the harbor. But it hadn't even turned full circle afore George an' I started makin our goodbyes. The men shook hands, but Mis' Caroline an' I hugged each other real hard. "Please come back," she whispered in my ear, an' then my husband had me by the arm an' hustled out of there.

He said to our cab driver, "You got any good Southern cookin in this town? Not too fancy?"

Thet colored boy flashed him a grin, showin more teeth than I thought could be fit in a human face. "Yessir! This place I know--down near the container port--isn't even close to bein fancy, but my momma sometimes cooks there an' it's clean. You game?"

We laughed. Somehow it felt like we'd been let out of school. "Take us to it," George said.

Now, we were both thankin fried chicken, mashed potatoes or grits an' gravy. Course there'd be some green beans or fried okra an' some biscuits too. What we got instead was ribs, red beans an' rice, an' gumbo. But then, I reckon Louisiana has got to be called Southern too.

42

I can't tell you how much we enjoyed thet food, though. There wasn't one thang on the menu written in French or sautéed in olive oil an' lemon juice. Not one waiter tried to put a napkin in our laps. George lined up two empty beer bottles afore he even started to eat.

When we were done, it was jest gettin dark. We stood outside the little restaurant an' looked up. Even with all the street lights, you could see the stars. It had turned into a real purty night.

"Can you walk for awhile in those shoes, Marilue?" George asked.

"Sure," I said, lookin down at my little blue suede pumps. "What you got in mind, honey?"

"Well, I think I got the direction to the hotel straight in my head, so I thought we could stretch our legs a little, clear our minds. Let the food settle."

"Sounds good," I said, lockin arms. "If it's farther than we thank or or I get footsore, we can jest take a cab." Shows how dumb I was.

Well, this next part is branded on my brain so clear, I can tell you ever detail. But I won't. I'll jest say thet there aren't the same number of street lights or cabs in ever part of Seattle. An' thet, afore long, we were walkin up a steep hill, mostly by moonlight, the cracks in the sidewalks makin it hard not to trip.

There were broken bottles an' trash everwhere. I had a good grip on George's arm though an' was traipsin along yakkin 'bout my day, like I do. I was right in the middle of tellin him how they sometimes had a beautician at the Yacht Club to fix up the ladies' hair an' even their makeup, after sailin, when it happened.

This big colored man jumped out at us from the shadows, grabbed George 'round the neck, pulled his wrist half way up his backbone an' jerked him so thet I went sprawlin. I got as far back up as my knees, sorta shakin my head, tryin to figure what was goin on, when I saw this skinny blonde woman standin right in front of me, hol'in a knife.

"Don't move, bitch!" She spit the words at me real mean-like, like I was trash.

It was kinda dark to see thangs clear, but I could sure see her an' thet knife. I heard awful gaggin sounds behind me an' I knew it was my George. Then I heard him scream. To my death, I will carry the sound in my heart; it had thet much pain in it. Made me come off the ground like a rocket an' bury my head square in the middle of thet skinny woman's brisket.

I felt somethin give, heard the air whoosh out of her. Then she was droppin like a rock, out of sight, over the edge of this little stair railin behind her. But I wasn't there to see her land. I was clawin my way up the backside of thet big colored man like a mad, wet wildcat. I ended up with one arm 'round HIS throat, the other punchin him wherever I could reach. I even had my teeth busy tryin to gnaw off his ear.

He let go of George then, an' set 'bout tryin to get me off, hollerin an' cussin like a crazy man. The next thang I knew, he'd tripped on some of the bad cement in the sidewalk an' fell straight forward. I rode him all the way to the ground. He slammed, face first, onto thet sidewalk with its cracks an' broken glass. Knocked hisself out plumb col'; driven by 144 pounds of Tennessee fightin woman.

I had some trouble gettin the arm thet was 'round his neck pulled free. Had to take some hide off to get 'er done, but I didn't notice it right then.

"George, honey," I was hollerin, "you okay?"

Now, I reckon you know cities are real noisy places. Not then. Afore it happened we had seen a few people in lighted windows. Not now. Now the windows were empty an' the only thang I could hear was me. Seemed like everthang an' everbody within seein an' hearin distance must have been hidin an' hol'in their breath.

I picked myself up off the ground, feelin some pain in my neck, but it didn't come to me thet I'd been knife cut. I started cussin country style at the lack of light, knowin my husband was right there in some shadder, needin me bad.

I could hear sirens then, but I couldn't hear George. I reckon I said, "George, you sonofabitch, answer me!" jest afore I heard the little moan an' him callin my name real weak-like.

44

You can't know, unless it's happened to you, how the starch goes out when you find thet your man isn't dead after all. Thet's when I started to cry.

Well, thet's 'bout it. By the time the law got to us I was awful shaky. I knew I was bleedin purty bad by then, but I had my George laid out as best I could to protect his hurt arm, my new raincoat folded up under his head. His shoulder was dislocated, I could jest tell by lookin.

Right away there were folks hepin. A man from the emergency van took a look at the slice on my neck an' shook his head. First thang I knew he stuck a needle in my arm. I heard some lawman with a big flashlight whistle real low an' say, "Harry, look here, these folks beat the living shit out of the Madison Street Muggers."

He had turned the man over an' was shinin the light on what was left of his face. An' I heard a deep voice say, "Well then, God bless em."

Thet was the last I saw or heard 'til I woke up in the Harborview Hospital, a genuine heroine, accordin to the newspapers, radio an' T.V. stations.

Seems like some reporter was listenin to a police scanner when the report was called in to dispatch. He made a big deal of the fact thet a housewife from Tennessee captured two of Seattle's most wanted, singlehandedly. Made it sound like I had 'em all hogtied an' ready to hand over when the lawmen come screamin up in their squad cars. Well, thet wasn't at all true, but thet's the press for you.

When I come to myself, a nurse was leanin over me, tellin me I was fine but had lost a lot of blood. Thet explained the needle taped to my arm an' the maroon-colored poke hangin by my bed; they were givin me more blood.

I looked 'round. My room was full of flowers. The nurse said a whole flock of reporters were in the waitin room. George had his arm "relocated" an' tied tight to his side. She said he was out there braggin to people on how I'd saved his life. Course, I thank he got most of what he knew from the law, since it was purty dark an' he was in such terrible pain. But, thet's George. A lot of men would have felt like they were less 'cause their

45

woman come out on top. Not George. I don't reckon thet sort of thought would ever even enter his head.

When the reporters talked to me, I laid the whole thang at the feet of my forbearers who go back in this country more'n 200 years. Asked em, did they know why Tennessee was called the "Volunteer State"? Told 'em it was 'cause our men fought hard in any war called by this country. Told 'em my great, great, great grand mammaw had a letter written by General Grant hisself, thankin her for the lives of seven strong sons. Said thet we had a quilt back home thet told the whole story. Said the good thang 'bout the attack was thet neither of us was done permanent harm an' two real bad pieces of trash were off the street. Said the worst part was thet we'd had to cancel our flight home so we could go down to the lock-up an' identify our attackers, give depositions an' such…an' thet I was really missin our youngens bad. I really was too. Homesickness was hurtin me worse than thet knife slice.

Later on, I kicked myself for tellin thet the letter 'an quilt were in Mammaw an' Pappaw's cabin. Should have known better after jest gettin a first-hand experience on the way some folks behave. I reckon it was jest thet ol' homesickness thet made my tongue wag so. Still, what with Pappaw's hounds an' the rifles over the door, he an' Mammaw weren't exactly defenseless.

I did get some carried away talkin, I will admit. But it is a fact thet my side of the family is uncommon proud of its history. I'm teachin my youngens the old stories, jest like my momma an' daddy taught me. Like I been tellin you, both pride an' roots run deep in our blood.

Seemed like, with us not flyin out for a couple of days, everbody wanted to put us ON the news or IN the news. High school teachers were callin up, askin would I come speak to their students. Daughters of the American Revolution wanted a lecture on the importance of quiltin in pioneer America or some such thang. Mis' Caroline told me a man from the Seattle Yacht Club wanted to name his new sailboat after me. Bill asked me, did I want to turn the whole mess over to Boeing Public Relations. It seemed like a fine idea at the time. It must have been the drugs.

I'm generally not one to want to stand up in front of folks, but thet PR man had George an' me scheduled to go on the television thet same day, with me jest out of the hospital. Then I found out thet he had scheduled some speakin engagements for when we returned in September, promisin folks I would show the now famous quilt.

"George," I said, "What does he mean, 'when we come back in September'?"

George ducked his head. "Honey, they have been puttin a lot of pressure on me, but I haven't promised a blessed thing."

I sighed. He was gettin thet look of misery on his face again. The hand writin was on the wall an' I knew it.

"I know, George," I said. "You thank I've been blind to the fact thet all these well-heeled women have been so special nice to me from the get-go? Not even a twinkle in anyone's eye 'bout the way I talk? You been courted one way, I been courted another."

I paused, thankin on the people we had met. "Now, Mis' Caroline, she's the real deal. I reckon she's jest a naturally kind an' generous woman...but, you wouldn't want to get on the bad side of her. She'd hand you your hat with the top punched in," I said an' saw he was grinnin at me.

"Well, then you make a pair, Marilue. Folks don't want to get too far on the wrong side of you, either." He grinned an' leaned close to kiss me, mindful of his bad arm, an' whispered in my ear, "You go ahead and ask those two muggers if what I say isn't true."

In the one T.V. interview, afore we left the hospital, the cameraman had his camera real close on us. Guess he wanted show folks how George was all strapped up an' where the hide was gone from my arm. He even made the doctor half mad when he asked him to pull the bandages away from my neck so he could show viewers where the knife had made the slice.

The reporter made a big deal of thet slice, the one the hog sticker made as I come under thet skinny woman's arm an' into her brisket with my head. Guess I broke her breast bone an' a rib or two when I thunked her. But truth is, though I got the credit, she knocked her own self out, fallin over into thet stairwell an'

47

hittin her head. I tried to tell 'em thet. Like I said, thet's one thang I learned 'bout the press; they got a deaf side.

"Momma," Billy said over the phone, "we all saw you on the T.V. I've already got you promised for 30 autographs at fifty cents a throw and that's without a bit of advertisin."

Junior got on. "Momma, my Civics teacher says if there were more people like you in this country, we'd all be a lot better off. Oh, and, I almost forgot, our principal asked if you would come and speak at a school assembly. 'Do us all good,' he said."

Vikki Ann was the last to get on the phone. We didn't say much, jest listened to each other sniffle. "I sure love you, honey," I finally got out.

"Me too, Momma," she answered so soft I could barely hear. Daughters are such a comfort.

When George an' I finally got on thet 727, you'd thought we were plumb crippled the way the United Airlines folks come rushin up to hep. Treated us like we'ns were royalty; nothin was too good for us. Got asked for my autograph a whole bunch of times an' so did George, though he had to decline 'count of his writin hand bein strapped down.

It's a wonder I didn't get the big head, what with thet PR man tellin us he was organizin the Marilue Perkins fan club after takin my picture with the airplane behind us. He took pictures of me, then of George, then both of us together. "Course, thet airplane was made by the Boeing Company.

As we settled in our seats, I found I wasn't a bit nervous. Felt like I was real different from the Marilue Perkins of a week ago, flyin west with her knees knockin, but I really wasn't.

"George, honey," I whispered into his ear, "only one thang makes me sad 'bout this whole business."

He looked at me, puzzled for a second, 'til I gave him 'the look" an' lifted an eyebrow. Then he started to grin. He knew exactly what I was thankin. "I know. Me too," he whispered back. "But look here, Marilue."

48

He slipped his hand inside his suit jacket an' pulled up the packet of Herbal Essence with his left hand. "I reckon our own bathtub will just have to do," he said.

CHAPTER FIVE
MAY

Jest like George an' I tol' the youngens afore goin' out to Seattle, we would decide together as a family whether to go or not. To their credit, our youngens wanted their daddy to get his chance. We sat 'round the dinin room table thet night an' George told 'em 'bout the Boeing Company, how much he liked the folks he met an' how much our weather was like theirs. He was still some excited.

"What is it exactly that they want you to do, Daddy?" Junior asked when he could get a word in.

"Well, they didn't exactly have a job description written for me yet, son. But they showed me a couple of things they've been workin on in their research and development department; top secret things--I had to sign a confidentiality form before they could even let me see." He looked 'round the table at our youngens, his blue eyes shinin an' happiness sorta bubblin out of him. I looked over at Vikki Ann an' her eyes were glued on him, her face solemn as a country judge.

"In fact, what they are workin on makes that gizmo I designed for Andy look like kindergarten work. Still, they think I can be of use in helpin see other ways to approach some of the problems they are havin."

He sat back in his chair an' pushed away his plate with his left hand, his right arm bein still strapped to his side on count of the stretched tendons needin their own time to mend. He hadn't even finished the piece of the chess pie I'd taken the

50

trouble to make. I saw our children noticin too an' I reckon thet's when they knew how much their daddy wanted this job. When the vote come, we all voted for George's dream; Vikki Ann's hand bein the last an' slowest to go up.

Turns out afterwards thet it was somethin our heads knew, but our hearts didn't. So, it seemed natural to me thet there were such heavy rains, off an' on, for most of the month of May. They matched the gray mood of everbody in the Perkins family jest fine. Everbody 'cept George, thet is. For 'bout two weeks, George was flyin kite-high. Kite-high-- 'til he got the contract to sign.

Last thang Mr. Johnston had told him thet night at the Space Needle, when they were shakin hands, was thet the Boeing Company would be makin him an offer. The last thang George said to Mr. Johnston was, "If the offer is good enough, my family and I will sure consider it." As far as George was concerned, the deal was all but done, should the youngens vote with him.

Now, our youngens an' I were workin hard to be happy for him. We laughed at his jokes an' listened to all his airplane talk 'round the supper table, but the not knowin whether we were really movin out to Seattle was givin us fits.

It could a been worse for Junior an' me I reckon; what with him gettin ready to graduate an' presents comin in steady-- an' me, the "local celebrity," gettin my picture in the paper, talkin at the high school assembly an' all thet other folderol. So what I'm sayin here is thet Junior an' I were some distracted at first.

Right away, it was Billy an' Vikki Ann thet showed the strain most--Billy bein sensitive in the first place an' peevish in the second on count of all the rained-out ball games. He started takin it out on his little sister. Teasin, hittin, thet sort of stuff he was way too old to be doin.

When my daughter wasn't actin' like a two-year-old, cryin an' complainin, she was bein real quiet. Spent more an' more time up in the ol' black walnut tree in the front yard, her baby quilt wrapped tight 'round her for comfort.

51

The day George took a nose dive back to earth I was in the kitchen rollin out bakin powder biscuit dough an' watchin from the sink window while Vikki Ann climbed higher an' higher in the walnut tree. I could barely see the yellow of her rain coat in the thick leaves. Thet's when George come pilin through the swingin door wavin this thick pile of contract paper with his good hand.

"Hell's bells, Marilue, you know I'm not dumb, but I can't make heads or tails of this 'terms of employment' stuff.' Seems like what they're sayin is anythin I invent, even on my own time, while workin for 'em is theirs lock, stock, and barrel."

He held the fistful of papers up under my nose, like I was supposed to drop everthang an' sort thangs out for him right then an' threre. I was wearin my, "MAMA AIN'T HAPPY, AIN'T NOBODY HAPPY!" sweatshirt, which should of told him what sort of mood I was in to start with. But, he didn't notice. *Wasn't much he IS noticin these days, bein up there in the clouds with his airplanes,* I thought.

"George, honey," I said, my voice drippin with acid-laced sugar, "kindly don't wave thet small print in my face while I'm tryin to roll out biscuits for supper."

I grabbed his wrist with my floured-up fingers like it was some sort of crawly bug an' moved his arm real firm to one side. I was glarin. He finally glanced down to what I was wearin an' right quick backed up a step, looked at me hard then sighed real deep an' frustrated.

"Sorry, Marilue," he said. "Maybe you could take a look at it later."

He turned an' walked, all slump-shouldered, out of the kitchen. I didn't say a word to stop him. I was lookin out the window at Vikki Ann again. Now, all I could see among them beautiful new leaves was her yellow rubber rain boots an' the rag tag ends of the quilt hangin down.

Rain kept on fallin steady. Meant I still couldn't take the Rototiller to my garden for prolly what was goin to be the last time. Meant Billy's ball game had gotten called off again. Meant thet Junior couldn't pick him up after his part time job at the Alcoa plant.

52

There was a frozen spot in my stomach 'bout the size of one of them baseball-sized hailstones we sometimes have here in Tennessee. Seemed like my husband was askin way too much, wantin me to hep him understand pieces of paper thet likely would be the cause of us all movin clean across the country. Seemed like everbody was needin chunks of me all of a sudden. Seemed like I wanted to trade places with thet ol' walnut tree. Nobody was ever goin to ask it to pull its 150-year-old Tennessee roots up an' move clean across the country.

I washed the flour off my hands, grabbed my ol' raincoat from the rack an' headed out the kitchen door. "Vikki Ann, honey," I called up into the tree, "I've got to run get Billy. Would you come cut the biscuits an' put 'em in the oven?"

"Sure, Momma. I was comin in anyhow," she answered. I was struck by how sad-toned both our voices were. I waited 'til she had unwrapped hersef from thet soggy, ol' quilt an' pulled it after her as she scrambled down. Then I grabbed her in for a hug.

"Thank you, darlin," I said. "Mind you don't forget to put Quiltie in the dryer."

She looked at me with them iris-colored eyes so much like my moma's an' my own. "I won't, Momma," she said. "Anythin else you want me to do?"

I smiled, put my hand under her chin an' kissed her wet cheek. She didn't taste like sweet Tennessee rain though. She tasted like tears. "Jest the table like usual. An' don't bother your daddy unless you need him. He's tryin to figure out some paperwork."

I hugged her again, Quiltie an' all. "You are such a blessin," I whispered in her ear.

Thet night it was like eatin supper at the morgue. Thangs were thet quiet. I'd given Billy a terrible scoldin on the way home in the car. Told him if he said or did one more mean thang to Vikki Ann, I'd give him a lickin, fifteen years old or not. I meant it too. Shows how I wasn't myself. I knew on my inside thet he was jest showin the signs of how cranky an' blue the rest of us were feelin. It was jest lucky I didn't give him the laughin fits like he sometimes gets when he's too tense.

53

When we got home, he jumped out of the station wagon an' went to his room without a word. Showed up for supper, not lookin at me, but right on time. Junior wasn't though. He come in 'bout half way through the meal.

"Sorry, Momma," he said as he slipped into his chair, chin ducked so none of us would notice thet he was lookin like a beat hound. I wondered if he an' Bonnie had finally called it quits. He'd hinted thet it was likely. His troubles made all three of my children down in the dumps. Seemed like on top of my own sadness, theirs was crushin the life right out of me.

When George said the blessin his voice was real low. I looked hard at him. *Welcome to the cellar with the rest of us,* I thought, feelin real righteous. Felt like thet ice ball had moved right up into my chest. Then, as I watched him tryin to manage his fork with his left han', his head down, his shoulders slumped, even though I didn't want it to, the thought come to me, *after his family, there isn't a thang George loves more than inventin. He likes it even better than fishin an' he's a fishin fool. No wonder he is so upset by thet contract.* My sigh come out of nowhere, an' clean up from my toes. He hadn't looked at me once durin the whole meal. Enough was enough!

I'd read in one of my woman's magazines 'bout it bein like an elephant in the room when folks didn't talk 'bout thangs thet was botherin em. Well, it felt like this elephant was sittin in the middle of our dinin room table an' the whole Perkins family was jest plain ignorin it.

I put down my knife an' fork. "I haven't seen this family so blue since Pepper died," I said real soft an' quiet. The youngens all stopped chewin an' looked at me--but not George. He keep right on eatin, one left handed forkful after another, too steady to be real.

I sighed again, took a sip of sweet tea an' leaned back in my chair. "Only this doesn't feel like sadness altogether. It feels all mixed up."

Everbody started lookin interested—'cept George. He jest kept on chewin like he hadn't heard.

"What exactly do you mean, Momma?" Billy finally asked, breakin the silence he'd kept since his scoldin.

54

"Well, I'm not sure, honey. I reckon I'm thankin thet this time, instead of jest bein straight sad, like we were when ol' Pepper died, some of us are sad/mad...or mad/sad. Maybe some of us are mad thet others of us are sad. Maybe it's the other way. Or maybe it isn't thet at all."

My voice wilted away in my throat. I wasn't makin sense even to me. Vikki Ann looked at me, her hands flat on the table beside her plate, rubbin the table cloth back an' forth.

"Are you sad, Momma?" she asked, like she really needed bad to know.

I took a deep breath an' looked at her. "Honey, one second I'm feelin one thang, the next second I'm feelin somethin else. I got thet many feelins bumpin 'round on my insides. Sometimes, when I thank of maybe leavin Tennessee I get real sad an' start feelin some sorry for myself."

She nodded, eyes glued to my face. I gave her a puny smile an' shook my head. "Then I get real mad, mostly at myself, but sometimes, even though it isn't fair, at your daddy. Thet's generally when I recollect we come to the agreement to go, all of us, sittin right here. So then it feels like I'm lettin your daddy down, like I'm bein a selfish, scaredy cat. Don't mean to be. But thet's the truth."

Billy let out his own deep sigh. "Reckon we know what you mean, Momma," he said.

I looked at the top of George's head, like I was memorizin the shape of his bald spot then closed my eyes an' thought how to tell 'em more of what was in my heart.

"I do believe the decision we all come to was right. Your daddy should have a chance to spread his wings. Everbody on this earth should get the chance to use the gifts the good Lord gave em."

The boys looked real serious. George wasn't chewin any more. Had put his fork down an' was lookin straight at me. Then he looked 'round the table at our children afore lookin back at me.

"Well..." he said. Then he cleared his throat like he does. "Well," he said again, "thank you for that, Marilue. There's no way of knowin how this whole thing with Boeing is goin to turn

55

out after all. I thought it was mostly a done deal, but right now it isn't lookin so good."

He paused an' nodded a sad little smile at me, then 'round the table at the youngens again. "Or it isn't lookin so bad, dependin on your point of view."

"What happened, Daddy?" Junior sounded worried. Looked like he'd made up his mind 'bout not attendin the University of Tennessee an' was ready to go. *Prolly a whole country between Bonnie an' him seems jest 'bout right,* I thought. Course, at the time I was jest makin all thet stuff up, like I do, thankin I know my youngens inside an' out.

George didn't look at him though, he looked at me. "I called Mr. Johnston while you were pickin up Billy. It seems like that part of the contract I told you 'bout is standard. No inventin things on the side. If you're workin for Boeing, you're supposed to be a company man. If you invent somethin, even if you do it on your own time, they own it."

Junior whistled. "That means all the doohickeys you keep on tinkerin with out in the garage would belong to them?"

George nodded. "Workin in Seattle they would."

Junior, our tightwad, didn't like the sound of thet one bit. "Why, Daddy, that doesn't sound fair at all. What if you invented somethin worth a bundle of money that had nothin to do with airplanes?"

"That was my first thought too, son. But it isn't really a matter of money. Mr. Johnston said it's a matter of 'cre-a-tiv-i-ty.' If they hire an 'in-no-va-tive genius,' they want all his brain cells thinkin 'bout airplane things. I can still keep on tinkerin on things in the garage, but I 'have no financial rights to them.'"

His voice was sad, maybe even a little bitter soundin. He smiled like the joke was on him. "It's why they offered me almost three times what I'm makin here, Mr. Johnston said."

I noticed George wasn't callin Mr. Johnston, "Bill" anymore. It made me double sad.

"It's a lot of money, but I have to decide if it's worth enough to this family, for me to give up all those crazy notions on how to make things work better. I don't know that I have it in me to be a straight company man. I sure do like thinkin that I might come up with somethin someday that would put us all on

56

easy street and maybe do some good in this world at the same time."

Junior had gotten his glassy-eyed look when his daddy had talked 'bout the big bucks. His head was doin calculations. He whistled again. "It seems like before long we'd be on easy street anyhow, Daddy. You wouldn't have to invent somethin to make us all rich. We'd BE rich!"

George nodded. "Yes," he said, "what with the way your momma manages money, seems that would soon be so."

We were all quiet for a bit. Then Billy said, "You know, Daddy, my baseball coach is always sayin, 'You play for me, you walk, talk, eat, think, read and dream baseball. I don't want players who aren't dedicated.' That's what Mr. Johnston is sayin too, isn't it?"

George shook his head. "It isn't Mr. Johnston, Billy. It's company policy, no exceptions and no compromises. The fact is, Mr. Johnston sounded real sad 'bout it. He said he'd talk to the top brass but he didn't hold out much hope. He also said he'd be real disappointed if I decided against this job because of those contract words. He even said again how the company needed new blood like mine."

He looked 'round the table. "He said they needed people like your momma too."

He smiled at me then. "His wife, who I guess is real picky 'bout her friends, said your momma was 'courageous and a breath of fresh air.'"

Vikki Ann spoke up, real proud-like. "Everbody likes Momma."

I smiled at her, but my mind was gallopin. Sounded like we maybe weren't goin out to Seattle after all. I was waitin for the gladnesss I expected to feel. But it didn't come. Instead, them col', sad, mad, scared feelins jumpin 'round on my insides left me jest like thet. I had this giant suckin feelin come through my body. It was like them deep tied ol' roots of mine had jest popped free of the top soil an' I was filled plumb up with righteous indignation.

"George Everett Perkins," I said, feelin it so hard my voice wobbled, "this isn't 'bout money."

57

I shot Junior a "keep your mouth shut" look. "This family didn't vote to go to Seattle jest so we could get rich. We voted to go so you could make full use of the special inventin talent God gave you. Best you be thankin on thet. Thet company might not be the one for you. If this one can't bend enough to give you what you want, find one thet can. Find one thet will give you a job where you can use thet brain of yours AN' doesn't care if you invent somethang thet makes us rich on the side. We're people, not trees. We can pull up stakes an' go anywhere. It doesn't gotta be Seattle."

I leaned back an' folded my arms across my chest. "But no matter what, this family is goin to stick together. Isn't a blessed thang in the world can't be solved if we are all workin on it together."

I looked 'round the table, which was easy to do since thet ol' elephant had taken his leave. Our children were lookin at their daddy an' noddin their heads.

I can't say thet the talk 'round the table thet night cured thangs, but it did hep some. Felt like nobody was playin pretend anymore. The rain kept fallin off an' on. Vikki Ann kept climbin the walnut tree. Only now, sometimes Billy joined her.

Junior finally told me Bonnie was wearin the letterman's jacket of the football team captain. George told Mr. Johnston he reckoned he'd have to take a pass on becomin a company man. Andy was tickled half to death. Thangs seemed to be gettin back to normal at the Perkins house.

A week later the phone rang. "Marilue, this is Caroline Johnston."

I was plumb happy to hear her voice. "Why, Mis' Caroline," I said, "How are you doin? It's sure good to hear your voice. An' thanks a heap for sendin thet picture of me an' the *Minnow*. I got it on the fridge."

She'd called once afore to see how George's shoulder an' my cut an' scrapes were healin. So, I expected this was another one of them friendly calls an' was gettin set to tell her the stitches were out of my neck but George's shoulder was bein real slow to heal on count of the torn tendons, but she set me straight real fast.

58

"Marilue, I'm fine, but this isn't really just a social call," she said. "Last night, Bill told me George had declined to work for Boeing. Then he told me why. Well, I told him I didn't blame George one bit, and that if Boeing wanted to survive this century, they'd better stop trying to make workhorses out of thoroughbreds!"

Well, she lost me there. I could tell she was some distressed we'ns weren't comin an' for some reason, thet was quite a comfort.

"Whoa, Mis' Caroline," I laughed. "Slow down. I kinda lost your drift."

I could picture her in my mind's eye, gettin her purty black hair with its streaks of gray, touched up after sailin, laughin, complimentin me on how fast I had caught onto thangs. For two such different women, we'd had a real good time together.

"Marilue, what I'm saying is: Boeing doesn't deserve George. They say they are looking for unconventional thinkers. Then they find one and want to put a harness on him and turn him into a workhorse."

I finally caught her drift an' a lump come into my throat. Seemed she did truly understand what made my husband tick.

"Why, thank you, Mis' Caroline. I'll pass your words on to George. He was some disappointed with the whole..."

She interrupted me then; something I hardly ever heard her do in the time we were together. "I want you to do more than that, Marilue! Listen! This morning I had the very best idea in the world! It has to do with your husband working with my younger brother, Louis."

I gripped the phone real hard, tryin to follow her on this "best idea in the world" thang.

"You see," she said, "ten years ago my younger brother, who lives on the other side of Lake Washington from us, organized a group of associates into what he calls a 'working man's think tank.' Since then, he has attracted a few special minds from around the country. Not everybody in the company can invent, but everyone who works with him can grasp a problem and find a solution. They work independently, but share as a team."

59

"Are you thankin my George has thet sort of mind?" I asked.

"Yes, indeed I am," she said. "I've already called Louis. I told him what I knew 'bout George. He called Bill as soon as we finished. Bill backed every word I said and told Louis he would be glad to give George a recommendation. Now, here's the reason I'm calling you--Louis plans to call George tonight at seven o'clock your time."

"Why, Mis' Caroline Johnston," I said sorta thunderstruck, "what a kind thang you have done. I don't know how we can ever begin to thank you."

She laughed thet real happy, satisfied-with-life laugh she has an' said, "I suppose we shouldn't get our hopes up, Marilue. But you just make sure your husband is within phone reach tonight. I need my sailing partner back!"

"Yes," I said. "I sure will. An' I won't say a thang to him in the meantime. I reckon he might like to hear thet sort of talk straight from the horse's mouth."

She laughed. "A thoroughbred's mouth at that, Marilue. I believe George and Louis are really going to like each other."

I was plumb tickled thet she got my joke. "Thank you again, Mis' Caroline," I said. "You are the best friend a body could have."

"My pleasure, dear! And you know the feeling is mutual. Goodbye now."

I was grinnin like a fool when we hung up an' thet surprised me some. I looked at my watch. *Only three o'clock-- time enough to fix somethin a little extra special for supper*, I thought, rememberin the catfish I had thawin. George an' the boys had caught quite a mess of 'em over by Knoxville, on Douglas Lake—which was really a reservoir built by the Tennessee Valley Authority back in the '30s.

I pulled out the recipe I'd wiggled out of Suzy down at Aubrey's Restaurant, an' thet night, after we'd finished a supper of peanut-crusted catfish fingers with hush puppies an' were startin on a pie, fresh made from some peaches I'd canned in the fall, the phone rang.

"Would you mind gettin thet, honey?" I said right quick to George, jest as calm as could be. He looked a little puzzled

60

thet I hadn't asked one of our three youngens, but got right up an' went to answer it.

Course, since the phone is right round the corner from the dinin room, all of us heard his end of the conversation. It was a true pleasure to hear the life come back into his voice.

We heard him say, "Is that a fact?" Then after a pause he said, "Well, isn't that nice? I sure liked him too."

Thangs were quiet for awhile after thet. Finally, George said, "Why, yes, I believe I would be."

By then, I was grinnin like a fool again an' the youngens were all lookin at me plumb puzzled. "What's goin on, Momma?" Junior whispered.

"It's your daddy's to tell. Jest you wait 'til he gets back to the table."

We could hear George make his goodbyes an' hang up the phone. Seemed like a long time afore he come back to his chair. Even then, he didn't say a word; jest looked at all of us, blinkin his purty blue eyes.

"Daddy, are you all right?" Vikki Ann finally asked in a worried voice.

Thet roused him. "Well, yes. I believe I am, Vikki Ann." Then he grinned an' shook his head. "Did you know," he said with pure hope singin in his voice, "that they have places where a man can work on inventin things all day long? Only they don't call it inventin, they call it 'problem solvin,' and they don't care diddly squat what a man does on his own time."

The youngens shook their heads. "Well, your momma knows 'bout it. Her friend, Mis' Caroline, told her this mornin. But what she doesn't know is that in a couple of days, a fellow from such a place is flyin to Florida--but he's stoppin here, comin in to our very own McGhee Tyson Airport to tell me more 'bout such a job."

61

CHAPTER SIX
JUNE

When George brought Mis' Caroline's brother, Louis, in from the airport, I sorta looked at him with the fish eye. He didn't look a thang like her, what with his tallness, horn-rimmed glasses, long tangled curls an' bell bottom pants. But he wasn't much interested in the rest of us anyhow; he was zeroed in on George. Even as they come in the house an' headed to the garage after introductions, he was pepperin George with questions I didn't begin to understand—stuff 'bout ratios, tolerances, tensile strength an' such. But George seemed real calm, took his time thankin afore answerin. I did notice thet Louis didn't seem put-off by thet slowness one little bit.

I hardly got 'em back in the house in time for Louis to have a bite of my fresh-made double apple pie with corn meal crust afore George an' he were off for the airport again. He said he sure liked my pie an' I reckon he did, the way he went at it. But then, everthang Louis did was fast. I'd noticed thet when we were out west; folks talked an' moved a whole lot faster than what I was used to.

Thet night, supper was plumb interestin. George was real hopeful 'bout this new deal, we'ns could tell. "Louis said companies contracted for their engineerin team to come up with solutions to what look like unsolvable problems. Not everyone who works for him works together all the time. He pulls the folks he needs from what he called his 'talent pool,' if he thinks that

62

person has got what it takes to get the job done." He looked 'round the table, wavin his piece of corn bread. "Louis said their best customers were the big ones like Boeing. Turns out, they pay real well." There was satisfaction in his voice. I could hear it.

"Means I'll be travelin some." He looked at us. "Fact is, I got to go out to Seattle in two days and meet the rest of the team. They don't like me, the deal is off."

I took a deep breath. "Well, them not likin you might happen when hell freezes over, George Everett Perkins. Even Andy says you got a way of gettin everbody on the same side of an idea."

"Everbody likes Daddy," Vikki Ann added. Thet girl was sure one loyal child!

After Louis's visit with George, seems like thangs started happenin real fast. Junior got graduated an' school was over for the summer. I put George back on the airplane, takin his hopes an' dreams out west one more time.

Then the next day, Vikki Ann an' I headed on out to pick up Momma an' Daddy in Pigeon Forge. All four of us were gonna visit with Mammaw an' Pappaw Campbell in the foothills of Mount Le Conte in the Great Smokey Mountains. It's where my kin have lived since 'round the time Scottish folks migrated to the area in the 1700s.

Some of the old families got moved off their land when it was made into a national park, but thet didn't happen to us. Partly I reckon 'cause we were jest barely inside the park boundary an' they didn't have any hikin trails wantin to be cut through our land. Never mind thet our deed to the land went way back afore Tennessee become a state, the government would of taken it, had they wanted to--jest like they did with Daddy's kin in Blount County.

For now, at least, the government agreed to leave us be so long as we kept the land in the family an' didn't do other than farm it. They didn't care 'bout Pappaw's carvin, thank the Lord. Nowadays, his little monthly social security check was the only cash comin in steady. But with that an' the occasional money for his carvins, the sellin of hound pups an' jars of honey, they got by jest fine.

Vikki Ann, Momma an' I had a special reason for wantin to visit our grandfolks. We women were gettin set to stitch Junior's graduation quilt together an' do a little gossipin like women will do 'round a quiltin frame. I already had the stitchin pattern chalked on.

When George an' I were sittin at the airport waitin for his flight to be called, I said, "I owe this visit with Mammaw an' Pappaw Joe to myself, honey." It was sorta my excuse for goin to visit without him.

Thangs hadn't always been easy between Pappaw an' George jest 'cause George was originally from Atlanta, Georgia. It didn't matter thet his folks had moved to Maryville 'bout the time mine had. Pappaw had a hard time forgivin him for marryin a granddaughter of his without bein "mountain-born."

When we would visit, he'd treat my husband like he was all but the invisible man, not talkin to him straight on, not callin him by name, sayin instead, "Thet feller you'n is married to had best be treatin you proper," an' stuff like thet.

But thet was all in the past. Seemed like after Junior, whose baptized name was George Joseph Perkins, was born an' layin on Pappaw's knees, all fancied up in a little outfit Momma had crocheted an' wrapped in a baby quilt Mammaw had made all by hersef, he lost them crochety feelins.

I still can recollect the day Pappaw forgot hisself enough to talk to George. He looked up at George, who was standin there right beside him on thet mountain cabin porch an' lookin down at his son real proud-like. Pappaw said to him then, "By dad gum, hain't he somthin, George? Looks, jest like a Campbell, don't he?"

"Yes," George said, smooth as silk, "I believe I can see that he looks a little like you."

"Well...," Pappaw said then, "I reckon, after I git done a lookin at this h'yar wonder, we'uns had better han' him off to his momma an' have us'ns a sip of my finest to celebrate, son. What'd you'n be say'n to thet?" An' thet was the end of it. None of us ever heard anythang but kindness come out of his mouth towards George ever again.

64

Momma an' I always wondered if Mammaw Ada had had a hand in it, or if he had come to forgivin George on his own, but we never said a word to either of em. Some questions are best left unasked.

George an' I had been passin the time at the airport while we were waitin for his airplane, by talkin 'bout little thangs, prolly to keep from talkin 'bout the big thangs left unsaid between us. He smiled at me real tender after I told him I owed myself a trip to the mountain. "I reckon you do," he said. He touched the scar on my neck. "Be just what the doctor ordered. Reckon your sons and fans can live without you for a most of a week?"

He was pokin a little fun at me, but I nodded real serious like, ignorin the "fans" part. Vikki Ann an' I were takin our sleepin bags in the back of the wagon. We were pickin up my folks an' then we'd all be stayin with Mammaw an' Pappaw an' get the quilt done; Momma an' Daddy in their spare bed an' Vikki Ann an' I sleepin in the back of the wagon.

But there was jest no way the boys could come to the mountain with Vikki Ann an' me, much as they wanted to. Junior was workin the day shift, an' some overtime too, at the Alcoa aluminum plant. Billy was up to his ears in a fancy baseball camp thet was by invitation only an' still doin his part-time work. Wasn't any way they could shake loose. "Be good for em," I said. "Besides, Billy has got to walk Mis' Adel's dog 'til Vikki Ann gets home."

After our neighbor, Mis' Adel, had been knocked down an' her leg broken by her crazy Irish Setter, Hattie, she had finally admitted the dog was some hard to handle an' hired our girl to walk the dog an' teach her some manners; stuff Vikki Ann had learned from her great pappaw, Joe. Folks'ud tell you he had the best mannered hounds in the Smokies, even though he couldn't hunt in the park; had to haul 'em outside the park boundary in his ol' truck to even hunt a coon.

I looked at George, real close. "You still feelin okay 'bout lettin Junior use the truck while we are gone?"

He scratched his head like he does; only usin his left hand, bein his right arm was unstrapped but still purty sore. "This

65

same boy was feelin grown up and responsible enough to get married a few months back. I reckon our truck is in good hands."

He grinned. "Anyway, I guess I told him the drivin rules enough times that he'll remember them."

I laughed, "Shoot! I'm guessin all of us know them rules by heart." I held up my fingers an' started tickin 'em off jest to pass the time:

1. Besides church, drive to work an' back, period.
2. Only stops: the grocery store, the gas station an' the baseball field.
3. Only passenger, Billy.
4. At work, park it in a safe place.
5. At home, put it in the garage.

They were callin George's flight jest as I finished recitin. I hugged him, havin a care for his arm. "'bout goin to the mountains," I said, "I promised the boys we'd go again afore we left."

George got real serious then. "As a whole family next time, honey."

I nodded an' said, "You be safe, you hear? Don't go walkin in strange places." I smiled as best I could, but I meant what I said.

He nodded. "Tell Vikki Ann not to be gettin fleas from all those hound dogs."

Thet made me smile a little. Vikki Ann was plumb foolish 'bout Pappaw's bluetick hounds. Our Pepper had come from him. "I'll tell her," I said an' turned real quick so I didn't have to see him get on thet airplane without me.

The next day, Vikki Ann an' I left real early. It wasn't so hot we couldn't leave the air-conditionin off an' roll down our windows. We put one of Dolly's cassettes in the wagon's tape deck an' listened to "My Tennessee Home" 'bout five times; her pushin the rewind button, me concentratin on gettin us through Maryville an' headin for Pigeon Forge.

I was double glad to be goin. I hadn't liked sleepin alone in our bed a bit! Couldn't even recollect the last time it had

66

happened, 'cept for when I was in the hospital havin our babies an' then the hospital in Seattle, if you wanted to count thet. Seemed like thangs were changin way too fast 'round our house. I was lookin forward to goin to a place thet never changed much at all.

Vikki Ann an' I picked up Momma an' Daddy an' dusted our way through Gatlinburg, turned right onto U.S. 441, headin south towards Mount LeConte. Daddy started grumblin beside me. "Lookit all 'em tourist traps, Marilue! Lookit all this traffic! A body can't hardly go no place but what you run into some folkses' elbow. We'uns are a gittin like sardines in a can!

He had a point. Pigeon Forge was still growin like a weed. What used to be wheat fields was now shoppin centers. Farmland was still bein bought out an' strip malls an' strangers movin in. Traffic in town had been bumper to bumper. When I lived there as a girl, all thet terrible growth was jest fixin to happen. In 1964, cause of the Smokies, U.S. Highway 441 was improved an' designated for "tourist use." The handwritin was on the wall clear back then.

"It sure does seem crowded for May, Daddy." I said. "You would thank the through hikers would want to shy clear of the rain an' the col'--day hikers too, come to thank of it.

"I'll tell you, little girl, all them tourists is enough to give a man the frights, drivin so dingle-dang fast an' parkin ever which where. Sure didn't use to be like this. Now there's rumors a goin 'round thet somebody's puttin in a big shoppin mall."

I looked over at him. He was starin at his hands, lookin glum as a preacher with an empty church. "It's them Herschend Brothers," he said. "Them's the ones thet come over from Branson; turned the ol' Gold Rush Amusement Park into Silver Dollar City. Already, you cain't put your eyes on thet parkin lot an' not see more cars than a body can count; most from outta state. Them boys'll be behind a shoppin mall, an' thet's a fact!"

"Now, Daddy, it's not like you to be listenin to rumors," I said.

He sighed. "I wisht they was. But I got me a feelin 'bout this. Thangs is a changin an' I'm a gettin too ol' to change with em. I liked it fine the way hit was."

Vikki Ann was tucked into her Mammaw Mildred's arm in the back seat. She took Daddy's bait. "How'd it used to be in the ol' days, Pappaw John?" Like she hadn't heard the stories a million times afore. I could of stopped the car an' kissed her! Nothin my daddy liked more than talkin 'bout the Smokies afore they become a park.

"When I was a boy, couldn't go a mile without scarin up a bear, deer, squirrel, turkey or somethin else fine for the stew pot. They was even an elk or two left. Couldn't put your line in a branch without some fish or other grabbin aholt your worm." He paused an' looked over his shoulder at her. "Course, the cottonmouths was awful bad along the water, a feller had to be real careful."

I looked over at him. His eyes had thet faraway look, rememberin...some of it truthful an' some of it stretched out like half-pulled taffy. "Yep, a boy had to be some careful...unless they was a lot of king snakes thet year. Them king snakes make a habit of killin poisonous snakes. The venom don't seem to bother 'em a'tall. My daddy an' your Pappaw Joe, never let no one harm a king snake on their propity." He turned an' looked at her again. "Didn't let a black snake be harmed either. They was better'n a cat at keepin varmints out of the corn crib."

Daddy's family was all mountainfolk on both sides too. They didn't maybe have our history, what with thet letter from President Grant, but jest like Momma's kin, the southern Appalachians held a lot of Cable family bones 'round Cade's Cove where they lived 'til the Park Service moved 'em off the land.

I looked out the window. Daddy was sure right 'bout the people. Seemed like the closer we got to Mount Le Conte, the more campers an' hikers we saw. But, if I looked out an' up into the foothills, seemed like rhododendrons an' azaleas were splashin purple, pink, yellow, orange an' white everwhere. We were gettin the best of the Smokies. A light fog was driftin in the hollers makin the mountains look real soft an' blue.

It got even better after we left the highway an' started across farmland on a little gravel road. A sign on the highway, put up by the Park Service, had said, "Private! No trespassing!" It looked real official, but we knew it didn't mean us.

On we went, uphill out of the bottom land. As the trees started closin in 'round us, I started seein the scarlet of red bud an' the purple of chickory, but I liked the white splash of a dogwood tree light'n up the woods with its star-shaped flower best. I can't tell you how soothin it all was…sorta like a sore throat feels when you sip on lemon juice with honey in it.

Ever now an' again we'd rumble over some little, bumpy bridge, the water beneath, rushin towards La Conte Creek like it had bees in its britches. Everbody was lookin. Nobody was talkin. I looked in the rear view mirror at Vikki Ann. She was snuggled up against her mammaw lookin out the window of the wagon, more at peace than I'd seen her since the whole thang with George's new job had come up. Momma was smoothin her hair like she was pettin a pup an' ever once in awhile she'd plant a kiss on top of her head, jest like she used to do me.

We hit a little fog-filled holler an' the road got narrower an' rougher. I had to start payin close attention an' stop gawkin. No way I wanted to high center our Impala wagon or worse, slip a wheel off the track. Was no way I wanted Pappaw Joe to have to hook up his ol' mules to come an' rescue me.

"You are a 'comin up to the turn-off," Daddy said, like I didn't know it.

I shifted down to low an' pulled real easy onto the track leadin to the cabin. It was steep an' rutted like always.

"Afore we leave, Daddy, you'd best thank 'bout hepin Pappaw hitch the mules an' drag this thang," I said, after I'd bottomed out for the third time. He didn't say a word; he was watchin my drivin like a hawk.

When we come out of the trees, sunlight soothed us like a blessin. We could see the cabin up ahead then, its hand-hewn timbers bleached to silver, its chestnut logs older than anyone could recollect. We could hear the hounds start in to bayin an' my heart started in to singin at the normalness of it all.

I looked at thet cleared holler thet had been farmed by my kin for mite near two hundred years like I was starvin an' lookin at supper, memorizin ever detail to take with me to Seattle, I was thet sure we were goin, 'specially oncet the sign had come to me that George's middle name an' the name of the city where he was to be workin were one an' the same.

69

Pappaw Joe had let most of the cleared land go to pasture for his two mules. I could see 'em in the distance, fenced in by an ol' split rail fence, their red hides gleamin. Now, all he plowed was a nice-sized plot of corn for his "you know what" an' Mammaw's garden spot. I could see frost glitterin in the shady spots an' imagined Mammaw's garden was still covered against it, even though it was mite near ten o'clock.

"Betcha fifty cents they been sittin in their rockers, a waitin better'n an' hour," Daddy said.

Momma laughed. Already she was gettin her thangs together in the back seat. "Maybe my Paw, but not my Maw. Not Ada Campbell. She's been a makin us a dried apple pie. Thet's what I'll bet on."

By some folks' measure, I reckon my grandfolks' house wouldn't be much, old an' smallish as it was, perched above the cleared holler on a knoll. But it wasn't a shack. Everthang was in good repair, includin the roof.

They had a real thick forest of Frasier fir trees standin close on the north side thet protected 'em some from the weather. But it is true that their water still come from a spring up behind the cabin. It was a good, sweet, clear-water spring with a little house built over it to protect both the spring an' the thangs they put inside to keep cool.

Nowadays, thanks to my husband, they had water in a gravity-fed pipe thet didn't freeze an' went to Mammaw's kitchen sink all winter long. Meant she didn't have to go to the spring for her water. Made it special nice when the snow got deep. Still, thankin' on it, I reckon it might seem a bit backwards to some. Hounds slept under the screened porch thet ran the length of the house an' there was an outhouse in the trees. Course, the whole thang had never seen a lick of paint, but then most of the old cabins in the Smokies never had.

It somehow gave me a heap of comfort to know thet Mammaw's chickens still poked 'bout an' roosted in the trees. The garden was fenced tight with chicken-wire to keep them an' other critters out when the hounds were out in the hills with Pappaw. It was a house thet brought up seven generations of Campbells with only a little addin on. Only thang newish was the sign at the foot of their track thet Pappaw had carved. It said, jest

70

what the sign down below had said: "Private Property, No Tresspassing," on account of all the visitors comin to visit the Great Smokey Mountain National Park these days, as he said, "pokin their nose ever which where."

But Pappaw didn't complain 'bout the visitors down in Gatlinburg an' Pigeon Forge like Daddy did. 'Cause them folks were the ones buyin up his carvins, fast as he could get 'em made. These days, one of us took 'em to a real nice fella who had a folk art gallery in Gatlinburg for him. But ever once an' awhile, Grandaddy wouldn't send 'em all. Sometimes, he'd look at one of his carvins an' say, "I reckon I'll hol' onto this'n. It's got a special callin."

Momma had lived in this same cabin with five brothers an' sisters 'til Daddy come courtin. I can't tell you how right knowin all thet felt; how I loved the sameness of everthang. I quick put the wagon in park, grabbed the big black plastic poke with the part finished quilt thet was lyin on the seat between Daddy an' me, jumped out an' beat everone else out an' up the steps.

"How do? Howdy do?" Pappaw Campbell was callin, one hand grabbin tight to a porch post.

Mammaw Ada barely had time to wipe her hands on her apron afore I flung myself into her arms. She started pettin my hair jest like Momma had been pettin Vikki Ann's.

"Well," she said, pullin me back so she could look at me. "Don't look like no permanent harm's been done you. Gonna carry thet neck scar likely, unless you'n'll take some of my doctorin cream home with you."

I heard Momma laugh out loud behind me as she walked on up the steps. "I might of knowed she'd stew 'til she got a look at you with her own eyes, Marilue. She always was thetaway."

When I hugged Pappaw, felt like he was made out of bird bones. Not a lick of fat on him. But he was all shined up--had shaved an' put in both his teeth an' his hearin aids in honor the occasion--not thet the hearin aids did much good for him at all anymore.

"Great Granddaddy Campbell," Vikki Ann said comin up beside him an', raisin her voice like she knew she had to as she hugged him, "Where's Charlotte's pups?"

71

He looked down at her. "Why, child, they growed up enough to be sold." He looked troubled. "'Cept fer one. Cain't believe ol' Charlotte could throw such a no-count pup."

I looked down the steps at Charlotte. Seemed like she hung her head when Pappaw said thet.

"Never you mind, Charlotte," I said an' walked back down the steps, sittin to take her big gray muzzle in my hands. "I expect you've raised more good pups than any other dog in Sevier County."

She waved her threadbare tail an' moved forward to put her 'ol head in my lap afore the other hounds could move in to crowd her out.

Charlotte was our Pepper's full sister. People wanted to be put on waitin lists for a pup from one of her litters. Generally, Pappaw's hounds would hunt anythang you set 'em on the trail of, so the pup, if she didn't like to hunt, was some unusual.

"But, Pappaw Joe, what happened to the no-count pup?" Vikki Ann's voice sounded real worried. *Seems to me thet her voice is soundin like thet a whole bunch of late,* I thought.

Pappaw scouted the knoll an' his eyes come to rest on a big black oak tree at the edge of the clearin. He jerked his thumb. "Over yonder, a watchin. She left the pack the minute she heard you'ns car. She don't take up with nobody on a purpose. I can call her over an' she'll come nice as you please, might give you a little tail wag, but hit hain't like she means hit. If'n she gits the chanct, she takes her leave. I cain't interest her a'tall in trackin spoor. Reckon if there's somethin thet dawg likes to hunt, I hain't found it."

We all looked over to where the pup was watchin us. It was a purty little thang, 'bout three months old, black an' white hairs of her coat mixin jest right to make her look plumb blue; was hardly any tan color to her at all.

"Never mind thet pup," said Mammaw Ada. "'Come on in an' have some coffee an' dried apple pie, fresh made."

Momma an' Daddy looked at each other an' smiled. "I reckon I'll do jest thet," Daddy said. I noticed he was lookin 'round real careful to see if there was any chores needin doin. "You'ns still got any spare oak rails? Seems like the garden could use a few new ones on the far side," I heard him say to

72

Pappaw as we all sat down 'round the old pine table. It was scarred from generations of use but polished to a shine with bee's wax from their own hives.

My Aunt Mary, Momma's youngest sister, an' her husband lived in Gatlinburg. They come up ever week or so, brangin groceries an' hepin out, but Daddy an' Momma liked to do their share when they could. They were the ones who generally took 'em into town when doctorin was needed.

Vikki Ann whispered into my ear thet she reckond she'd stay out an' pet the hounds for awhile. I knew what she really had on her mind was thet pup.

"You want to uncover Mammaw Ada's garden for her on your way to see the pup?" I asked. She looked at Mammaw to see if thet's what was wanted an' got her nod an' smile of thanks afore slippin off.

Once we'd finished our pie an' coffee, Momma got her purse. "Lookit these'uns," she said, an' pulled some newspaper clippins out of it. I couldn't hep but groan when I saw em. Seemed like I'd put the whole thang behind me when I left Maryville. Momma read ever one of 'em while we were sittin at thet ol' table. Several of 'em mentioned the part where I gave credit to my fightin ancestors an' told of the quilt, but the one thet was in the *Seattle Times* thet I'd given her had gone into some detail.

Pappaw's far-away sight was still good, though he couldn't see much at all up close without the thick glasses he used for his carvin. But he took thet clippin an' smoothed it real careful with his rough wood-carver's fingers, lookin hard at the page.

"Them's shore fine words, honey. You done us all proud."

Mammaw Ada said to Momma, "Mildred, honey, I reckon I'd like to hear the part 'bout the quilt again."

Momma took the clippin back from Pappaw Joe an' read:

"Mrs. Perkins attributed her quick action during the attack to the blood of her ancestors. In an interview with this "Times" reporter, she indicated that her relatives had

73

fought, with honor, in every war, starting with the War for Independence. Her capacity to relate oral history was inspiring. When personally complimented by this columnist, Mrs. Perkins gave credit to the fact that their history has always been preserved by the women in the family through the art of quilting. As an example, she related that in 1866, General Ulysses S. Grant wrote a letter consoling her great, great, great grandmother, Grace Page Pitts, for the loss of seven of her eight sons. Mrs. Perkins indicated both the letter and the quilt made to honor the fallen sons still exists and is currently stored in the trunk of her 84-year-old maternal grandmother, Mrs. Ada Ramey Campbell of Gatlinburg, Tennessee.

It was real quiet 'round the table; all of us lost in our thoughts. I was wonderin how thet reporter made what I'd said sound so educated an' real glad thet I'd made it sound like Mammaw an' Pappaw lived in town. In the back of my mind, I was still worryin a little 'bout sayin Mammaw had the letter an' the quilt at home. Course, like I said afore, they weren't your average defenseless senior citizens what with the hounds an' the huntin rifles hangin over the cabin door.

"My," Mammaw Ada said, "who'd ever a thought to see my bible name in a newspaper from clean across these United States."

Pappaw smiled. "Why, I reckon it's proof of the puddin, hain't it?"

"What do you mean?" I asked.

"Well," he said, noddin at Mammaw, "thet's why her great, great Pappaw had to lose all his brothers, don't you see, to keep these states united durin the Civil War."

He stood up, like he was unkinkin one joint at a time, his blue eyes were twinklin when they fastened on Daddy. "John Grover Cable," he said, "I do reckon this calls for a celebration."

Daddy shot to his feet. He did love sittin with Pappaw in the porch rockers sippin corn likker. Sometimes, Pappaw got out his carvin wood an' Daddy heped him do rough cuts on the pieces he'd had blocked out for his figures.

74

Mammaw said real quick, "Hol' tight, ol' man. You hain't a goin off to no spring house without first riggin my quiltin frame." She stood, hands on her hips like she was Wonder Woman. "An' then ye go fetch down the trunk with the quilt from the attic. Seems like Marilue'd best have it. Likely them folks out West would 'preciate seein it."

With her words, said like she was talkin 'bout the weather, I practically knocked over my chair jumpin to my feet an' rushin to give her a hug. "Mammaw," I said, "I can't hardly believe my ears! I've been worryin some on how to ask you for the lend of it. I'll take special care, I promise."

"Why, child, I know thet. But it hain't a lend. I'm a givin it to you'n. I already talked it over with your momma. We'uns agreed thet it's time. The letter though, I'm a keepin. You can make a copy of it, but the original stays here on the mountain."

Well, I'll tell you, them words went deep into my heart. I looked at Momma, wonderin. Did she really not mind havin the quilt passed on directly to me? It was her right to have it after Mammaw, bein the oldest daughter, but I couldn't hep but wonder if she really wanted it passed on dreckly to me.

She was noddin, lookin real satisfied. "You really don't mind, Momma?" I still had to ask.

She shook her head. "No, honey. It feels real good to know you're goin to make good use of it, maybe hep folks to recollect their history some. It's not like you have sisters to fight with 'bout it."

Her voice sounded real croaky. We women all sat back down at the table an' jest looked at each other for the longest while, words stuck tight in our throats, recollectin the number of times she'd had to carry babies to get even me, bein I was the only one live-born.

"Well," I finally got out, "I sure do thank you both with all my heart. Knowin' that ol quilt is goin west with me is goin to be a heap of comfort."

We were sittin' there shiney eyed, not sayin' a word 'til I got myself up an' said, "Well, I'd best go see what my girl's up to, an' get the pins an' thread from the station wagon, if we're gonna to get anythin done."

75

I stopped at the top step. Jest since we'd been there, the sun had warmed thangs up. I saw Vikki Ann had rolled the black plastic cover on Mammaw's garden back jest as nice an' neat as you please. She an' the pup were both under the oak tree, only she was on one side of it an' the pup was as far as she could get an' still have shade, on the other. I walked on over.

"Momma," she said as I walked up, "I made up my mind to make this pup take up with me. So, I'm jest a sittin here talkin an' singin songs. I'm not payin her a bit of mind." She sighed. "Cain't tell if she's even interested though, the way she keeps thet ol' tree trunk a tween us."

I had to cover a smile at Vikki Ann's way of talkin. Seemed like once we got here, she started talkin jest like hill folk--like she was doin Pappaw an' Mammaw Campbell one better. Then I thought to myself, *Shoot, I haven't paid much mind to it, but we all do it, even George, after he's been here awhile, starts soundin mountain-born instead of Georgia Tech-educated; trades thet Georgia drawl fer mountain twang.*

"We're jest fixin to start quiltin, honey. Want me to brang you your new square so you got somethang fer your hands?"

She shook her head. "No, thank you, Momma. I reckon I'll take a little stroll along the trail to the branch; see if I can spot some of them little wild orchids. Then I'll come on in directly to hep."

I looked at the pup. Her long hound ears were perked, like she was listenin, but her head was on her paws, facin the other way. She hadn't looked at me even once.

"You go ahead then, but take one of Pappaw Joe's sticks in case of a snake," I said an' went back to the wagon for the thangs I'd come to get.

I don't know where our tradition of makin a quilt for a son to mark the end of his bein a boy an' the start of bein a man come from; none of us did, but I was real glad for the ancestor who thought of it. I know for sure our Junior seemed pleased as punch to be gettin his.

When I got back to the cabin, the quilt frame was on the hooks let down from the cabin ceilin an' the dark indigo blue cotton backin an' the battin stretched. Momma an' Mammaw

76

were tryin for patience. They hadn't gotten to see all the squares sewn together yet but were waitin for me afore we rolled it out over the quiltin frame.

I got it out of the plastic poke an' smoothed it onto the frame, fillin my eyes with it like I hadn't seen it afore. There they were, all the important dates an' events of Junior's life: The piggy bank, for how proud he was when he'd opened his savins account at the bank, the red two-wheel bike he learned to ride on, the eagle carryin a blue ribbon to honor his becomin an Eagle Scout...I touched the first square with the blue baby rattle sittin on a big puffy cloud made with a bit of material from his first bib. I'd embroidered the date, April 2, 1962, under it--seemed like yesterday.

"Why, Marilue, I reckon your stitchin has gotten even finer," Mammaw said when she looked at my squares.

I laughed. "Thet seems a mite unlikely. Since I hit 40, my eyes are givin me fits." I got my half-glasses out of my purse.

Momma smiled. "Your work is fine, honey, an' I do admire this last square of thet graduation cap with the star behind it. I hain't seen it afore. When did you do it?"

"On the airplane to Seattle," I said. "Kept me from gettin a case of the nerves."

We could hear the rockers bein pulled into the shade of the side porch. We had the windows an' front door open an' it was makin a nice breeze. We could hear the men on the porch talkin of huntin an' hounds an' debatin the importance of plantin by sign. Then Daddy got back on what was botherin him an' started tellin Pappaw the rumor he'd heard 'bout the shoppin mall goin to be built in Pigeon Forge.

"I reckon it's thet damned World's Fair a comin to Knoxville thet's 'causin the prices to go up like they're a doin. Them Herschend Brothers, thet come over from Branson an' bought thet ol' amusement park an' turned it into Silver Dollar City, are seein dollar signs, what with all the people a comin to their amusement park headin to or from Knoxville."

I heard a glug of the jug an' Pappaw laugh. "Shoot! Looks like I'd best get to carvin, John Grover. I'm thankin I can likely git myself a little piece of thet tourist dollar."

Thangs were real peaceful as we bent over the quilt, stitchin the quilt top an' battin to the back with tiny, careful stitches. Peaceful thet is, 'til we heard Vikki Ann's scream.

I heard the thump of boot heels an' Pappaw holler, "Git the rifle, John Grover." I was barely untangled from the quilt an' to my feet when Daddy had grabbed the gun from over the door an' was gone, poundin down the cabin steps with me right behind him, but I co uldn't begin to keep up. He was headin down the trail to the branch, his long legs chewin up the ground. Pappaw was bellerin at his hounds thet took off ahead of Daddy, callin 'em back. "Luke, Charlotte, Jilly, Dagger, Jolly, durn you, get to heel!"

I could hear a frantic high pitched bawlin bark, but didn't pay it much mind. I was jest tryin to get to my daughter.

"Vikki Ann, don't you move a muscle!" I hollered, tryin to follow Daddy. Seemed like my legs had turned to molasses an' were stickin to the ground, he was thet much faster.

Well, by the time I got there, Daddy was standin quiet, the gun cradled in his arms, breathin hard, watchin Vikki Ann. The only sound I could hear besides our breathin was the gurgle of the branch. I took his lead an' stopped to watch what looked near to bein a miracle unfoldin.

My little girl was sittin in a patch of ferns with a part-grown roan pup half in her lap, tryin to wash the tears off her cheeks with a big pink tongue. Vikki Ann looked up at us an' pointed, without makin a sound, towards the branch trail. When I saw where her finger was pointin, my legs turned from molasses to jelly.

At the edge of the water was a big cottonmouth water moccasin, bit mostly in two right behind the head, but still wigglin, its jaws snappin. I rushed over an' leaned down, lookin her over good. "Are you bit anywhere, honey?" I asked real gentle, fearin the worst but tryin for calm.

She shook her head, arms glued real tight 'round the pup, her jaw wobblin an' her nose runnin.

Pappaw come puffin up then with the hounds behind him jest like they were trained to do. He had a hoe in his hand; it was his favorite snake-killin tool. Sometimes, he has premonitions

78

'bout thangs. I wondered if he had this time, what with his stoppin to grab it.

He took it all in, let out a low whistle an' then told the hounds to "git down." When they'd dropped to their bellies, he warned, "Don't nobody get near thet haid or you'ns'll get snake bit fer sure."

He walked slowly towards the snake, the hoe low in front of him. It set his hounds to whinin an' moanin but they stayed put. With a quick move of the hoe, he finished choppin the head from the body an' pitched both pieces into the branch, its jaws still snappin like they sometimes do when they're fresh dead an' don't know it yet.

Momma, with Mammaw on her arm, was comin down the path, some winded, Mammaw Ada soundin like a horse with the heaves. "Everthang is fine," I called. "Slow yourselves."

Pappaw walked back an' praised his hounds afore lettin 'em get up. Ol' Charlotte went right over to her pup, touched noses an' then sniffed the two of 'em over good, both hers an' mine, like she was reassurin hersef.

Everbody else sat down on logs or in the ferns to sorta collect 'emselves. We were stayin peaceful, not makin a move to touch the two, still bundled closer than bark to a tree trunk.

In a little, Vikki Ann loosed her hol' an' began to stroke the pup's neck an' talk in a whisper of a voice. "I didn't even know the pup had come along, she was thet quiet. First thing I knew the snake was makin down the path straight for me, its ol' white mouth wide open. I screamed an' got my stick ready, but quicker than you could believe, the pup was there. She was a yippin an' a divin an' a stayin outa reach. Then so fast I couldn't barely even see it, she grabbed thet ol' cottonmouth snake an' give a hard shake, tossin it to jest where you saw."

Pappaw looked at the pup with surprise. "By dad gum! Thet's what she is then. She's a snake dog! Ol' Left-hand Cobb had one when I was a boy. Only thang it liked to kill was rattlesnakes an' cottonmouths--though it was a redbone hound, as I recollect. Never knew of a bluetick to do such a thang." He was shakin his head in wonder.

79

Vikki Ann lifted her head an' looked square at her great pappaw. "She ain't a no-count hound now, is she, Pappaw Joe? Not after what she done."

He shook his head. "No indeedie, child. Thet she hain't."

Somehow his words satisfied her. She gave a real deep wobbly sigh an' looked down. The pup's tail was beatin a steady rhythm on the soft, mossy ground. "I reckon she's took up with me alright," she said, real proud-like. "I thought she might not, but she did."

Pappaw nodded an' smiled down at her. "'Pears thet she has. But, child, how be you gonna convince your momma to let her to change up homes when you'ns go back down the mountain?"

Well, the stars come into my daughter's eyes then. She looked at me, hope I'd say "yes" was fightin fear I'd say "no" on her face.

"Vikki Ann, honey," I said, pullin a hankie out of my pocket an' goin to wipe her nose, "I sure got to apologize for yellin at you not to move. I can't thank what made me say it. I sure coulda made thangs worse for you. Hadn't been for thet pup…" I closed my eyes an' felt a shudder go straight on through me.

I looked at the pup an' reached out my hand for her to sniff an' then handed Vikki Ann the hankie. After she gave her nose a good blow, I touched her cheek. "Why, honey," I said, "it doesn't appear to me thet we got much choosin to do 'bout it. Look at thet tail go. Seems like you been adopted."

My, them words felt right. "Besides," I said, "we end up out West, seems like it'd be right nice to take a part of ol' Pepper's bloodline with us, doesn't it?"

80

CHAPTER SEVEN
JULY

"I'll be comin in tomorrow at three o'clock, Flight 124. Louis and I just finished workin out the details an' doin the signin."

Hearin George's voice made me miss him real bad. "I've sure missed you, honey," I said. "I'll be at that airport with bells on."

"I've missed you too and my arm's feelin nearly mended. Get out that Herbal Essence, Marilue!"

I laughed in his ear. "They don't lose your luggage an' your flight's not late, you got a deal. Junior an' Billy don't get home 'til 'bout five-thirty an' you know Vikki Ann is still at Mammaw an' Pappaw's with her pup."

I'd told George 'bout Vikki Ann, the snake an' the new pup the day before. He took the news 'bout havin a new dog in the family real pleasant like.

"Wouldn't be Christian to turn away a pup who'd saved your baby's life," he'd said as if it were the simplest thang in the world.

I'd also told him his pickup was fine, but I didn't tell him what a sad state I found the house in when I got home a day earlier than the boys had thought I would. *No sense in makin him disgusted with his sons when he is clean across the country*, I thought.

Course, over the years, I'd heard tales from our friends 'bout the mess teenage boys will make of a house when their

81

parents are gone. *I'm lucky my boys are bein brought up better,* I'd thank to myself, feelin puffed up 'bout what good youngens they were. So to say I was some surprised when I got home an' found my kitchen in a mess would be understatin thangs. I mean, a hog wouldn't have eaten a single bite off the linoleum, it was thet tracked up what with stuff bein spilled with no care for moppin it up.

I opened the refrigerator's freezer first thang. Right away, I saw they hadn't eaten a single casserole I'd left frozen for em. The counter was plumb covered with open jars thet had dinner knives stuck out the tops. Milk cartons, bread crusts, banana peels, apple cores--even the bologna skin, where they'd peeled it off, was lyin there, makin a real feast for a swarm of fat blow flies lookin for a place to lay their eggs.

They'd got in our mail, but it was lyin helter skelter in piles 'round the kitchen. I glanced through the swingin door. Not a crumb on the dinin room table. Not a thang out of place in the livin room either. I felt some relieved as I walked, 'til I peeked in the den an' it looked like a pack of animals had been livin there. Empty pizza boxes, empty Millers an' Pabst Blue Ribbon cans an' full ash trays were everwhere. One of my hand-quilted couch pillows had a big red-orange smear of what looked like it might have been pizza sauce on it.

I sat down the suitcase I was still carryin an' I rubbed my eyes, jest like you see folks do in the movies when they are plumb thunderstruck. When I took my fists down an' looked again, I saw it was even worse than I thought. Thet's when I saw the white rings on the hand-rubbed pine coffee table my pappaw had carved an' a big cigarette burn in plain sight on my brand new, wall-to-wall blue shag carpet. Some of the cigarette butts in the ashtrays had lipstick marks on em, an' it wasn't pale pink like nice girls wear, either.

My first thought was thet gangsters had tied up my boys an' taken over the house. My second thought was to wonder where the razor strap was. Them boys had enjoyed quite a party, of thet there was no doubt.

I'll tell you, I was near in a state of shock. My mind was buzzin like all the flies in the kitchen had been put in one jar. Right away I dialed up the personnel department of Alcoa an' asked did George Perkins Junior report for work thet day. He had. Thet was a relief. I figured if he was at work, so was the pickup. I brushed a pizza carton off the couch an' sat down for a thank.

After a little, I looked at my watch. Four o'clock. Junior didn't get off work for another hour. It was clear as crystal glass thet he an' Billy didn't expect their momma to be home so soon.

I went into the kitchen, ignorin the flies, to look at the calendar. Sure enough, the arrow runnin through the days Vikki Ann an' I would be gone ended on Tuesday by mistake. This was Monday.

My, my, I thought to myself, *them two sneaky Petes thank they can come zippin home this afternoon, clean this whole place up slicker than spit an' their momma won't know the difference.*

I looked 'round at the mess. One thang for sure, their momma wasn't goin to do any cleanin up for em. I got to my feet an' went to hide the station wagon up the street a ways. After thet, I took my suitcase upstairs. Time was gettin short. I wanted to be ready when they pulled into the driveway.

I unpacked my suitcase, took a quick shower an' washed my hair. Then I got into my robe an' set watch in our bedroom window with *The Ladies' Home Journal* for company. When I saw the pickup come up the street, I got out a quilt square to keep my hands busy an' settled myself, door closed, jest in case they come up to go to the bathroom or somethin.

They didn't though. They got right to work, Junior in the kitchen; Billy in the den, I could hear 'em hollerin back an' forth to each other. After awhile, I crept out to hide at the top of the stairs so I could listen better. Purty soon most of the clankin, an' gruntin sounds were done an' I could hear the vacuum runnin in the den. Then I heard Billy's voice to fetch Junior from the kitchen. They met at the bottom of the stairs.

"Look, pizza sauce on one of Momma's good pillows. How should we clean it?"

"Dunno," said Junior. "Throw it in the washer I reckon. Give it to me, I'll do it."

"How 'bout them white rings on the coffee table?"

"Get the brown shoe polish." Junior's voice sounded real confident.

83

"Great idea!" said Billy. "An' I'll get Momma's sewin scissors an' cut the burn mark off the carpet."

"You be danged careful," our oldest warned his little brother.

Well, thet did it for me; it was time for my grand entrance. I stood up an' marched down the stairs. When I rounded the lower landin in my black robe, my hair still done up in a black bath towel, I hoped to God I looked taller than life.

"Howdy, boys," I drawled.

I expect to them I looked like a witch, but you'd a thought they'd sure as shootin seen a ghost, they turned thet pale. I come on down an' pushed between 'em, snaggin the pillow as I walked on past, first to the kitchen an' then in the den. Thangs were lookin a sight better.

I turned on my heel, an' headed back up the stairs, stoppin at the landin. George's sons were still lookin at me, plumb slack-jawed an' silent.

"Your daddy will want to have a talk with you 'bout this whole deal when he gets home. In the meantime, forget tryin to hide the damage you done an' finish cleanin up this pig sty."

I pointed a finger at Junior. "You! You make sure an' certain thet ever speck of food left out on thet counter for flies to blow has been thrown into the garbage an' out of my sight. An' them counters had better be scrubbed clean enough to eat off of. Do it once an' then do it again."

I turned to look at Billy. I was some surprised he didn't have his hands over his mouth, laughin an' figured it might have been the shock. "An' you! Soon as you're done in the den, get your butt out of here an' go walk Hattie. An' you might as well take one of them casseroles thet weren't good enough for you to eat, down to Mis' Adel when you go. As for me," I said as I started up the stairs, "I'm goin to go do my hair."

Come Wednesday, I got myself all fixed up in a nice skirt an' blouse with little stacked sandals on my feet an' went to get George off the airplane. Course, I wanted to talk 'bout the boys first thang, beins I was sorta proud of how I'd handled the whole deal. But what he wanted was to tell me all 'bout his new job.

84

"They won't pay movin costs, Marilue, but they will advance me six month's salary money until I get my feet on the ground," he said.

"Your boys had a beer party while Vikki Ann an' I were gone," I said. "Made a real mess of thangs at the house."

"Those fellows I'll be workin with are real sharp, Marilue. Some of the stuff they're workin on, I can't say I quite understand."

"I told the boys we'd wait an' talk 'bout it when you got home. Thangs have been real quiet 'round the house since."

"Mis' Caroline put me in touch with a real nice real estate lady she knows named Mis' Estelle. I got lots of house pictures for y'all to take a look at. But real estate is sure expensive out West."

"Food rottin on the counters, pizza stain on the couch pillow, burn-hole in the carpet an' such."

George got my point then. He thought for a little while then said, "Betcha Junior talked Billy into payin for the pizza and beer." Then he laughed in a "boys will be boys" kinda way.

Thet's when I clamped my jaw shut tighter than a snapped mouse trap. George sighed real deep like he does an' covered my hand with his. When he gave it a squeeze, I didn't squeeze back.

"I'll have a talk with the boys," he said. He didn't say another word 'bout the new job, jest patted my hand.

When we got home, first thang he did was open his suitcase an' pull out a signed autograph picture of the Mariner's baseball team for Billy; a packet of information on the University of Washington, an' a purple tee shirt with an Eskimo dog on it for Junior; an' a purple collar for Vikki Ann's pup thet said, 'ONCE A DAWG, ALWAYS A DAWG', all the way 'round it in yellow letters. For me, there was a coffee cup sayin, 'I ♥ Seattle,' filled with chocolates.

"Thank you, honey," I said, real polite. I can't tell you where I wanted him to put thet ol' cup, chocolates an' all-- wouldn't be ladylike.

Then he handed me the pictures of houses for sale. "Here are some of the places listed for sale, Marilue, I reckon some will do."

I quick put 'em into a drawer. "One thang at a time," I said.

He looked at me an' shook his head, "There isn't much time, honey. We've got to be moved, lock stock and barrel by September. Youngens start school. I start work. We need to get this place on the market, right away."

Well, there he'd said it, straight out--one of them thangs thet had been left unsaid between us afore he'd gone off to Seattle. Me hopin we could somehow keep the house; him prolly knowin when he signed the contract thet we couldn't. Both of us knowin thet with the three acres, the place would sell quick as a minute to some developer who'd likely tear down the house an' put up apartments for folks workin at the Alcoa plant.

The silence in my kitchen was thicker than fog in a Smokey Mountain holler. We looked at each other, George knowin his words had been some blunt. Me knowin he'd said what needed sayin, but feelin real mad at him anyways. I leaned back to rest my backside against the drawer with the house pictures in it an' crossed my arms, glarin at him.

I finally unclamped my jaw enough to say, "No way we're sellin this house, George!"

My! I can't tell you how good it felt to say them words. So good, when he got this queer, blank look, I said 'em again. "I mean it, George. No way we're sellin!"

"How's that?" he said then. "What do you mean, Marilue?" He walked over an' stood in front of me--like if he got close up he could make sense of my words.

"Jest what I said, George." I felt pure joy rushin through my veins. "It would be plumb foolish to sell the home where we brought up our babies to have it be torn down an' my garden buried under an apartment house afore you know if you even like bein a full-time innovative genius."

"But, Marilue, honey, what with all the house remodelin, there isn't the money to get us and all our stuff settled in a new place out West unless we do."

86

I leaned forward 'til we were nose to nose, blowin ice crystals all over him with my breath. "Thet is NOT my problem, George. You wanted this job, you figure it out!"

Then I turned my back on him an' started slammin cupboard doors an' drawers like I was lookin for somethin, 'til I heard him sigh real big an' leave.

After he was gone, I sat at the kitchen table, thankin little, mean thoughts, fingerin the thangs he'd got for the youngens. I didn't throw the mug, but I sure had a mind to.

The swingin door between the kitchen an' the dinin room was propped open, so I could see all the height marks we'd made for the youngens over the years. It was a thang we did ever New Year's Day. I recollected thet Junior had only been a one-year-old when we'd moved in.

I turned an' looked at the double row of coat hooks by the back door. It was one of George's inventions. He'd designed it so thet each year the youngens got older the bottom row could be moved a little higher. Now the rows were right close together, the top hooks for caps; the bottom row for coats.

But I was recollectin when the bottom row was as low as it could go an' filled with their little kid coats an' caps. I could mite near see the newspapers there under the boys' muddy little red rubber boots an' Vikki Ann's white ones with the rabbit fur on top. I squeezed my eyes tight, picturin ever room in the house.

We'd bought the place more for the land than for the house, but now with the new blue carpetin thet brought out the rich brown color of the wood moldin, an' the new soft cream color paint on the walls, I decided I liked the house best; even better'n the land.

Thet sorry thought made me get up. I decided maybe what I'd do was go take Mis' Adel Calhoun another one of the leftover casseroles I'd made for the boys an' walk her dog for her.

I knew I should talk to George an' tell him I was goin; say I really didn't mean it 'bout the house. But I didn't. Instead I wrote a note on the kitchen blackboard. "Taking casserole to Mis' Adel and walking Hattie. Be back by 5:00," it read. No "George, honey," at the start or "love, Marilue," on the end.

Didn't even sign my name an' draw a heart over the "i" in Marilue like I usually do.

I looked down at my feet. *No sense tryin to walk a crazy Irish setter in these sandals,* I decided an' went upstairs to find my tennis shoes.

Once I got upstairs, I took the time to go to the pot, put my hair up into a pony tail, fix my face an' check the boy's room for dirty clothes. I stayed a little to admire how pin-neat they were keepin thangs since they'd landed themselves in the dog house. The whole thang didn't take very long, but I could hear George on the phone as I come down the stairs. The swingin door was still open, so his voice came to me plain as day.

"Well, yes, I am plumb serious, Hap. You have been pesterin me for years 'bout havin that old truck to drive in parades and such, so I'm givin you first chance."

There was a pause then an' I held my breath, stayin still as death at the bottom of the stairs 'til I could make sense of the conversation. After a wait, I heard George say, mild as milk toast. "Not a damn thing wrong with it, Hap. Seems like I just don't need to take it to Seattle when we go."

I squeezed my eyes tight, picturin, plain as day, thet tub of lard Hap, who had more money than brains, slobberin over finally ownin my husband's1938 fully-restored, straight-pipe Ford pickup truck with its new candy-apple red paint job. 'Cause sure as it never rains in Blount County on the Fourth of July, George was aimin to sell his baby…an' I was the reason why.

I tiptoed back up the stairs past the landin so I couldn't be seen from the kitchen an' sunk down on a step to thank. Sure as shootin, George had read my chalk message, thought he had the house to hisself, an' was goin to make a quick deal on the truck without me even knowin. I tried real hard to work up a good snit over the fact thet George was bein so sneaky. But this sneaky voice inside me was talkin real hard an' fast. It said, "*You're to blame, Marilue, an' you know it. He's jest doin what you told him to do, figurin it out. He knows he has to raise cash. For all your brave words to your family, you been sittin so tight on the pity pot you got a butt ring.*"

"*Do not!*"

"All right then, you go right on down them stairs an' show yourself. Talk 'bout bein a sneak! You take the cake!"

Well, I knew thet voice was sayin the truth. But I didn't do what it said. Instead I jest sat there, hidin. Then I heard George say, "All right then, I'll just bring the truck on down so you can take it for a spin and see for yourself."

Next thang I heard was the shuttin of the door thet leads to the garage from the kitchen, the same one George come through with the champagne an' Fredericks of Hollywood box. Then I heard the firin up of the pickup.

I got up from where I was hidin an' strolled on down them stairs jest as purty as you please. The casserole for Mis' Adel was sittin on the counter, but George prolly hadn't even noticed it. I picked the thang up with steady hands. When I turned, the blackboard caught my eye. George had been doodlin while he was talkin. $8,000.00 CASH-FIRM was written an' underlined over an' over in one little corner.

He'd added my name to the note an' above the "i" in my name he'd drawn the missin heart. It didn't even make me blink. I went on out thet door, head up, jaw tight, lookin proud, an' feelin righteous.

Halfway to Mis' Adel's my feet stopped. I looked down. Seemed like of their own will they were turnin 'round an' startin to run. They had me in thet station wagon an' zoomin down the street toward the Ford an' Lincoln dealership Hap's daddy had left him, casserole lid rattlin on the seat beside me.

Hap! Made me grind my teeth to thank of him. Hap! The man who drove a brand new Lincoln Continental with dealer's plates an' could pay $8,000 cash for a 42-year-old pickup, made his wife drive any ol' used car he couldn't find a sucker to buy.

A grinnin Hap was likely jest now settlin in behind the wheel of thet sweet little truck thet George an' his brothers had taken years to restore proper.

Fat, greasy, sweaty Hap, strainin them poor 42-year-old seat springs an' grindin the gears. I pushed my toe harder on the gas pedal. Billy was walkin up the street with his bat an' glove over his shoulder. He waved. I waved back but I didn't even slow. I saw his eyes get wide, his mouth open in an "o", then I was past. Didn't even look for him in the rear view mirror. I had

89

to concentrate. Wouldn't be any sense in killin a pedestrian or gettin thrown in jail for exceedin the speed limit by 30 miles jest 'cause I aimed to squash a deal. Truth to tell though, I didn't have a bit of a plan on how to go 'bout it.

Sure enough, there they were, George in the process of openin the door on the passenger's side, Hap openin the door on the driver's side when I come wheelin into the lot, nearly clippin Lenny Barnes, the lot boy in the process.

"Howdy, Hap. Hi, Honey." I kissed my flabbergasted husband on the cheek, but I couldn't look him in the eye. He had to know right then an' there thet his wife was an eavesdropper. Course he knew it already from me tellin him the story 'bout listenin in 'til the boys got set to throw my couch pillow in the washer.

"Reckon if we squeeze real tight, the three of us can fit in? Kinda feels like this might be my last chance for a ride."

Without waitin for an answer, I scooted past George an' settled myself, straddlin the gear shift.

Now, I patted the seat on both sides of me. "Come on, boys, let's take a little spin. Course, Hap, I'm goin to have to do the shiftin," I said real playful like as he got in an' shut his door, but tryin to make it clear I didn't want his hands anywhere NEAR my legs.

"Otherwise you'll end up gettin your face slapped," I added, soundin not so playful, to be double clear. I didn't add, "jest like you did in high school." But he an' I both recollected thet he did, an' thet I was the girl who did it.

Even as a boy, Hap had been a dirty ol man. Used to take all sorts of liberties with girls in the name of shiftin gears, passin in a crowded hall, slow dancin an' such. Then he'd laugh an' tell stories in the locker room.

"My, isn't this fun?" I said as George got in, handed Hap the key an' shut his door.

I can tell you, it was a fit tighter than sardines in a tin. Like I told you afore, even losin them pounds, I wasn't no little bitty thang an' George had done his own spreadin over the years. An' Hap? Well, Hap was jest a plain fat slob.

Now, I don't know if you recollect, but there wasn't a way to slide the seat on thet age of truck an' the steerin wheel

90

was good-sized. Hap could barely get his pork barrel gut behind it. I looked down to where his hairy belly peeked through on both sides of a strainin shirt button an' felt a touch sick to be sittin so close.

When he leaned 'round the wheel to put the key in the ignition an' I felt him leanin hard into my chest an' belly, then sorta rubbin with the back of his arm, I nearly called it quits—'specially since I still didn't have a plan.

Come to find out, I didn't need one. Sittin squeezed into thet truck, it come clear to me thet maybe the house had to go, but not to a developer. Maybe the truck had to go too, but not this way. An' not to this man!

George an' I hadn't had a chance to really talk 'bout much what with thangs happenin so fast an' me flyin off the handle the way I did. An' we sure weren't talkin now. George had stayed real quiet after he shut his door, even when Hap ground on the starter motor some. I put both hands on the shifter knob.

"Tell me when you got the clutch in, Hap," I said.

Well, to make a long story short, we never did one smooth shift. Gears were grindin left an' right an' it wasn't me. Hap wasn't a long legged man, which he needed to be, with a belly like his. He never did get the clutch in proper, even though he told me it was. But George never said a word even then. He jest looked out the window, his mouth tight.

Once we got into third gear, headin west on State Highway 73, thangs went a touch better. The truck ran real fine. Hap started to whistle. He rolled down the window the rest of the way, put his arm out to signal a left turn into Tellico Lake, then reached over to down-shift into second an' put his fat sweaty hand right over both of mine on the knob.

"I'm doin the shiftin, Hap," I said sorta sharp.

He laughed. "Why, Marilue, you don't mind us doin it together do you? I kinda want to get the feel of this."

Thet's when he made a big mistake. Second gear was bad enough, but when he mashed George's baby out of second an' his fat, hairy paw with mine in tow disappeared under my skirt to hit third with me hollerin, "I'm doin the shiftin here, Hap, turn me loose, right now!" George had had enough.

91

"Stop this goddamned truck!"

My husband is not a shouter. Never has been. But right thet second he sounded like a thunder clap from God. I craned my neck to look at him. He was glarin straight ahead, not lookin at Hap, his jaw clenched, blue lightnin sparkin from his eyes. Lordy, but thet man was mad!

Hap's hand shot out from under my skirt an' back onto the steerin wheel where it belonged. He hit the brakes without puttin in the clutch an' the little truck gave a lurch, a cough an' a shudder. Then it died.

It got real quiet 'til Hap giggled. "Heh, heh, got so excited there by golly, I sorta forgot myself. Heh, heh. Seemed like I was right back in high school all over again."

George opened his door an' got out, right there in the middle of the Tellico Lake turn 'round. He looked at me. "I can't do it, Marilue," he said, real quiet.

I nodded an' scooted over on the seat to put some room between Hap an' me. George shut his door an' walked 'round the truck to open Hap's door.

"Get your fat ass out of my truck, Hap." He said it mild, like he was tellin the time.

Hap's eyes opened as wide as eye buried in pig fat can span. "Your truck? Just tell me what you want, George, then it's my truck."

"Hap," said George, still soft-voiced, "You can't afford this truck anymore. Now, get out."

Thet's when Hap started to whine. "I couldn't drive it proper, what with Marilue bein there in my way."

I swear he sounded jest like he was sixteen again, tryin to get his hand between my knees. "Hap, you make me barf," I said. "You never could drive! Now do like my husband says an' get OUT!"

What with thet, I turned, braced my back against the door an' gave him a shove with both tennis shoes. Caught him unawares. He went slidin off thet leather seat an' if George hadn't sorta caught him, he'd of landed on his fat backside— which would have suited me jest fine, bein I was somewhat riled myself.

92

"Hap," said George, "You want a ride back to town, you'd best get in the back."

What with them words. George hopped in beside me, shut the door an' started the engine. I snuggled into my place beside him an' put my hand on the shift knob. George put in the clutch an' I found first, smooth as silk.

"Last chance for a ride, Hap," George said out the window as we started to roll forward.

Well, you should have seen thet fat man scramble to heave hisself over the tailgate then. By the time he got settled, we'd shifted into second an' were headin for third, George's hand coverin mine, not 'cause he needed too, jest 'cause thet's the way we've always done it.

"I know we gotta sell the house George," I said as I put my head on his shoulder.

CHAPTER EIGHT
AUGUST

You ask most anybody in Maryville, they'll tell you when Mis' Marilue Gracie Perkins makes up her mind, jest look out. "Best either get out of the way," they'd say, "or plan to get run over." I reckon it's prolly the truth. I know, after I got done pitchin my hissie fit 'bout not sellin our house an' nearly causin my youngens to disown me for gettin the truck sold out from under us, I buckled down.

Not the first night though. Thet first night George was home, after the prayer at supper an' the passin 'round of the fried chicken an' other stuff I'd made in the way of celebration, we were mostly quiet out of respect for the sermon George had preached to the boys 'bout not respectin our home or 'emselves. He told 'em not to come apologizin to me 'til they could feel genuine 'bout it. Said they'd better get their bicycles tuned up 'cause there was no way two boys acted like thet could be trusted with the family vehicles.

Both of 'em were purty hang-dog, slantin shifty eyes at me in their shame. I mostly ignored 'em an' talked with George 'bout the new job. It come to me again how much he needed such a challenge.

I also finally told 'em all the details 'bout Vikki Ann's close call with the cottonmouth water moccasin an' how I'd hollered for her not to move a muscle. "Coulda got her kilt," I said, "'cept for one of Charlotte's pups." Their eyes got real big when I told 'em the story an' thet Vikki Ann now had a bluetick pup called Shadow.

"Likely Shadow won't take up with us like Pepper did. She's more'n likely a one-person hound an' I reckon we got to respect thet. Besides, you aren't havin as hard a time leavin Maryville as Vikki Ann is. I figure thet pup will be a whole lot better than Quiltie for comfort."

It was the next day, after I went to Momma an' Daddy's an' brought Vikki Ann an' Shadow home thet I went into super organizin mode. By the time my men had gotten home from work, I was ready. They hadn't even gotten their clothes changed or their showers taken when I said, "Look here."

I'd made a big calendar on butcher paper. Spread it right out on the kitchen table so we could see it easy. It showed where we were now, at the end of July, the whole month of August an' the first two days of September.

"We got to be packed up, lock stock an' barrel, moved an' settled in enough to get you two," I said lookin at Billy an' Vikki Ann, "off to school by September 8th. Thet's when school starts out west. I'm fixin to get back on an airplane to go house huntin somewhere close to your daddy's new job. Seems to me like you two don't need to start school here; likely I'm goin to need your hep."

I looked at Vikki Ann an' Billy to see if they were payin attention. They were starin at my finger pointin to the square thet said '8.' I could see they were thankin hard 'bout what I'd jest said. I wrote in black ink, 'SCHOOL STARTS.' Then I moved my finger backwards 'til it landed on August 25th. "I figure we got to have more'n a week to make it clean out there over all them mountains, an' do some sightseein on the way."

I wrote, 'LEAVE' on the 'August 25th.' The words looked real black on the white paper--final somehow.

"Thet means we got a little over a month to get shed of 20 odd years of collected junk, get packed an' make our goodbyes."

It was as quiet as the bottom of a six-foot grave 'round thet table. Everbody's eyes were plumb glued to them empty squares with the little numbers countin off the days.

95

I squinted at George an' said. "Thet Al from RE/MAX called to say you'd listed the house an' wanted to start showin it startin tomorrow. I asked him to wait for a couple of days."

George didn't say a word, jest nodded, understandin I'd rather be across the country than hangin 'round watchin strangers poke through my house like they already owned it. He would have to do thet part.

"Now," I said, "what I figure to do is get myself out to Seattle day after tomorrow. Stay 'til I find us a place." I wrote 'M.L. TO SEATTLE' on 'July 30th.' "Mis' Caroline says she's cleared her calendar for me. With her hep, shouldn't take more'n a week, maybe less. Tomorrow, I'm goin down an' put all our savins into our checkin account so I got down payment money."

I looked at George. He had a look of pure amazement on his face, eyebrows clear up to his hairline. I said real gentle, "I got to go. How else we goin to get this done, George?" He knew there wasn't any way I'd let someone else pick out our new nest.

I turned back to the youngens. "Means your daddy an' you are gonna have to fend for yourselves. Try to eat stuff from the freezer. We sure can't take it. You can get boxes from behind the Krogers or the Piggley Wiggley for packin. By the time I get back, I'm expectin you to have your rooms packed up, an' stuff sorted out for the garage sale we'll be havin here."

I was already writin 'GARAGE SALE' under 'August 15th' an' '16th' when George said, "Garage sale? Did I know about a garage sale, Marilue?"

He was runnin his hand through his hair like he does, makin it look all spiky 'cause of the humidity. I shook my head, still writin. "Prolly not, honey, since I jest got my brain in gear today. Thet's when I thought 'bout everthang includin the garage sale AND the party."

"The party? What party?" George was standin on one side of the table, me on the other. Youngen's heads were swivelin like baby owls as they tried to keep us both in sight.

"Why our goodbye party, of course. 'Bout ten different folks have called, wantin to throw one for us'ns. I figure the only good solution, so as not to hurt anybody's feelins, is to throw it ourselves, in the park after Sunday services."

96

I wrote 'PARTY' in the square under the number '17.' "The church ladies are goin to hep." I smiled at my family then, real satisfied like. "So, thet only leaves the weekend of the 23rd and 24th of August free for the family reunion."

I looked at the calendar again. "But thet date works fine. We'll be all loaded up an' ready to roll from there. I'm gonna call up Momma an' tell her," I said.

George started feelin for a kitchen chair like his knees were weak. He slid into it, "Both sides of the family comin?"

I nodded real serene, like I hadn't had my ear glued to the phone most of the day, talkin to my momma, George's momma, the airlines, the real estate lady in Seattle, the church ladies who were hepin with the goodbye party an' the Baptist Clothin Ministry, who had promised to come an' get whatever all we couldn't sell at the garage sale.

"Yep. Momma's in charge of everthang. It'll be at Pappaw an' Mammaw Campbell's, of course."

The "of course" meanin, Baptists, which we were, don't hol' with drinkin, or dancin but for sure an' certain, any Campbell/Cable/Perkins reunion was goin to have a fair amount of both goin on. Everbody 'round my kitchen table was noddin their heads, knowin like I did that Maryville jest wouldn't suit. There'd be horseshoes, log splittin, knife throwin an' target shootin, besides. Fact is, there prolly wasn't any other place thet would have us. I wrote the word 'REUNION' on the paper.

"It's a heap to get done," I said real cheerful, as I looked at the calendar, proud-like. "But I figure if the Lord made the world in six days, the Perkins family can get 'emselves moved in a month."

I grinned at 'em an' sort of dusted off my hands. Nobody grinned back, they were starin at the calendar, but I could tell their mind wheels were churnin' like a bogged down car. I sighed an' went on. "Billy Dean," I said, "tomorrow you start plannin our trip west. Figure out the road numbers, mileage we'll need to cover ever day an' sights to see. See if we can do some campin to save us a little money."

He looked at me, nodded an' hid a grin then, likin the responsibility, I could tell. He an' his brother were both back in my good graces after a real sincere soundin apology.

"Vikki Ann, honey, I hate to do it to you, but you an' I got to tackle the attic tomorrow. It's goin to be like takin a steam bath up there, what with this humidity, I'm afraid. We'll have the menfolk tote on down what we sort. Then, when I get back, we'll tackle the cellar, which shouldn't be near so bad." I smiled at her. "An', when I'm gone, I'd sure appreciate you spendin time thankin on how to organize our garage sale, maybe get some signs made."

I looked at Junior. "Son," I said, "I'm thankin you might as well give your two-week notice at work. There's a sight to be done thet'll take both you an' your daddy."

He looked at me real funny then. "Momma," he said, real steady, "I haven't decided for sure, but I'm thinkin on not movin with y'all."

It got so quiet the only sound we could hear was Vikki Ann's pup pantin from where she was under the table, an' the hummin of the air conditioner an' the refrigerator.

Finally, George said, "How's that, son?" I could tell he was as surprised as I was.

"Well," Junior said, not lookin any of us in the eye, "I read that catalog you brought on the University of Washington, Daddy, and I'm not goin to be able to attend their fall quarter. It's too late now to get enrolled. Besides that, bein from out-of-state, I'd have to pay a bunch extra in tuition with no scholarship chance at all. Since I've already been accepted here, I figure to stay with Pappaw and Mammaw Cable, work part-time in Knoxville and go to school usin that scholarship money."

"Son," George said, "I was countin on you to help with drivin one of the three rigs west."

"I know that, Daddy. I figured I'd drive that old pickup truck on out for you, since you'll be drivin the U-Haul and Momma'll be drivin the station wagon. I aim to look around some, see those fine fishin rivers for myself, and then I'll fly on back here. Course I'll help with the unpackin too."

Butter wouldn't have melted in thet boy's mouth. With his first words, I'd had to find my own chair an' was sittin there feelin flat as day-old soda pop, already missin my oldest. But, when he said them words, my ears perked up. Somethin wasn't quite square. Thet boy was sittin on a card or two. "You mean

98

you aim to buy your own airplane ticket?" I asked jest to make double sure I was hearin right.

"Sure, Momma," he said. "I know you and Daddy have got to watch your pennies until things get settled. Seems the least I can do."

Then I caught sight of Billy. He was lookin tense. Had his eyes fastened right square on his big brother.
There was some secret here all right, an' Billy knew what it was. *Thangs get any tenser, he's bound to start laughin,* I thought.

I quick looked at my daughter an' there was a little pink splotch on each of her cheeks an' seemed like she was hol'in her breath. Likely she was in on it too. My husband, on the other hand, didn't have a clue somethin was amiss.

"Why thank you, Junior," he said, real sincere. "We do appreciate your help. We'll sure miss you, but I reckon you thought this through with what's best for your future in mind. Best call up your Mammaw Mildred and ask her what she thinks 'bout havin a boarder after we get done here."

I heard Vikki Ann's breath let loose with a whoosh. George didn't notice thet either. Instead, he looked at his watch an' smiled. "But for right now, we'd better stick to the subject of gettin moved, if we want our supper anytime soon."

He looked across the table at me. "You got any more plans to share, honey?"

I shook my head. Felt like, with Junior's news, a huge eraser had been wiped over the blackboard in my brain. One look at me an' George could tell all the steam was gone from my roller.

It was a touchy situation an' he knew it. If he gave me one drop of sympathy 'bout maybe havin to leave our first-born behind when we moved west, I'd break down bawlin. If he gave me a pep talk, 'bout boys becomin men an' needin to make their own way, I'd get wet-cat mad. So, he jest sorta took the floor again an' ignored me to give me time to get myself together.

"We sure have to thank your momma for gettin us so organized," he said to our three. "Now, here's one way we can help her. If y'all recall, where I'll be workin is north of Seattle in a city called Everett. They've got lots of places for sale, some in

99

the city, some in the country, so we'd best be thinkin on what we want your momma to be lookin for when she goes out there."

He got up an' pulled the pictures he'd brought from the real estate lady out of the drawer where I'd stuck em. "Go get your tablet, Billy." he said. "We'll make a list for your momma." They did too. Sat at our kitchen table doin it while I went ahead an' fixed our supper same as always. The boys waited 'til after they ate to get their showers. Already, thangs were a little up-side-down in the Perkins' house.

When I saw Mis' Caroline waitin for me when I got off thet airplane, I can't tell you how my heart lifted. I'd done real well so far flyin west, but I wouldn't want to say I hadn't been worryin some 'bout landin at Sea Tac an' not findin anyone at the gate to tell me what to do next. I practically ran to her, dropped my carry-on suitcase an' gave her a hug thet coulda busted a rib. "You are a sight for sore eyes, Mis' Caroline Johnston," I said.

"And you as well, dear!" She said takin both my hands, givin 'em a squeeze an' smilin her purty smile at me. "Estelle is waiting for us in her car. We've got your whole day planned and then Bill is taking us to the club for dinner." Jest like thet, she took charge and hustled me out of there and into Mis' Estelle's car.

After introductions, I dug in my purse an' pulled out the "want list" my family had made an' read it. "George wants a good, big shop. Billy wants his own room an' to be within bike-ridin distance of a baseball diamond. Vikki Ann wants her own room an' a fenced yard for her dog, Shadow. She'd also be partial to some big trees."

"And what 'bout you, Marilue," Mis' Estelle asked? Her voice was real gentle, so I figured Mis' Caroline had told her 'bout my not jest dyin to move west. "I reckon I'll know it when I see it. I would like it to be in a good school district an' not too far from where George works. A small town sounds good."

"Would you prefer a newer home?"

"No." I shook my head. "Not new. I don't mind doin some fix-up work. Be good to keep myself busy."

100

"Did you like any of the pictures your husband brought home?"

Fact is I'd hated most of em. Not a one of 'em had enough character to write home 'bout, what with their postage stamp lawns…an' neighbors so close you wouldn't dare cough, sneeze or scold your children without someone hearin. "Hard to tell from a picture," I said. I expect she could tell by my voice thet she had her work cut out for her.

Mis' Caroline said from the back seat, "She loves flowers, Estelle. She has a big flower and vegetable garden at home."

"Not this year," I said, feelin a pity-lump come into my throat. "I never got the chance to get it started."

Mis' Estelle had been drivin us north on the Interstate 5 Freeway. Like afore, I saw more cars on the way into Seattle than I saw in a year back home. As we come over a rise in the road, there was the city spread out afore us. It was a sight, all them tall buildins an' the water with the mountains behind it.

"Welcome back to the Puget Sound, Marilue. We should be sailing. It's a perfect day." Mis' Caroline said.

Even I could see thet she was right by the number of boats doin thet very thang, white sails stretched tight to catch the wind on the Sound.

I said, "Recollect when I thought it was called a 'sound' 'cause it made noise, Mis' Caroline?" I turned an' we smiled at each other an' she reached forward to pat my shoulder. I took a deep breath, an' blessed the Lord for findin me such a good friend.

Drivin with one hand, Mis' Estelle handed me a map an' pointed her finger. "Here, Marilue. Today, I'm going to drive you to where George will be working in Everett. Then, I'll show you how easy it is to drive to the little town of Marysville, which is just on up I-5. There are some nice listings in that area. If we don't find something you like today, tomorrow we'll visit some small towns a bit southeast of Everett. There's Lake Stevens, Mill Creek and Snohomish for starters."

I was real glad when she put both eyes back on the road an' I grabbed onto the name of the first town she mentioned. "Marysville?" "Why I live in Maryville now," I said. "Take out

101

one little 's' an' they'd be the same name." It seemed like a good omen.

But, there wasn't a thang in Marysville thet caught my eye. Seemed to me the price folks was askin for them cracker boxes was highway robbery. In fact, in two days of house huntin 'til we were all cranky, I was thet close to givin up on tryin, an' I reckon poor Mis' Estelle was real close to givin up on me. She did say, afore she dropped us off at Mis' Caroline's thet afternoon, "Caroline, I have an early morning meeting tomorrow that I hate to miss. Would it be possible for you to take Marilue out to Snohomish in the morning? That way, she could start looking around that dear little town. I think she'll like the character of it. I could meet you there on First Street at the John L. Scott Office by no later than 10:30. Then we could look at properties and I would be delighted to buy you both lunch for your trouble."

So thet's what Mis' Caroline an' I did. Next mornin we hopped in her purty gold Mercedes, drove on out of where she lives in Madison Park an' across the 520 Bridge over the lake. I read her mind as we drove over all that water. "I'm thankin we'd BOTH rather be sailin on a purty mornin such as this," I said.

Mis' Caroline was concentratin what with traffic bein bumper to bumper, an' movin slow, but she nodded an' said, "Except that I want you to find the house of your dreams, Marilue, and I actually have high hopes for Snohomish. In fact, the way I'm taking you there isn't the fastest way, but I did want you to see that we still have open land and two lane roads here."

Well, thet sounded real good to me. Already, I was wonderin how I was ever goin to learn to negotiate four lanes of traffic like she was doin. After awhile, she turned off the 405 an' traffic got some better. Purty soon, I was seein lots of nice farms with big green fields, some of 'em had hay on the ground or hay bein baled. I could feel my insides settlin at the sight.

"Thank you for this, Mis' Caroline. I sure am enjoyin myself," I said, my head swivelin to take it all in.

She looked over at me. "Whether or not we find a house, I think you'll like the town of Snohomish, Marilue. It's quite historic and over the years, the people who live there have

102

fought to keep it so. That's what Estelle was talking 'bout when she mentioned several times that it had a lot of character. There are a number of lovely old Victorian homes and the downtown has many of the original historic, brick buildings. You can still see how lovely it must have been in its day."

Turns out, she was right. Practically the whole town looked like a lady who'd been rich, but was down on her luck. Still, the quality was there. I could see it. Plenty of places had good-sized lots an' the trees were real big. She was right 'bout the buildins downtown too. Quite a few were built out of purty red brick an' there was a nice-sized river 'long one side of the town. I saw lots of antique stores, a big hardware store an' even an old-fashioned ice cream parlor. I liked it. I liked it a lot.

We parked, wandered through a few of the antique stores an' then met Mis' Estelle at the John L. Scott storefront on First Street where she was waitin. We got in Mis' Estelle's car an' right away both Mis' Caroline an' Mis' Estelle were talkin so much 'bout the beautiful Victorian homes, pointin 'em out, an' oo'n an' aah'n over their potential, thet I mite near didn't recognize our house when I finally saw it.

But there it was, big an' sprawly, two stories, sittin on this little rise in the ground. It had a real big yard with a fallin down picket fence, held up only by pink climbin roses. There were three chimneys. I reckoned one for the livin room, an' one for the kitchen. I'd have to wait an' see 'bout the third one.

I could see a clothes line out back an' plenty of space to plant a garden. There was even the original squatty one car garage an' another, newer garage hooked on it an' a couple of sheds set back from the house.

In the front yard were two great big "climby" maple trees. One of 'em had a rope an' tire swing on a limb. The way the deep front porch sagged in the middle made the ol' house look like it was smilin at us. I smiled right back at it as we walked up the walk. Mis' Caroline tripped on a spot where one of the tree's roots had lifted the cement.

"Marilue," she said, "what on earth are you seeing here that I don't?"

Mis' Estelle was keepin real quiet. The house had been on the market for awhile. I could tell by the age of the 'FOR

103

SALE' sign an' the way the grass had grown up 'round it. She fished a key out of the lock box an' let us in. "I think it looks worse than it really is," she, tryin hard to sound hopeful, peerin in her file.

"No one has lived here for some time." She read some more. "It was inspected again this last May, and the foundation, electricity and plumbing were declared sound. The roof isn't though. Evidently, that transaction fell through because the sellers didn't want to both come down on their price and replace the roof, which is what the buyers asked them to do."

Now, I will admit, the place was past its prime. To spruce it up, someone had thrown ugly yellow paint at it. But the windows still stuck, the doors sagged an' the whole place smelled like a wet dog inside, prolly 'cause of a leaky roof. It had hardwood floors though. *More'n likely maple*, I thought. I couldn't tell 'cause they had been painted an ugly reddish brown. "This floor would have to be sanded down an' refinished," I said, like it was nothin to worry 'bout. I was already in love.

The kitchen was big an' would have been sunny an' warm with clean windows an' a fire in the hearth. I walked slowly through the rooms. There was a feel I'd get from time to time. It sounds foolish to say it, but it was like the ol' house was talkin to me.

Like the floor, the bannister had been painted. But there was beautiful hardwood under there, I could tell. I ran my hand over the curves of it an' got the feelin again. "What year did you say this place was built, Mis' Estelle?" I asked.

"The listing sheet says in the 1910s," she said.

I nodded. "You got to thank a lot of livin has gone on here in them seventy odd years," I said, mite near to myself, picturin it all.

When I climbed the stairs, boards creaked under the worn carpet tread. "Be careful not to catch a heel, Marilue," I heard Mis' Caroline warn. Seemed like her voice was comin from a distance.

There were four bedrooms, one small, like it could of been a nursery an' only one big bathroom upstairs. I sighed, already missin George's an' my new, private bathroom back home. Mis' Estelle had her handkerchief over her nose.

104

"Oh, Marilue, I only brought you here because the listing mentioned a shop. I see now, this place couldn't even be made livable in six months, much less one." Her voice echoed through the empty master bedroom.

I had found the reason for the third chimney. "My," I said, as I turned to her, "won't it be romantic havin our own cozy fire up here."

Over the phone, Mis' Estelle had our house bought afore noon, at my price with the sellers agreein to carry the contract 'til our house in Tennessee sold. I promised I'd take care of the roof. They were plumb tickled to be shed of it, I could tell.

I called George, straightaway. "Honey," I said, "unless you say no, I'm buyin our house an' writin the down payment check today. It's a little run down right now, but thet jest means we can afford it. Prices here are uncommon steep."

I could tell he was tickled thet I was excited 'bout a house. "Marilue, honey, I can't even believe you got it done. You are sure somethin else! You go right ahead and sign!" he said.

Mis' Estelle bought us'ns lunch at this cute little café an' then dropped us off at Mis' Caroline's car so she could go on to her office to write up the deal to make everthang legal. Said the owners were waitin to sign. Said she'd be done in an hour or so an' did I want to meet with her at Caroline's or back here at the house?

Mis' Caroline looked at me. "You're dying to go back to the house, aren't you, Marilue?"

I jingled the key from the lock box. "You are a fine sport, Mis' Caroline. I sure would like to start writin down what needs fixin, if you got it in you to go," I said. Then I grinned at her. "Besides, it's too late to go sailin."

Mis' Estelle didn't blink 'bout drivin back out to Snohomish. "I'll see you as soon as I can," she said out her car window.

Afore we went back to the house, we walked on down the street to the hardware store. I introduced both myself an' Mis' Caroline to a man by the name of Bud. Told him I'd bought a house an' would be needin some cleanin supplies. He

105

welcomed me to the community in a real nice way an' said he hoped I would like livin here.

I said, "The place I bought is needin some work, but I have an idea 'bout gettin it fixed up at a reasonable price. Do you know the name of the shop teacher at the high school?"

He laughed, lookin back an' forth at Mis' Caroline an' me. "Well, yes, I do. As a matter of fact, he buys some of his supplies for his shop class here. His name is Jeff Adams and he's a fine young man."

"Well, thet's a good thang then. I'm hopin to talk him into hepin me get the place right for livin' in time to get my family settled afore school starts, beins we have two youngens needin to start. There's a sight to be done what with a new roof, gettin thangs unstuck, propped up, sandin the floors and such."

I smiled at Bud who was leanin back against the counter behind the cash register lookin at me, takin in what I'd said. I could see he was thankin 'bout the hunk I'd bit off an' how short the time was. I sure didn't want him tellin me he thought it couldn't be done. Then he grinned an' stood up straight. "I think you'd better see if you can get him on the phone then, Mrs. Perkins. Let me look up his number for you. If anyone can do it on such short notice, it would be Jeff."

It turned out to be my double-lucky day. His wife answered the phone an' she put him on. I said, "Jeff Adams, you don't know me from a door knob, but Mister Bud here at the hardware store where I'm callin from says you might be the man to hep me fix up this ol' house I jest bought here in Snohomish."

He was some surprised at the call, but after we talked a touch 'bout George gettin the job in Everett an' us movin the family from East Tennessee, he settled down some. Mis' Caroline had found a stool to sit on an' was jest lookin at me, shakin her head an' smilin, listenin to ever word, jest like Mister Bud was.

After thet nice, gettin-to-know-you kinda talk, I got dreckly to my point. "Mister Adams, I want to hire you an' if you got some boys from your shop class thet need summer work, I'd like to hire 'em too, if you'd be willin to supervise."

106

He was some surprised at thet too, but he got over it in a hurry when, takin the advice of Mister Bud, I told him what I'd pay.

"You know, Mrs. Perkins, being a teacher, I can always use the money. Besides, I'm getting a little bored anyway and I do know for a fact that some of the boys would jump at the chance to earn pocket money before school starts. This might work out for all of us."

"As soon as I get the signed paper back in my hands, we got a deal," I said an' gave him the house address. "My friend, Mis' Caroline, an' I are leavin Mister Bud's an' goin to the house, should you want to meet us an' see what kind of work you got cut out for you. We jest got to buy some cleanin supplies from Mister Bud an' we'll be there."

We thanked Mister Bud 'bout a million times afore we left. "Mrs. Perkins, I like people who can 'think outside of the box' like you are doing," he said as we walked out the door.

"Reckon I learned it from my husband, George," I said over my shoulder. I couldn't wave him a goodbye carryin' buckets, scrub brushes, a mop an' such.

Jeff Adams beat us to the house. He had a yellow pad in his hand an' was walkin 'round on the front porch, lookin up. After introductions, I said again, "Mind you, we only got 'til school starts to get this place livable. An' I mean jest thet; it sure doesn't have to be perfect."

I showed him inside the house an' then we went out to have a look-see at George's garage.

"I was a mite fearful you would have to get George's shop in shape afore you could start on the house," I said. "I'm plumb tickled to see it lookin' this good."

'Til then, I hadn't taken the time to have a look in the garage. It was like the Lord was on my side. It was in need of some cleanin, but somebody had already made the little ol' squatty garage into a first class work space. Jeff whistled long an' low when he saw it. He ran his hands over the dusty laminated wood counters an' looked into the row of empty cubby holes, admirin the craftsmanship. Then he smiled at the pot-bellied stove in one corner. "There's a story behind this, Mrs.

Perkins," he said, wipin his hands on his pants. "Why would someone do such a good job on their shop and slap paint on turn-of-the-century, fine-grain maple hardwood floors in their house?"

"Call me, Mis' Marilue," I said. I couldn't keep the grin off my face.

He took out his pad. "Mis' Marilue, I'm going to make a list of everything I think needs doing. Then you can number the order you want them done. If you don't want it done, cross it out. We can't do the roofing, liability's too great, but I'll get you a name."

I nodded. "Write a cost estimate behind ever single thang so I'll know what I can afford."

Jeff nodded. "I'll call the roofer tonight."

I turned to go back into the house when he went for his tools. Then I remembered. "Where's the nearest place to play baseball?" I asked. He grinned over his shoulder.

"The high school is a half mile north of here. You got a baseball player in the family?"

"Yessir. You got a good team?"

"Not bad. In fact, this whole town is crazy about baseball."

We smiled at each other. "Look for dry rot," I said.

Mis' Caroline was standin on the front porch with a scarf on her head an' a rag in her hand. "Marilue," she said, "I think I'm beginning to see what you see. That foot rail in front of the big fireplace is brass, not cast iron. And that bow window in the living room is going to be absolutely stunning."

When I got on the airplane to go home, ever bone in my body ached. I'd spent twelve-hour days on the house, good ol' Mis' Caroline right beside me. I owed her big time.

We'd used enough ammonia to float a boat. We'd scoured an' sanded, chipped an' chiseled, stripped cabinets an' did anythang else we were strong enough to tackle. I even gave George's shop a once over. Jeff an' his crew swarmed over the place like army ants.

"Mrs. Perkins, my mom said to ask you if you were the woman from Tennessee that captured those muggers in Seattle."

108

I looked up from where I was scrubbin. Tony, one of the boys, was standin there some embarrassed.

I smiled. "What do you thank?"

He smiled back. "I think you are."

Mis' Caroline said, from where she was varnishin a windowsill, "Of course she is, Tony. But just try to get her to talk 'bout it; she's entirely too modest."

"Well, my mom has your picture on our refrigerator at home. She'll be impressed to know it's really you."

I sighed. "Tony, you tell her the newspaper folks made way more out of it than it was."

He shook his head. "Actually, she liked that part of the story, but it's the quilt and your family history that interests her most. She's the town librarian and a quilter."

By the time I left, the porch was level, the kitchen linoleum stripped off, the moldy carpetin gone, the broken plaster patched an' the roofers were startin on the roof.

"You mind the roses when you're replacin thet fence," was the last thang I said to Jeff as Mis' Caroline dragged me to the car.

"I'm going to get a speeding ticket or you're going to miss your flight as it is," she said, plumb riled up.

"Friends don't come better'n you, Mis' Caroline," I said.

We smiled at each other. "I am spending tomorrow at the spa," she declared.

I slept practically all the way home on the airplane, my purse with all the paperwork sayin the house was ours, tucked tight under my arm.

George, Billy an' Vikki Ann met my flight. They were all hollerin an' cheerin, from their side of the fence when I walked down the stairs an' onto the tarmac. Seemed like I'd been gone forever. I'd no sooner got through the gate an' into the arms of my family, when Junior come runnin up towin a girl I'd never seen before.

"Howdy, Momma, welcome home," he hollered, givin me a hug thet reminded me how sore I was. He pulled the girl towards me. For a minute, I swear I thought it was Farrah

109

Fawcett, what with her mini-skirt an' mane of hair, bangs all curled back from her face like Farrah does.

"Momma, meet Darlene. Darlene, this is my momma."

"Howdy, Darlene, real nice to meet you," I said, noticin how they were standin hip to hip, his arm draped real comfortable 'round her shoulder. Then I noticed the red lipstick an' it come to me sudden an' clear that maybe there was more than one reason our son had decided the University of Tennessee was the only school for him.

"Nice to meet you, Mis' Perkins," Darlene said. "How was your flight?"

"Why, thank you for askin. I reckon it was fine. Truth is I slept most of the way."

"Momma," Junior said, "I bought a little old Honda Civic, used."

I turned to him. "My, my, son," I said, "Aren't you jest full of surprises?"

Out of the corner of my eye, I saw my husband lift an eyebrow. He'd picked right up on my tone. I sighed down to my toes an' then said, "Good for you, Junior. I'm real happy for you…long as you didn't buy it from Hap."

"No, ma'am. I bought it dirt cheap off the man who wants to buy our house."

Behind me, I heard George groan. Then I heard Billy start to snicker. I turned quick to look at him. Sure enough he had his hands over his mouth. I knew any minute he was gonna embarrass hisself in front of God an' Farrah Fawcett.

"Billy," I said, takin his shoulders in both my hands, realizin I had to stand tall to look him in the eye. "No sense gettin tense now, the secret part is over. We all knew the place was goin to sell real fast. Haven't real estate folks been buggin us for years?"

I hugged him real hard 'til he hugged me back an' I could feel the tension leave him a little.

Junior's face looked like somebody had painted him with whitewash. "Aw, Momma, I'm real sorry to spill the beans that way. Reckon I got too excited…"

"Son," I said, interruptin, "Nobody in this family ever got scolded for tellin the truth."

110

I looked dreckly at Darlene, then back at him. "Life is gonna run better for you if you tell it like it is, Junior. Tell the whole of it, I mean. Not jest the parts thet's convenient."

His face went from white to red, jest thet quick. Even his ears glowed, so I knew he got my drift.

I sighed an' looked at my husband. Vikki Ann had slipped her hand into his an' it looked like they were both 'bout half inclined to run.

"You can relax. Truth is I'm feelin some relieved by Junior's news 'bout the house. Havin to make all them decisions an' spend all thet money on the house in Snohomish sorta took the starch out of me. Right now, sellin our house jest feels like one more detail to worry 'bout has been crossed off the list."

I looked at my oldest, forgivin him. "You givin me a ride home in thet car of yours, son?" I asked with a smile.

CHAPTER NINE
SEPTEMBER

By the time we made it across the Washington State border, the Perkins family looked a sight. Our nearly new Chevy Impala station wagon looked like somethin the Clampetts would have driven west, it was thet dirty. It had campin gear all bundled under canvas, but hangin cattywampus off the roof.

Billy's an' Vikki Ann's bikes were strapped over the campin gear an' lashed real good to the roof rack, so we knew nothin was comin off; jest lookin like maybe it was tryin. On top of the load was the only place we could thank to put them bikes, what with George's pickup, the little trailer it was pullin an' the 26-foot U-Haul truck, the largest U-Haul had for rentin, were all packed tighter than a tick.

Turned out we didn't use the campin gear 'cept at Mount Rushmore. We had terrible thunderstorms crossin from Missouri to Iowa. Second-best quilts were flappin 'round the stuff packed in the back of George's pickup. Then everthang thet had gotten dusty drivin through the dirt roads at Mount Rushmore, got muddy in the rainstorm thet hit again in Montana, includin us.

"We'd better be pullin into Snohomish after dark tomorrow," George said, squintin at us when we stopped for gas. "Else they'll be pullin up the welcome mat, and that's a fact."

He was half serious; we were all so travel worn. My children looked like they'd been pulled from somebody's rag poke. I couldn't see myself, but figured I was the worst of our lot. My hair felt greased to my head under my fluorescent green

Badlands ball cap. Somewhere, I had spilled chocolate shake on the front of my last clean peasant blouse an' my britches were too dirty to talk 'bout.

The trip had taken its toll, but, my, we'd had ourselves a time! Course Vikki Ann an' I had bawled our heads off when we pulled away from our house in Maryville. Then we bawled when we waved goodbye to everbody at Pappaw an' Mamaw's after the reunion. We even bawled again when we crossed over the state line. It was the "Leaving Tennessee" sign thet did it to us. But we sure hadn't cried since.

I reckon Shadow was real glad. It sure made thet little pup nervous, all thet cryin. Seemed like there wasn't time for even a sniffle, what with Billy lookin at his trip plan an' crackin the whip. Seemed like I'd sure done a good thang, assignin Billy the job of gettin us across the USA. We started callin him "the wagon master."

Back in Maryville, one night, when we were all sittin 'round the dinin room table eatin our supper, same as always, he said, "That first day, we've got to get up and get ourselves gone from Mammaw and Pappaw's before the sun is up. We've got 8-9 hours drivin time to get to Saint Louis. I got us into a Best Western Motel there pretty cheap."

I can tell you, ever fork paused in mid-air, includin mine. "How's that, son?" George asked like he either didn't hear or didn't understand.

"Just what I said, Daddy. First day's our hardest drive. That's why we're goin the fast food route for breakfast and lunch."

George nodded. "Sounds right. But why the motel? Thought we were campin?"

"I figure we'll get in so late it would be foolish tryin to set up camp with Momma drivin all day and then havin to do the cookin. The Best Western has a restaurant, plenty of parkin and it allows dogs."

"Thet's real thoughtful of you, Billy," I said. "I reckon after drivin thet far, it doesn't stretch my mind too far to know I might like to fall into somebody else's clean sheets after supper."

113

He nodded the same way George does. "Next day's just 'bout as bad, only it's mostly flat land. That first day, IF we behave ourselves at the family reunion, it should go fine, 'cause we'll be rarin to get goin."

Junior looked ready to get gone on the spot. "You got this whole trip already planned out, little brother?"

"Yep. I got us booked into the Best Western in Sioux City, Iowa. We kids gotta sleep in sleepin bags on the floor both nights; cheaper that way. And, Momma, we can have fruit and cold cereal in the room if you'd rather. I just thought fast food was easier." He frowned. "Campin is just too big a risk. The weather report says we got a good chance of gettin real wet to the tune of thunder claps in both southern Missouri and Iowa."

"Do we now?" said George, hidin a smile behind his hand. "Is that a fact?"

Billy nodded seriously. "It's a sight of drivin, 'bout eight hours both days. But once we leave Sioux City, we only have a little over five hours to get to the Black Hills. I got us booked into the campground at Crazy Horse State Park for two nights. They allow dogs and got a lake to swim in. I figure we can spend the whole day, do all the monuments includin Custer's Last Stand."

"Why, Billy Dean Perkins, you have outdone yourself," I said. "Thet all sounds fine!"

He looked pleased. He ran his hand through his hair, jest like his daddy does when he's thankin. "And I got it figured, Momma, all that drivin makes you tired, I can take a spell. Once we hit Highway 90, it's string-straight and flat as this table headin on west."

His Perkins blue eyes held steady on mine. He'd gotten his learner's permit the last part of June an' George an' he had been doin some practicin both in the pickup an' the wagon.

"Well, your daddy says you're doin fine, so thet might be jest the ticket to get some experience if the weather's good." I couldn't hep but wonder how long he'd been hol'in thet drivin thought in his mind, thankin on how to present it to me so'd I'd agree.

Seemed like ever day our rigs headed west, thangs got better. It was awful flat thet second day. Vikki Ann said, "I never

114

see another corn stalk in my entire life, that's fine with me!" I had to agree. It was actually a blessin to let Billy drive us for awhile after we hit the I-90. I could rest my eyes from the stalks whizzin by an' Vikki Ann was real happy to ride in the big truck with her daddy, Shadow on the seat beside her.

Then, once we hit the Badlands, thangs started gettin down right interestin. Them folks thet had carved the Presidents on Mount Rushmore an' the feller doin the carvin of Chief Crazy Horse sure knew what they were doin. We were some impressed.

Day before, after campin right near thet huge statue of Crazy Horse, we'd had to drive through a herd of buffalo to get back to the highway. Some of 'em ornery lookin, enormous critters were close enough to make us real nervous; they were thet big an' mean lookin with little bitty, wicked lookin' eyes. Lots of places sellin food were advertisin buffalo burgers; so we figured they had to be good eatin.

Vikki Ann had quite a time with Shadow who was standin on her lap, lungin, snappin her jaws an' snarlin through the rolled-up windows. You'd of thought she was dyin to tear into em, but I thank, if the pure truth were known, thet half-growed pup was glad she couldn't get out of the wagon. Made Vikki Ann real proud--even though by the time it was done, her legs were some scratched from Shadow's claws, bein as how she had on shorts.

"She's sure some dog, isn't she, Momma?" she said, after thangs had quieted down an' we'd gone through a couple of fences with pipes laid across the road afore bumpin back onto the highway. Come to find out, they were called cattle guards.

Other than the stretch that Billy drove, Shadow and Vikki Ann had shared the front seat of the wagon all the way, Shadow mostly lookin out or gettin down an' curlin up at Vikki Ann's feet.

"Yes," I said, "she sure is."

Now, standin in thet gas station, I looked at my rumpled, dirty children. "Billy," I said, "I know you planned it careful, but would it hurt your feelins if we didn't camp tonight? Found us a motel with a nice little pool, had us a swim, some supper, a hot shower an' a good night's sleep instead?"

115

Well, I can tell you, oncet them words sunk in, a cheer went up. Thet's what we did too. Stopped 'bout two o'clock on the west edge of a town called Spokane in Washington State. Found the El Rancho Motel. It was real nice, what with its little pool, split rail fence an' "Pets Welcome" sign.

Asked the lady there, would she direct me to a Laundromat an' on the spot she said thet there wasn't one reason not to use the motel's washer an' dryer. I thanked her proper. Then told her I aimed to wash an' dry myself first an' then I'd take her up on it.

I can't even begin to tell you how fine thet shower felt. After I got a wash goin, I come out an' settled myself on a chaise lounge in my bathin suit, lettin my hair sun dry, listenin to my children hootin an' hollerin in thet pool an' changin a load of wash ever now an' then.

It sure was different than home, what with the dry air, the bright blue sky an' a whole bunch of big pine trees with real purty red bark but no brush underneath. There was a biggish bird with dark blue feathers an' a top knot on its black head, hoppin 'round in the trees. I wondered if it was a cousin to our blue jays back in Tennessee.

George come up carryin a brown paper poke. He smiled. "Man at the mini-mart said we only have 'bout five hours drivin time tomorrow. Billy sure called it right."

I smiled. "Thet means we got more than three days to get ourselves settled afore the youngens start school."

He handed me a soda an' pulled hisself out a beer. "Want some chips?" he asked.

I shook my head, "No, thank you, honey. Youngens will though."

"Cheers, Marilue!" he said.

We clicked cans, lookin at each other real deep. "That new house got a bath tub?" he asked.

I'd been real close-mouthed on the house details, wantin to surprise em, but now I nodded an' said, "With claws for feet."

"My, my, that's fine," he said, movin my legs a little an' settlin hisself on the end of the lounge. "Tell me again 'bout that old shop with the laminated counters and pot-bellied stove."

116

I smiled an' glanced to where the pickup sat. Behind it, in the little box of a trailer, were the innards from George's shop back home. Each an' ever piece numbered an' packed jest so. He'd sold Andy, his ol' boss, his drill press an' heavy lathe, but even so, there were thangs he couldn't leave behind...like his precision lathe and some of his special measurin equipment. He'd had to do some real fancy packin to get it all in and warned us not to mess with the latch on it, cause thangs might come spillin out.

Now, lyin all scrubbed clean with a load in the washer and another in the dryer, I said, like I hadn't said it all afore, "For one thang, you got a hand-pegged hardwood floor. There's a bank of good lightin, counters of different heights, cubby holes, a big storage area thet can be locked and room enough for a couple of chairs in front of thet pot-bellied stove come wintertime. The shop teacher, Jeff, says there's got to be a story behind the way the place was fixed, 'specially thet floor and them counters."

George was buildin a mind picture with my words. He smiled and took a long last swallow of his beer. "Almost there, honey," he said, as he patted my leg and moved to the other chaise lounge.

He settled back and tipped his Mount Rushmore ball cap over his eyes. I nodded and said, my own eyes feelin heavy-lidded. "Yep, I aim to get up energy and go call up Jeff; tell him we'll be in 'bout noon tomorrow. Make sure everthang is set and the phones got hooked up."

George didn't hear me though, he'd already started sawin logs. Sounded jest right.

I woke up from my own nap hearin a camera go click. Knew afore openin my eyes, it was Billy and his Kodak. He'd bought hisself one afore we left. Made a pest of hisself all the way across, catchin us at the oddest times. Ever night he wrote down stuff in his tablet thet he wouldn't let us see.

I sighed and sat up. "You sure do like to waste film," I said real quiet, givin him a look. He grinned at me and I thought again how he'd grown. I softened what I'd said with a wink and added in a loud whisper, "You sure did a fine job plannin this trip, Billy Dean Perkins."

117

Junior and Vikki Ann were sittin on the edge of the pool takin the last of the sun on their backs, eatin chips and drinkin soda from cans. "Take a picture of thet," I said, pointin.

But he didn't. He took a picture of his daddy all sacked out, instead. George didn't even move. I got up and motioned for the youngens to follow me. We'd decided to get two rooms, a single for the "girls" and a double for the "boys."

"I got a last load to put in the dryer, but you get your showers now. There'll be clean clothes laid out time you're done," I whispered.

Once we were out of earshot of their daddy, I said, "The clerk at the mini-mart agrees with Billy thet we're 'bout five hours out from Snohomish."

"'Bout five and a half to six, more like," Billy said, correctin his own estimate. "We've got the Cascade Mountains to get over yet. That big old U-Haul's goin to slow us some. They're not the Rockies, but they're plenty big."

I smiled at him. "Your word is good with me. I'm fixin to call up Jeff and tell him what you got figured."

Billy hit the nail square. Took us jest a hair over six hours to make it to Snohomish. My heart was givin me a thump by the time we crossed thet Snohomish River and traveled the last few blocks up the hill to pull up in front of the house.

Everbody piled out of our different rigs and jest stared for the longest time. Faces looked like they were playin poker, they were thet hard to read. Made me real nervous.

"Recollect, I only had Jeff and the boys tackle the thangs thet had to be made safe or useable afore we could move in," I said, sort of makin apology for the oldness, ugly color and overgrown yard.

Like Charlie McCarthy, they all nodded their wooden heads, blinked their puppet eyes and turned their stiff necks, lookin and lookin, but nobody talkin. Second thoughts and "what ifs" were 'bout chewin me up on my inside.

"Well, come on then, let's have a look-see inside," I said, keepin my voice bright, tryin real hard not to recollect Mis' Caroline's first impression.

Truth was it didn't look like I recollected, what with the new roof and the "smile" gone out of the porch. "Be mindful of the sidewalk," I said, pointin to where the roots of the big maple tree had lifted it. I pulled the key from my pocket, leadin the way to the front door. When the front door didn't creak or drag when it opened, I was thankful to my toes.

Everbody stood in the entry, still actin like dummies. I walked over and put my hands on the big ol' carved post at the foot of the stairs. "I figured, I could strip and varnish this myself, but the floors look mighty good, don't they?"

Seemed like once I'd said thet, I couldn't get a hol' of my tongue. I took George with one hand, Vikki Ann with the other and was towin 'em through the rooms, tryin to show 'em what the house was goin to be. I showed 'em the fireplaces, the fancy carved moldins, the bow window in the livin room, and the French doors in the dinin room.

"Day like today, we can open these up an' once we get this verandah rebuilt, maybe even have us a little table and some chairs out there."

Junior and Billy had jumped the tour and had gone upstairs, without us. Both of 'em come back down slidin on the banister. "Momma," my oldest hollered, "why didn't you let on you'd bought us a mansion?"

"Why, it isn't!" I said. "What makes you say such a thang?"

Junior laughed. "How many folks in your personal acquaintance have a fireplace in their bedroom?"

Beside me, I heard George chuckle. "You sure got us, Marilue," he said, like I'd done it on purpose.

"George," I said, real riled up, "this is NOT a mansion!"

He chuckled again and put his arm 'round my shoulder. "Maybe it isn't by today's standards, honey, but I reckon the fella who built it back in 1910 thought it was."

He was lookin up to where the paint and wall paper were peelin off the wall. "My, my," he said, "you got your work cut out, Marilue, but I sure do get a good feelin just standin here. It's like the house is talkin to me."

I put my arms 'round his middle and hugged him tight, feelin some relieved. "George Everett Perkins," I said. "You do have a fine way with words."

119

He looked at me a little puzzled, but pleased, then hooked a thumb at the boys. "Best go on out and get the truck maneuvered so we can start unloadin furniture after your momma shows me the upstairs."

Vikki Ann and Shadow ran on up and we followed, walkin, hip to hip, arms 'round each other all the way. The old threadbare stair treads were gone. Not one board squeaked.

Upstairs, I saved showin our bedroom for last. "Well, well," George said, at the doorway, "this is somethin. Wonder if that old fireplace will draw?"

I smiled at George, walked over and ran my hand over the big river rocks above the openin. "You don't see any soot here, do you? Course it'll draw."

I dug a brass key out of my pocket. "Now, go on down and look at your shop. I know you been dyin to." He was gone afore I'd even finished my say.

I went to find Vikki Ann. She was sittin on the window seat in the bedroom thet was above the dinin room, eyes closed, Shadow beside her. I leaned against the door frame and watched her, knowin exactly what she was doin. A month ago, I'd been doin the same thang. "What color?" I asked, real soft.

She smiled, eyes still closed. "I'm havin me a time decidin. Can I have wall paper?"

"Why, sure, honey. What you got in mind?"

"I'm not sure yet. I been sittin here, tryin to think what this room was like when the house was new."

"Vikki Ann, honey, once we get ourselves settled, we'll go to the library, do some checkin on how folks were decoratin girls' rooms in 1910."

"Why, I'd like that Momma," she said, real pleased, openin her eyes.

"Well, we'll do it then," I said. "The librarian is the momma of one of the boys thet's been workin here. Maybe she'll hep us. But right now, we'd best get our tails in gear."

Vikki Ann and I had packed up our beddin and the thangs from our ol' kitchen jest the way I wanted. We'd stowed it in the back of the wagon so it would be real easy to get to. I figured if I got my kitchen set up and the "boys" got the beds unloaded and

120

put together, a trip to the grocery store and we'd be set for another day.

When we got outside, Jeff and the boys had jest pulled in and were standin 'round admirin George's pickup. Vikki Ann stopped on the porch like somebody had nailed her feet to the boards.

"Who are those folks?" she whispered.

"Why, honey, jest the folks thet worked on the house."

"I'm not goin out there," she said.

I looked at her over my shoulder in pure amazement. This was the same girl thet was tree climbin and leg wrestlin all takers at our family reunion, not a shy bone in her body. She had them little pink blotches on both her cheeks.

"Why, honey, you'll likely be seein a lot of them boys. Some of 'em'll be classmates of Billy's. Might as well get acquainted."

But, she was gone like a whisper; had slipped back inside jest thet quick. I sighed and walked on down the steps, tryin to recollect my own twelve-, nearly-thirteen-year- old self. "Howdy, boys." I said, reachin out a hand. "Everthang looks real good. I can't tell you how pleased I am."

"Mrs. Perkins," Tony said, "I told my mom what you said 'bout the paper makin more of that attack than it was, but she says I can't come home unless I get your autograph." He grinned. "Oh, yeah, and she said to say, 'Welcome to Snohomish.'"

I laughed and waved my hand. "Tony, the only autograph you're goin to get from me today is the one on your check. You tell your momma I'll be comin to see her for some hep on lookin up how to decorate this place. Tell her I'll be signin my "autograph" on my library card. But I do thank her kindly for her welcome."

Jeff said, "Marilue, I have your new washer and dryer in the back of my truck. It didn't come in until this morning. When we get that moved in and hooked up, I guess we're done with your list and out of your hair."

"You sure haven't been in my hair," I said, "you have been a blessin! Let me jest go get my checkbook."

I paid em, but they didn't leave. Stayed 'til ever last thang we owned, 'cept for George's little trailer, was empty. Way

121

George had planned the move, with unloadin in mind, everthang went real slick.

First thang off the top of the U-Haul load was our new braided rugs, one a goin away gift from our kinfolks, the other was one Momma had on her livin room floor where I grew up in Maryville. Since they'd bought the little house in Pigeon Forge, she didn't have a room thet would take it.

"'Spect it might as well be gettin some use," she'd said.

A body would have thought she'd braided it special for our new livin room, it looked thet good. Gave the big room a homey look if I do say so myself.

"Don't put anythin against walls," I warned everbody, "we'd jest have to pull it out again to paint and wallpaper the walls."

All the boys were gruntin and groanin, includin my own, tellin me I was a slave driver, but doin jest what I asked while showin each other who was the strongest. *There's nothin like workin together to make strangers into friends*, I thought to myself, watchin Billy and a boy named Richie maneuverin a bureau up the stairs.

I put Vikki Ann to work unpackin dishes out in the kitchen, thankin it would let her ignore everbody. Happened, all three of them high school boys worked up a terrible thirst, one after the other. Went to the kitchen. Took turns askin, would she mind if they had a drink, thankin her real polite. Then, on their way out for another load, they started sockin each other on the arm and makin funny sounds like they'd been watchin Tarzan movies.

I looked at George and he looked at me. I grinned and shrugged my shoulders like I was sayin, "Don't ask me."

Billy had taken it all in too. Went and got his own drink then. Come out of the kitchen with the funniest look on his face.

Purty soon, George and Jeff had the legs back on both the kitchen and dinin room tables and all the chairs set 'round em. I could hear Junior givin instructions on how to put beds together when I took a box of beddin up. I can't tell you how both them thangs cheered me.

122

Afore I even knew for sure, George and Jeff had taken the U-Haul truck away and come with sodas, potato salad and the biggest bucket of Kentucky fried chicken the store had. They'd even stopped for groceries like fresh milk, bear paws and col' cereal for in the mornin.

I watched the two men jawin as they come up the walk. "Thank you, men," I said, "thet was right thoughtful of you." I took some of the picnic and headed into the kitchen, the whole starvin crew followin me. Vikki Ann was nowhere to be seen, but she'd gotten a lot of unpackin done. There was a heap of empty boxes stacked in one corner by the side door.

George set his load down, looked at me and said, "Marilue, I haven't had the chance to say it to you yet, 'bout the shop, I mean. It's a ring dang dandy. Jeff kept on showin me things in there 'til he had me hoppin around, bayin like a hound dog under a just-treed bear."

Then afore I knew his intention, he grabbed me and kissed me proper, right there in our new kitchen in front of everbody. It flustered me some, I'll admit. But it pleased me too. I put my hand up to straighten my combs.

"Why, George, honey," I said, "You did put it on your list, you know." Then right quick, I put some chicken on a plate for Vikki Ann and went to use our new upstairs phone to call up Mis' Caroline.

Mis' Caroline! I was some behol'in to her generosity. Back home, I had been turnin over in my mind what to do as pay back for the sailin, bein my taxi driver and workin like a field hand to hep get the house ready, figurin it would come to me once I didn't have so much on my mind. Course when we'd been up on the mountain workin on the quilt, I'd told my momma and Mammaw all 'bout her. Mammaw had looked at me with a little smile on her face. "Well, she deserves more'n a little 'thankee kindly,' don't she?"

We bent back over our stitches. "I'm thankin hard on it," I said. But it was right then I got the idea to start on makin her a quilt 'bout sailin once thangs got back to normal in the Perkins family. I'd never made a quilt for anyone outside our own, but I reckoned for her I could do it. I didn't say a word though. It didn't feel like the time.

123

Fish stories were flyin by the time I got back downstairs. The chicken bucket was nearly empty. I grabbed a piece for myself. George was rubbin his hands together and I knew he had the fishin fever.

"Marilue," George said, as I passed 'round a poke of store-bought cookies, and opened the gallon of milk, "you found us a town smack dab beside one of the best steelhead rivers in the state of Washington."

Well, he had me there. "How's thet?" I asked, real puzzled. It set the boys to grinnin and rockin back on chair legs, sneakin sideways looks at each other, like boys will do.

"Fish. They're fish, honey," George said.

Jeff smiled, "Big, fighting fish that only allow themselves to be caught when the weather is at its most miserable. I've never even hooked one unless the wind is blowing snow or it's pouring rain."

"Why, thet sounds like jest a heap of fun, Jeff," I said, makin my voice sound like I didn't mean a word. Then I looked at my husband. "We're gonna be in church on Sunday, George," I said.

He grinned. "Lucky it isn't the season then, huh, Jeff?"

Jeff winked, then looked at how long the shadows were gettin and got to his feet. He whispered somethin in George's ear and made a motion for his boys to start movin. Then he shook Junior's hand.

"It's nice to have met you. I just wish you could stay around longer and get to know the country."

Junior grinned. "Reckon I'll be back. Don't know I would ever feel right 'bout my life unless I caught me one of them big steelhead."

They left then and it got real quiet on our porch as we waved 'em goodbye. It had come to all of us with Jeff's words, thet Junior wouldn't be with us much longer. When we took him to the airplane, Sunday afternoon, that'd be it. I was glad I had declared myself on goin to church. My family would pray together one last time.

We all went back into the kitchen. George took a chair like he was feelin old. Vikki Ann come down then. Billy looked

124

at her, then looked away. "You're only twelve," he said, real serious.

The pink spots come back to her cheeks. "I know how old I am, Billy Dean," she told him, col' as ice. "I don't need you tellin me."

"I told those boys that too, before they started thinkin different," he said.

She let out a gasp, stiffened like she'd been dunked in a starch bucket and then toed right up to him. "Billy Dean Perkins, you ever talk my business to those boys again, and you'll wish you hadn't."

She gave him a hard thump on the chest. "You aren't my momma or my daddy so I'll thank you to keep your nose where it belongs!" She was so mad it didn't take any imaginin to picture her fluffed up and spittin like a cat. Didn't seem to bother Billy much though. He shrugged his shoulders at her thump, like he didn't even feel it.

"Naw," he said. "I don't aim to."

He looked at his brother who was standin there some amazed. "With Junior leavin, I reckon I'm the only big brother you got close enough to do you any good."

Then he did somethin I had never seen him do. He made a muscle and pointed to it. "I was payin close attention when we were all totin things, and I reckon I can whip any of those boys in a fair fight."

Vikki Ann grabbed her carefully combed hair with both hands like she was goin to pull it out. "Fight? Fight? Have you gone plumb crazy?"

Vikki Ann and Billy had done their share of scrappin over the years, but nothin real physical, 'cept thet time jest afore we moved, since they'd been little tykes. I thought they'd gotten smarter with age. But for a minute, it seemed not.

I reckon if Junior hadn't finally picked his chin off the floor and waded right in with his own opinions, she'd have been on Billy like a burr in a mule's tail.

"Vikki Ann, Billy's right. He knows things you don't know. You'd better be listenin to him."

Well, I got to admit, Vikki Ann did me proud. Didn't back off one bit. She rounded on Junior, her eyes narrowed and

125

her fists clenched. "Let me get this straight," she said to him, her voice smooth and oozy as scum on a pond. "Billy thinks three high school boys that have come over to pick up their paychecks and help us unload, deserve to be beat up 'cause they come into the kitchen and asked me real polite, for a drink of water…and you agree with him?"

"Aw, that isn't it, Vikki Ann," Junior said, his own voice heatin up.

"Then you mind explainin to me what it is?"

I looked at the three of 'em all circled up, jaws clenched, glarin at each other. Right then was when George snagged Billy's comera off the kitchen counter and took their picture. Hearin thet familiar clickin sound sorta discombobulated em.

"What did you do that for Daddy?" Billy asked, real peevish like.

"Well," George drawled, "I figured if it didn't work, I'd have to douse y'all with water."

"Aw, George, honey," I said, "and here I was 'bout to start sellin tickets out front." I waved a hand towards the windows with no curtains, "no sense lettin our new neighbors see and hear how our children behave for free."

Nobody paid me a bit of mind. "Daddy," Junior said, spreadin his hands, lookin for understandin, "I reckon you know what Billy and I are gettin at."

"Why, no, son, I don't believe I do." George scratched his head. "I have been tryin to follow the gist though, and if I got it figured right, in spite of the fact that the three of you spent a couple of hours swimmin together yesterday, this is the first time you two boys really noticed that your little sister isn't so little anymore."

They both nodded, figurin they were finally gettin somewhere.

"Doesn't matter what she's gettin to look like, she's still just a little girl, and those fellas were lookin at her like she wasn't," said Billy.

George, seein how Billy's words fell on Vikki Ann, quick reached out and took her by the shoulders to keep her from flyin off the handle again.

126

He turned her 'round and looked her up and down, his face real serious. Then he stepped back and looked at his boys. "No," he said, "she isn't just a little girl any more. But that is not the point here. Point is you youngens are all growin up. Look at you, Junior, makin grown up decisions, fallin in love, buyin a car."

George scratched his head and turned to Billy. "And you, Billy. No one, old or young, could have planned our trip west any better than you did. And, right or wrong, here you are, takin a man's stand, sayin your piece straight. It doesn't appear that you even gave a thought to havin a laughin spell."

George's voice was full of so much softness and love, seemed like it put a spell on all of us. He bent down so his eyes were level with his daughter's.

"Honey," he said, "these boys are some misguided. I reckon they figure your chest starts to grow, your brain starts to shrink--that you've turned into this thing that can't think for herself and needs strong brotherly protection."

He shook his head, sad-like. "I reckon it's a habit with us Perkins men. Feelin some protective of our womenfolk, I mean. If they didn't love you, they wouldn't be actin like such jackasses."

He grinned at her. "Doesn't mean you have to forgive 'em though. Fact is, were I you, I'd be givin them the cold silent treatment for a long while."

Vikki Ann looked at him, thankin. Then she looked at her brothers. "Daddy's right," she said at last. "You ARE a pair of jackasses! I don't even LIKE boys!"

With thet, she turned on her heel and stomped out of the kitchen, headed upstairs.

George straightened up then and looked at me. "What are you thinkin, honey?" he asked, studyin my face. "You haven't said much."

I walked over and put my arm through his. "I was thankin," I said, plantin a peck on his cheek, "happened you weren't an 'in-no-va-tive genius,' you could of been a 'dip-lo-mat.'"

Then I turned to my sons. "I do believe you owe your sister an apology. You can't tell her, better thank of some way to

127

show her. But for now, best stay clear and start workin on unpackin some more boxes and get your beds made."

By Saturday afternoon, we were all startin to settle in. Breakfast 'round the ol kitchen table sort of set the tone. After, Vikki Ann took Shadow outside where she finally relaxed enough to peel hersef from Vikki Ann's side and explore her new territory. Vikki Ann climbed one of the big maple trees more to prove she could do it, than anythang else. She was talkin to her brothers, but barely.

"Reckon I gotta make peace with Junior before he leaves," she said to me while we were makin an airplane snack for him to eat, "but I sure DO NOT want to." I was proud of her for thet.

Junior and Billy asked for the loan of the pickup. Said Tony, Richie and Stu had volunteered to show 'em 'round the town. George told me he figured the truck was for girl bait and let 'em take it.

"Sure worked on me," I said, smilin at him.

We did some explorin of our own, found the First Baptist church, looked the town over and stocked up on more groceries.

Come Sunday, George woke up lookin double pleased with hisself.

"What's up, honey?" I asked.

"For me to know and you to find out," he said, real smug, pretendin like he was zippin his lips.

I groaned. "George," I said, "I don't need any surprises today, what with Junior's leavin and all."

Well, he got sober faced at thet reminder. Made me a little mad at myself for ruinin his mood. Church went real well though. Everbody was plumb friendly. Tony and his family were there. His mother made such a fuss thet I finally did give her my autograph. Promised I'd show her the Civil War quilt one day.

The preacher asked George how he liked livin in the Northwest so far. George allowed as how it was a lot more like Tennessee than most of the country we'd seen in between.

We didn't stay long to visit. I wanted ever minute I had left with my oldest. When we got home, Jeff was sittin on the

128

porch. "Howdy, Jeff," I said, "come on in and have a glass of iced tea." I'd already learned thet folks out west didn't like sweet tea, not even a little.

"No thanks, Mis' Marilue, I'll take a rain check though," he said, lookin at George and sorta noddin his head as he took his leave.

Thet puzzled me some, but I didn't have much time to thank 'bout it, beins my family was all rushin me towards the kitchen. Well, I didn't see it at first, which 'bout drove George and the youngens crazy. And when I did, seemed like I couldn't believe it. There it was, jest like in the old house, the measurin stick in the doorway. Looked like the writin had even been freshened up some.

"Why, George Everett Perkins!" I got out, afore a throat lump stopped me. I couldn't do a thang but stand there huggin thet doorjamb, fightin tears. Then I jest gave in. I was cryin, laughin and huggin everbody, not a word of thanks able to make it past my lips. They knew though, way their eyes were shinin.

"Momma," said Junior, "Look what else I got to put up before I leave." He was hol'in out our coat rack.

"And that's not all, Momma." Vikki Ann lifted my arm and put it 'round her shoulder, snugglin in like she does. "Daddy and I dug up some of those purple iris and put them in a black bag. He hid 'em in the little trailer with all his shop equipment. I'll plant them for you soon as you decide where."

After I got myself mopped up a touch and gave my nose a good blow, I finally said, lookin 'round at my family, "My, my, I reckon now it truly feels like the Perkins family lives here."

I couldn't brang myself to say "home." I'd tried to get thet word past my throat a couple of time, but it got stuck inside somewhere and wouldn't come. I reckoned I'd have to give myself some time on thet one.

CHAPTER TEN
OCTOBER

My husband once said to our son, Junior, "Gettin married is the easy part. Stayin married is the hard part." I got to tell you, the same was true of us movin. I mean, after George got hisself off to his job and the youngens started school, I had too much time on my hands. Thet's when I finally got to missin my Tennessee kin, the state of Tennessee and 'em ol' blue mountains to beat the dickins. But then I recollected thet the whole time I was in "super organizin mode" and then gettin the move made, I'd been okay. I decided I had to keep myself busy.

Once I'd thought the notion through, seemed like I couldn't fill my days full enough; most all of it out of our house, either at the library doin my research, speakin somewhere or sailin with Mis' Caroline. With Bill's coachin me at first, got so the two of us could take the *Flyin Tarpon* out on thet big sound and sail our pants off, all by ourselves. Seemed like with us always on the move, adjustin this and trimmin thet, I didn't have time to thank of home and wonder how everone was doin back there.

Now, I thought, real sad, to myself, *movin here was the easy part. Stayin here is the hard part.* I can't tell you how many times I wanted to call up Pigeon Forge jest to tell Junior, Momma and Daddy it was me and hear gladness come into their voices. But I didn't. It was like stayin on a diet. I knew better than to take thet first bite of sweetness. Besides, I knew they'd figure right away thet I wasn't steppin up to the plate like I

130

should. Cause sure as certain, when I heard one of their dear voices, I'd go plumb to pieces.

I did write letters, though; one ever week. *Dear Momma, Daddy and Junior,* I'd write, usin my special purple ink. *You should see how pretty it is here in September. Miss Caroline took me to a place called "The Pike Place Market" the other day. It was some sight to see all those fresh fruits and vegetables. Every farmer had his own stall for selling. Besides that, there was every kind of fresh fish a body could see in the ocean. I was some amazed. That's one thing real different out here. Folks eat a heap of seafood. Miss Caroline bought a big salmon from a man with a real deep voice. After she pointed to the one she wanted, he picked it up and threw it over the heads of everybody. It flew all the way to the counter where another man caught it, pretty as you please. Well, that other man had it filleted out and wrapped up ready to go, quicker than an eye blink. It was some amazing.*

Another week, I wrote: *Dear Momma, Daddy and Junior, I can't believe how hard it is to find decent grits out here. Mis' Caroline took me to a fancy grocery store called "Larry's" over in a town called Kirkland and they had some of the instant kind, but they wanted dear for it and I'm like you, Momma, I think instant is a poor substitute for good old-fashioned grits. Seems like you can't add enough butter, salt and pepper to make them taste like anything but mushy wallpaper glue.*

One thing's good though, Billy got a job in a grocery store and if I give him a list and some money, he'll bring home what I ask. One time, I asked for breakfast cereal, thinking he'd get me the Kellog's Cornflakes, the honey puffed oats or such. Instead, he brought home some granola cereal. I can't tell you how good it was. I reckon it's got bits of fruit, nuts and brown sugar in it. Even Vikki Ann likes it, and you know how she loves her Rice Krispies.

My letters were full of foolishness, mostly. I did tell them that everbody liked the house I'd found for us to live in real well and thet Shadow sure liked her yard with the climbin roses. I knew they would take my letters up the mountain to share with

131

Mammaw and Pappaw. Course, Pappaw would be wantin to know 'bout the pup. I figured I'd get Vikki Ann to write a special letter 'bout thet.

I'd told 'em that I'd planted the Iris from home, but I sure couldn't tell 'em thet I had my garden plot started or thet I was workin on the house, 'cause I wasn't. Instead, I was keepin myself real busy in other ways. For one thang, I spoke to anybody thet invited me, long as they wanted the speechmakin done on the east side of Lake Washington. I still couldn't force myself to tackle the traffic in Seattle. It gave me the all overs, and that's a fact.

Turns out quite a lot of folks on the east side were wantin to hear me. Thet surprised me some. Knowin how folks are, you'd have thought all the folderol 'bout the Marilue Perkins fan club would have up and run its course by the time we finally come west and it sorta had. But still, folks were callin and askin' would I speak. So, even if I didn't have a fan club like a movie star did, it seemed like I sure was popular at givin history lessons. I kept gettin asked real regular, even though folks had to call up information to get our number since it wasn't in the phone book yet.

I reckon it was partly on 'count of the court settin a trial date for the Madison Street Muggers makin the news thet brought me back to their minds. Course, the reporters had to say a bunch of times thet George and I were the prosecution's star witnesses.

I had my daily reminder calendar from the Hallmark Cards scheduled with speeches clear into 1981. Seemed like historical societies, quilters, guilds, ol' folks' homes, librarians, scout troops, 4-H clubs, and the schools were all interested in my family history, the Civil War and the South in general.

I learned real quick thet if I was talkin to children, the boys mostly wanted to hear me talk 'bout gettin mugged. Got so when I'd walk up front to talk, I'd say, "Now this speech isn't 'bout fightin off muggers, but, since some of you are interested, I'm gonna pick the best listener in the room when I'm done talkin. I'm gonna let thet good listener ask me one such question 'bout the muggers at the end." My, but thet little trick kept a whole lot of squirmers tryin their best to be good.

132

I was talkin a couple of times a week and mostly folks were real friendly, clappin some when I was done and wantin to ask questions. Some, especially the youngens, were even askin for my autograph. And of course, everbody wanted to see the ol' quilt I'd brought west with me. At first, I would hand it 'round. Then I caught one lady at an ol' folks' home settin to snip hersef a little souvenir off a frayed corner with her sewin scissors. After I got my heart started again, I decided maybe jest lettin folks look at it bein held up front was enough.

Mis' Lucille, at the library, and I got to be real good friends. "Mis' Lucille," I said one day, "the folks I'm talkin to reckon I know all this stuff I'm tellin 'em 'bout, but you know I don't. Reckon, thanks to your hep, I'm learnin more 'bout them ol' worn down Appalachian Mountains and the state of Tennessee than I ever thought I wanted to. Seems like ever time I get asked a question 'bout it, quiltin, or the South in general, and I don't know the answer, I jest got to dig into some book to find out. Seems like I sure don't like not knowin."

She smiled. "What you really need to do is use the library at the University of Washington, Marilue. Its purpose is mainly research." She paused and raised her eyebrow at me. "Now, you haven't forgotten you're coming here to speak to my quilting circle, have you?"

Even Mis' Caroline asked, if I would speak to the ladies in her hospital guild 'bout the history of quiltin. Said I could jest drive to the yacht club, which I had already done a bunch of times to go sailin. Said she'd pick me up, take me on into the city to speak; the city meanin Seattle. No way I was goin to turn her down.

"Mis' Caroline, if I had to rent a taxi, I'd do it for you," I said. Meant it too. I sure owed thet woman a heap.

"You gotta build a picture in your mind," I tol' the ladies thet belonged to the hospital guild, "how thangs were way back then, afore the Boston Tea Party was the straw thet broke the camel's back and started the Revolutionary War. Back then, England controlled ever bit of cloth made or imported to what they called "the Thirteen Colonies of the New World." Since England was broke from years of fightin, first with General

133

Napoleon Bonaparte and France, then in The Seven Year's War, they needed all the money they could get. Charged terrible prices for ever single thang, includin cloth, knowin the settlers had to have clothes, bed covers and such…"

I noticed they'd all stopped whisperin to each other and diggin in their purses by then and were listenin good. "Them poor women handmade everthang thet their families wore; so they had a fair amount of leftover scraps thet they could piece together. Often, thet's what they did at night; pieced them little hoarded scraps together. Then they'd get together after some woman's quilt top was all stitched into a rectangle and sew all them tiny stitches thet hol' the top to the battin inside and the fabric on the back."

Afterwards, Mis' Caroline seemed some impressed. "You are SO good at this, Marilue! You just be careful you don't get so booked up with speaking engagements that you can't do our Wednesday sail."

I laughed, still feelin some proud from all the ladies clappin and givin me such fine compliments on my talk. "Not a chance, Mis' Caroline. My Hallmark daily reminder calendar has Wednesday marked for sailin plumb through Christmas. The weather gets too bad, you got to tell me. Otherwise, you say let's go, I'll say, I got my slicker."

She smiled. "When the weather gets too bad for sailing, I'll teach you to snow ski."

I snorted. "And I'll teach you how to scald a hog." Me bein strapped to long skinny sled runners, headin down mountains as high and unfriendly lookin as these Cascade Mountains seemed 'bout as likely as Mis' Caroline hepin my kin turn a pig into picnic hams.

She caught my drift and laughed. "Now, Marilue, it isn't like you to shut your mind to something you haven't tried. A lot of people think skiing is fun."

We were walkin to her car. "Listen," I said, "what with all the house fixin, history researchin and doin double duty as the momma and the daddy at home, I got a full plate. I don't even want to hear 'bout an opportunity to break my neck."

Mis' Caroline stopped and looked at me. "Is poor George still working those long hours?"

I nodded, but clapped my trap shut. Wasn't any way I was goin to bad mouth my husband in front of anybody, even Mis' Caroline; and it seemed like them were the sort of words tryin to come out of my mouth.

Real truth was, I still hadn't got 'round to much house improvement. Hadn't been doin much real cookin lately, either. Seemed like homemakin had lost its appeal to me. Don't know why I said thet stuff to Mis' Caroline. Real truth was, I could barely stand bein home at all. Real truth was thet I was not only missin Tennessee and my kin, I was missin my husband real bad.

I knew in my heart thet it wasn't true, but it seemed like he might not care a lick 'bout me and the youngens anymore, he liked his new job thet much. Seemed like he hadn't so much as patted my fanny in more'n a month. Seemed like the new computer at his job was the one gettin all his attention.

Mis' Caroline looked at me for the longest time afore she put her key in the car door lock. "Well," she said, "all the more reason for you to keep busy. Why do you think I learned to sail?"

We looked at each other for jest a tad longer over the top of the car and then got in. Then I said, real quick, changin the subject, "I got to pay close attention when we drive by the University. Mis' Lucille, the librarian in Snohomish, says I'd better get to know the library there. Says they'll have a heap of books on Southern history. Says they got a new way of lookin up stuff usin a computer."

We were stopped at a red light. Mis' Caroline smiled and pointed at the street sign. "This is where you turn. The library is 'bout two blocks up on the right. You'll use the same freeway exit you use to get to the yacht club."

"Well, seems like I could do thet," I said. I memorized the trees on the corners of Pacific and 15th so I could spot the place again. "Maybe I jest will."

"What you should do is call the history department at the University and ask for an appointment with the professor who knows the most 'bout the South. It seems to me that might be the quickest way to get pointed in the right direction."

135

I reckon she was teasin me a little, sorta darin me to do it, but thankin I wouldn't. "Reckon maybe I'll do thet, too," I said.

"Momma," Vikki Ann said thet evenin while she was peelin potatoes for the pot roast I was fixin to put in the oven, "I don't believe these kids out here like me very much."

I asked, only half payin attention, "What makes you thank thet, honey?"

She shrugged. "They're real standoffish. I mean, the girls say 'hi' in the hall and stuff, but nobody asks me to sit with them at lunchtime, or even ask how I like things out here so far."

She put down her peeler and sat down. Shadow got up from under the kitchen table and buried her head in Vikki Ann's lap. Reminded me of how ol' Pepper used to do me.

"What 'bout the boys?" I asked, thankin thet they wouldn't be blind to how purty she was.

Vikk Ann's face turned red. ""They don't much count. Seems like all they know how to do is twitch my hair when I'm not lookin and say my name like it's got a million parts."

"My, my," I said, tryin not to smile. "Now how on earth could they do thet?"

She screwed up her face and crossed her eyes. "Vee-hick-kee-a-yan-Purr-rick-kins." She drawled the words out real slow.

I said, "Don't cross your eyes, honey, they're liable to stay thet way, then them boys wouldn't thank you're purty enough to tease."

She slid from her chair, gathered Shadow into her lap and said, her voice real sad, "Lucky I got Shadow. She's the best friend a body could have anyhow."

It passed through my mind to call up her school and talk to her teachers. Maybe get a girl assigned to be her friend. *Nope*, I thought, *she has to get this figured out all by her own self. Jest like I got to get what to do 'bout George figured out all by my own self.*

I wasn't only worryin 'bout the two of us, I was startin to worry 'bout his health. The man wasn't eatin or sleepin proper. I had finally come to see thet it wasn't only the likin his new job

136

thet was keepin him apart from us. Worry lines were takin permanent residence on his forehead. Looked to me like he'd bit off a big bite and was workin to get it chewed up enough to swallow.

Funny thang was, "Solution Quest," Louis's company, had been hired by Boeing to solve some wirin problems in the wings of their new 777 airplane. So, in a way, George was workin for Boeing after all.

This job was real different from the one he'd had in Maryville, no mistake 'bout thet. For one thang, they didn't keep regular hours at "Solution Quest." Louis figured their folks could get an idea for solvin a problem at any time, night or day, and they might want to go on in to the company to work on it; feed data to a computer, use the draftin equipment, thet sort of stuff. Sometimes they'd brainstorm with other folks in there workin too. Least, thet's what George told me.

All I knew was sometimes, in the dead of night, I'd hear him slip out of bed and into his clothes. If I heard the truck start, I knew he was headin for Everett. No engine sound meant he was workin out in the shop with his fancy new equipment.

Sometimes he'd come back jest afore gettin up time, pretendin he hadn't been gone; me, pretendin along with him. Me, noticin thet he'd taken up his belt a notch. Me, watchin the hollows under his eyes get darker as the days passed. Me, havin my own homesick dreams and wide-awake nights. Me, not sayin a word, jest keepin myself busier and busier 'cause I couldn't thank how to start, or even what to say, without it soundin wrong. Inside I was howlin with homesickness.

But then, one night when he was out in his shop, I got up and went on out. Stood at the door to his shop and from the darkness, I watched him standin there, his fingers strokin his precision lathe, eyes jest starin. It gave me the all overs. I knew jest what them fingers felt like. I am ashamed to admit thet it felt like I'd caught him cheatin on me. "George," I said, plumb disgusted, "you plannin on workin yourself to death afore the year is out?"

He jumped like I'd stuck him with a straight pin. "Why, Marilue, honey, what are you doin up this

137

time of night?" he asked in the voice he used when he'd been thankin hard.

"Lookin for you," I said, walkin on in an' givin him a real tight hug.

"You're goin to catch yourself a cold runnin around in the night air, dressed like that," he said, rubbin up and down my arms to warm me.

It felt real good. Octobers in the Northwest do have a chill to em. I looked down at myself. Had on my second best nightie an' robe set. The nightie was two layers, turquoise over green an' real purty, if I did say so myself. He had changed from rubbin my arms to hol'in me tight. Felt like he was hol'in on for dear life.

"George," I said real soft, strokin up an' down his back, "I do reckon you're right. I am col', 'cept for where you rubbed on my arms. Why don't you come on back to bed an' warm up the rest of me?"

His laugh had a funny choke to it, but I knew he'd caught my drift. "In a minute," he said, steppin back from me. "I got just one more little part to think 'bout."

He reached for a pad of paper an' a pen. "You go on in now."

I went, smilin all the way. But he never come.

Later, I heard the engine to the truck start. Seemed like I couldn't get warm for the rest of the night. Towards mornin, I figured if I didn't thank of somethin else besides my predicament with George, I was gonna go crazy. So I switched my mind off George an' got to puzzlin for the umpteenth time, on what I'd done with the little carvin Pappaw had asked me to give to Mis' Caroline.

Seems like Mammaw had told him what I said 'bout Mis' Caroline bein such a good friend an' what a hep she had been. I reckon you recollect thet ever once an' awhile my pappaw kept one of his carvins back when he sent the rest of 'em on down the mountain to the man who buys em. When he does keep one back, he says there's a feel to 'em when he carves the wood. He knows then thet the piece has got a special purpose.

At the reunion, he gave me such a carvin all wrapped in brown paper an' knotted up good with strang. 'Here, Missie," he'd said. "This'ns for thet friend of your'ns out in the west country. Tell'er to look close an' she'll see somethin of hersef in it."

Course, I'd fussed to see it, but he didn't pay me any mind. "Reckon it's right for her to see it first, honey. You go put this packet some'er safe now." He slapped me on the behind like I was one of his ol' mules. "Git now," he'd said, "put it away safe an' go find som'un else ter pester."

I was plumb sure an' certain thet I had done jest what he said 'bout puttin it somewhere safe, but for the life of me, I couldn't thank where it was, what with all the movin.

I lay in our bed squeezin my eyes tight, tryin real hard not to thank 'bout the empty space beside me, feelin more lonely than I could ever recollect--what with missin my kin, feelin sad 'bout the lost carvin an' losin my husband's interest.

Seemed like I couldn't stand to fess up an' tell Pappaw how careless I'd been. Pappaw! Clear as day, I could see his weathered, hickory face, ever detail plain, from the mole on his forehead, to the little, red, broken blood vessels on his nose an' cheeks. Seemed I could even catch the scent of him, or at least a whiff of the soap Mammaw washed his overalls in. He was smilin at me, the sapphire blue eyes thet time couldn't fade filled with so much love, it seemed for a second like he was really there. And maybe somehow he was. I was finally warm an' somewhat comforted when I didn't thank I could be. Not long after, I drifted off to sleep.

Next mornin, when the alarm clock jangled me out of bed, I knew exactly where I'd put Mis' Caroline's carvin. It was under the front seat of the station wagon, jest where I'd put it when Pappaw had shooed me off at the reunion.

I threw off the covers. Thet knowin an' the fact thet it wasn't rainin out, cheered me some. I woke the youngens, told 'em my news 'bout recollectin where I'd put the carvin an' started down to get 'em a real breakfast, not jest granola.

There was a note on the kitchen blackboard. It said, "Gone to the office, be back in a couple of hours. Love, George."

139

I had half a mind to run an eraser through the word "love." *You don't show it, so don't write it,* I thought.

The youngens come down. Billy looked up at the note, then fastened his bright Perkins blue eyes on me. "We sure haven't been seein much of Daddy lately, have we Momma?"

"Or you either, since you got that box boy job," Vikki Ann said, walkin up to do her own readin.

He grinned at the truth of her words, pleased with hisself. "Yep," he said as he slipped into his chair, "but I'm not Junior. I don't aim to bank all my money. I've got my eye on a 1956 Chevy two-door. I'm hopin to break Daddy free so we can go have a look."

If Billy was even a little bit homesick or at least feelin some unsettled by the move, he sure wasn't showin it. I stood in the kitchen, flippin eggs onto plates an' feelin real put out with him all the sudden. *He an' his daddy are jest two of a kind,* I thought, *not carin a lick 'bout what they left behind.*

Billy looked at me again an' I swear, he'd read my thoughts. "It isn't like Daddy wants to be away from us so much, Momma, you know that. He's just doin what he thinks he's got to do to make a place for himself out here," he said real calm an' went to eatin his eggs.

Well, I went from bein put out to wet-hen-mad in an eye blink. "Billy Dean Perkins," I hissed, shakin the spatula under his nose, "who do you thank you're talkin to? You thank I don't know thet your daddy is wearin hisself to a frazzle for us?"

Was a time, me doin thet would of made him start to giggle. Not anymore. Fact is, he hadn't had a spell since Junior's girlfriend socked him. He looked up at me real steady. "Sorry, Momma," he said, an' went back to eatin his eggs.

As I started for the stove, I heard Vikki Ann say, almost under her breath, "Least Daddy HAS to be gone."

Well, if I hadn't had thet metal spatula in my hand, I would have slapped her. I was thet riled up. I whirled an' asked, real col', "You care to explain thet remark, young lady?"

She got up from the table, eyes down, put her plate in the sink, ignorin Shadow, an' stood there with her back to me.

"No," she said, "I don't reckon I do. Things are just hard for me out here. Not havin Daddy or Billy or you around much probably makes it seem worse than it is."

I looked at Billy an' he was lookin at me. "She's got a point, Momma," he said. "I reckon I have been pretty scarce round here."

Got real quiet in the kitchen then, me lookin anywhere but at my son. All them words I wanted to say to square mysef to my children for spendin ever spare minute away from my family an' the house I jest had to have, died afore they hit my throat. I nodded slowly. Inside, I was shakin like I had the flu bug, but somehow I found a steady voice. "True." I said, finally lookin at my son. "She's got a point."

Then I turned an' walked over to Vikki Ann, put my arms 'round her from the back. "Perkins family IS runnin a little rough right now, honey. Prolly seems like you been patient with us 'bout as long as you could stand. Prolly you been waitin for us to gather 'round the dinner table so we could talk it out like we used to. Only we never got ourselves gathered."

She nodded her head. I couldn't hear her cryin, but I could feel the hot tears nearly burnin holes on my forearms.

I sighed deep. "Honey, go on up an' wash your face with col' water while Billy gets the bikes out of the shed. You two are runnin real late."

Before she went, I turned her 'round an' lifted her chin. "I got your drift an' I promise you, we'll find a time to get this talked 'bout afore the week is out."

Youngens got gone an' I changed into my clothes so I could go fetch the carvin out from under the front seat of the wagon. It gave me real pleasure to finally lay my hands on it. I put it on top of the refrigerator, poured myself a cup of coffee an' sat down for a big thank.

I looked 'round the kitchen an' thought how I'd fibbed to Mis' Caroline 'bout fixin up the house the day before. I'd wanted her to feel sorry for me, for bein so busy an' all. Instead, she seemed to feel sorry for George. I covered my eyes with my hands, recollectin when Momma an' Daddy an' I sat 'round the kitchen table in Maryville. I was real sure then, thet we should give George his chance. In the end, after nearly losin him his pickup, I'd done right by him. Even found us this house. Got us ready for the move; an' with Billy's hep, kept us all organized while makin tracks west. It hadn't seemed too hard. An' in the six weeks since George had started work, I hadn't complained once to him 'bout his long hours. Thet was worth somethin, wasn't it?

Or was it? Had I been keepin myself too busy? I got up an' got my daily reminder calendar from by the phone. Only thang in there was Wednesday's sailin trips with Mis' Caroline an' the dates of the speech-givin I'd promised folks. I closed it an' held onto it, like it was the Good Book. Somehow, I knew there was a truth, hidden in them pages, thet I couldn't quite see.

I got up an' poured myself another cup of coffee, knowin thet I shouldn't, an' went to let Shadow back in. She always stood on her hind legs at the fence corner to watch Vikki Ann ride out of sight. When I opened the back door for her, I saw George's truck was parked in front of his shop. I'd been thankin so hard, I hadn't even heard him come back. It struck me then thet he hadn't come to the house for his breakfast.

I walked down the steps an' headed towards the shop. Didn't mean to sneak up on him, like I'd done in the night, but I did. He was standin, all bent over his drawin table, hol'in onto the edge like he was in terrible pain. His eyes were shut an' it looked like he was prayin. Later, he told me he was.

I hadn't ever seen my man look worse. "George," I said, real soft, after I'd walked right up on him. "Are you sick, honey?"

He didn't even jump. I put my hand on his back an' he let out a groan from somewhere deep inside. 'Bout broke my heart to hear it.

"You never should have let me try this, Marilue," he said. "I can't even think now why I thought I could do it. Foolin 'round with my little home-built, *Popular Science* computer and inventin those machines for Andy made me think I knew somethin, but I don't know diddly squat."

He opened his eyes an' sighed. Then he reached out his hands an' took me by the shoulders. "I reckon old George is 'bout to tuck his tail, ask Andy for my old job back."

142

I looked at him. There were shadows under his eyes big enough to hide a swamp in an' he was 'bout the color of fresh tree sap. "When's the last time you ate, George?" I asked, as if I didn't know.

He shrugged. "I've got no appetite, Marilue."

"Well," I said, "it appears we got some talkin to do. You'd best come in an' let me feed you somethin in the process."

He looked at me like I was speakin in tongues. He hadn't been so tired; he'd prolly have gotten real mad. Here he was, feelin like the world's biggest failure an' his wife was talkin bacon an' eggs. I took him by the hand an' he followed me, not sayin a single word, Shadow walkin quiet behind us.

It did my heart good though, to see thet once he got started, he didn't stop eatin 'til he'd slicked up a stack of toast, six eggs an' 'bout a half pound of bacon. I filled his coffee cup for the third time, puttin my hand on his shoulder when I did the pourin. He sighed real deep an' reached up to cover my hand. "Thank you, Marilue. That tasted fine."

"You got to stoke the engine, George," I said. "Come on, get up now."

I led him up the stairs, pulled his boots an' put him under a quilt, clothes an' all. Since I hadn't yet got 'round to makin curtains, the sun comin through them tall windows had warmed the room considerable. It felt real friendly. He sighed again, only it seemed too sad an' worn down to be a sigh. I went 'round to my side, kicked off my own shoes an' snuggled in right next to him, strokin his head with one hand, usin the other to hol' him close.

"Don't let yourself thank now, honey," I whispered. "Lay your burdens in the Lord's lap for a little. You get some rest now an' you'll see thangs clearer."

"I've got to..." he said, but never finished what he was sayin, he was asleep thet quick. I held him, felt the muscles in his arms an' legs jerk like he was still fightin to keep on goin from somewhere deep inside. I watched him sleep for awhile, goin back over my mornin's thankin.

I can't say it come easy, or thet all my ideas were right. But, what I did come up with plumb riled me to the soul. George talked 'bout tuckin his tail. Well, he was second in line. I'd beat

143

him to it by a country mile. Only, when I'd tucked my tail, I'd run away from my own.

I tried to thank of the last time I'd made somethin special for dessert, done up Vikki Ann's hair in rag curls, or offered any sort of encouragement to George.

Billy didn't matter so much. He was at the age when his friends, sports, school an' his job come first. But Vikki Ann! I squeezed my eyes tight, thankin when she'd tried to talk 'bout how bone deep lonesome she was an' all I'd done was tease her 'bout bein purty.

Of a sudden, I knew what the secret in the little Hallmark calendar was. Everythang marked in there was a thang thet took me away from my family. I hadn't even started workin' on Mis' Caroline's quilt an' she was jest like family to me.

An' George! I couldn't even name the problem thet was plaguin him so, not even one detail. At first, he would want to talk 'bout it 'round the dinin room table, but the youngens an' I would try to get the subject changed quick as we could. Told him we thought computers were borin as a main topic of conversation.

"But we're makin history here. You can't talk 'bout it, but this is the very first ever, computer-designed airplane, bein made an' usin 3-D graphics to boot."

Billy looked a little interested in thet, but Vikki Ann an' I pretended to yawn. Reckon he got the picture.

But then, my suppers had changed too. Mostly we were eatin casseroles I'd thrown together ahead of time, easy stuff thet I didn't have to thank 'bout. If I had an afternoon speech, Vikki Ann put 'em in the oven. Then, after we'd rooted through our food, Billy would go to his job, George would go back to work, an' if I had a night speech, Vikki Ann got left doin up the dishes, all alone cept for Shadow.

I lay on my back beside George hurtin myself with my thoughts; thankin I'd rather take a beatin than come to grips with how I'd failed 'em thet I loved most. But I made myself keep on thankin an' decided thet the house was one more example of how I'd failed. I'd jest had to have it, had all sorts of grand plans for it, but hadn't really done a thang to it since we'd moved in.

144

"Mis' Caroline, you jest tell me when the weather's too bad for sailin. I'm plumb used to rain," I'd said. But jest one little drop an' I'd find an excuse not to work in the yard. Hadn't even turned my garden plot an' here it was the middle of October with the ground likely to get too muddy any day.

I hadn't put up a speck of wall paper, stripped that terrible paint off the staircase or made a curtain. Wind still whistled under the outside doors 'cause I couldn't get 'round to replacin the weather strippin. My thankin got so riled up, I slid out of bed an' back into my shoes, bein careful not to wake George, then headed straight for his shop.

For once, I really looked the place over, recollectin thet first day when I hadn't even come with him when he was seein it for the first time. Besides the fancy machines an' the draftin table with sketches an' scribbles I couldn't begin to understand, there was a shallow box-like thang on one counter with 'bout a million pegs connected with some sort of fine wire. Label in one corner read: "Advanced Flight Deck Wiring Concept Model."

Course, I didn't understand them words either. But, I sure knew somebody who did. I went back in to check on thet somebody. He was lyin so still he looked dead. Gave my heart a thump 'til I listened close an' could hear him snore the little soft whistlin sound he makes when he sleeps on his back. Shutin our bedroom door real soft, I closed my eyes an' asked the Lord to let him sleep the day away.

In the kitchen, I cleaned up the dishes, mopped the floor an' set a double batch of yeast to workin. My little girl was goin to come home to a momma an' a house full of the smell of bakin bread.

I left George a note on the blackboard. *Gone to library and market. Be back in one hour. I love you! Marilue.* I put a heart over the "i" in my name, like I do an' underlined *I love you!* for good measure. Then I wrote: *P.S. You had better be here!!!!*

At the library, I waved to Mis' Lucille, asked her, would she be so kind as to see if the library had a book thet would show house decoratin styles at the turn of the century. She told me right where to look. Then I passed right on by the history books, not even givin 'em a glance an' went straight to the books

145

on house decoratin. Got me an armload. One of 'em had a whole section on rooms for girls. From lookin at the pictures, I was purty sure Vikki Ann could get some real good ideas.

At the market, I asked the butcher to special thick-cut me some pork chops an' to saw the joint bone on a couple of ham hocks so I could do a good job on a mess of beans. I even remembered to get more eggs so I could make Seven Minute Frostin. There would be Devil's Food cake for dessert tonight.

Thet it took me more than an hour didn't matter. George had turned on his side, but he was still sleepin, Slept 'til mite near 2:00 o'clock. Thet was fine by me. When he woke up, there was fresh bread an' coffee waitin.

"George," I said after he got plumb awake, an' was workin on his third piece of bread an' butter, "we got a heap of talkin to do, but for right now, jest what is an 'Advanced Flight Deck Wirin Concept Model?'"

He let out a sigh an' looked at me. "It's what's drivin me plumb crazy, Marilue."

"How's thet?" I asked.

"Well, Boeing is havin problems gettin folks to put the wirin in the cockpit...that's where the pilots fly the plane. It's a real complex job of systems management. We're talkin electronics and hydraulics here."

He jerked his chin in the general direction of the shop. "You saw that model I made out there?"

I nodded an' he said, "It sure makes all your quiltin patterns look easy, doesn't it, honey?"

I nodded again, still chewin on his words, thankin I was way over my head, but wantin real bad to understand.

"You tryin to make the wirin more simple, George?"

He laughed, but it wasn't a happy sound. "No. Me and my big mouth..." He tipped back his chair. "That WAS the problem Boeing engineers handed us, but I got folks to thinkin we could teach a computer to do it."

"Can a computer do such a thang?" I asked, knowin now for sure how far over my head I was, but still listenin hard.

"Sure. It can do it quicker, cheaper and without human error."

146

I gave him a little smile. "Why, thet's fine then," I said. "So, what's the problem?"

He tipped his chair forward an' caught both my hands in his. "The problem is that your husband is the fella who has to design both the systems and the robotics for the computer program to do its job."

We both looked at our little pile of hands for awhile. Even I could see thet he'd gotten hisself in a pickle.

Finally, I said, "Well, George Everett Perkins, you might solve this, or you might not. But I will tell you one thang; you'd stayed back in Maryville, you wouldn't of had the chance."

He laughed a little bitter sound. "Now THAT IS the truth. And I wouldn't have moved my family three thousand miles from their friends and kin either."

I looked at him hard. "My, my, but we are a pair, both of us sittin tight on the pity pot. You, lookin to be a hero, work yourself to death so you got an excuse in case you fail. Me, gettin the big head, what with all my speakin, concentratin so hard on bein a star thet I plumb forgot my duties as wife an' mother."

George sat back. There was a glint in his eye. "How's that? What're you sayin here, Marilue?"

"Why, I reckon for you, I'm sayin you got to change your attitude. Louis said he'd give you six months to get your feet on the ground. You're feelin a failure 'cause you haven't done it in six weeks. For me, I'm not sayin I can't do my speakin. What I am sayin is…I got to do it for the right reason, not jest keepin myself busy 'cause you're so busy…an' not 'cause livin amongst strangers is hard…or 'cause when I get idle time, I miss Junior, Momma, Daddy an' the rest. I got to do it 'cause after bein the best wife an' momma I can be, I got time to give somethin back to the world."

It was a long speech. I was sorta breathin hard at the end, talkin so fast an' feelin it so strong. George jest sat there, struck dumb an' some battered under my hail of words. His blue eyes behind his glasses were blinkin hard. Then he leaned over an' took both my hands again. "Come on over here to my lap, Marilue," he said real soft.

147

I couldn't get there fast enough. We wrapped our arms 'round one another an' he buried his head in my chest for a minute. I could feel his warm breath. Then he leaned back an' I leaned down so our lips could touch. I can't tell you how good thet kiss felt. After a time, he said, real deep an' hoarse. "I've sure as hell missed you, honey."

"George," I whispered against his lips, "everthang's gonna work out jest right. But let's not talk 'bout it now. We got more than a half hour afore our youngens get home."

CHAPTER ELEVEN
NOVEMBER

I set so long on the pity pot thet I had never gotten 'round to callin the history department at the University of Washington. But finally, I got so dang tired of school youngens askin me why I talked funny an' sometimes catchin folks hidin their smile behind their hand, thet I called em.

The straw thet broke the comel's back come when I was at the library, talkin to Mis' Lucille. Now, I'll admit thet it was some past my lunchtime when it happened. I can get a little cranky when I forget to eat. But, right then, seemed like I'd jest had a craw full. This little boy an' his momma were standin there listenin to us like they didn't know it wasn't polite an' I heard the little boy say, "Mom, that woman talks funny. Is she an Okie?"

Well, I'll tell you I spun 'round from the desk, bent over an' looked at him, eye to eye. "I'm not an OKIE, I'm a HILLBILLY! There's a big difference. I come from the Smoky Mountains of Tennessee, not from Oklahoma. You got thet straight?"

I left his momma standin there with an open mouth an' marched past 'em out the door, leavin Mis' Lucille to clean up the hurt feelins. I sighed with the rememberin an' reached for the phone.

I didn't even make polite talk first, I just said to the woman in the history department who answered, "My name is Marilue Perkins, an' I'm wantin to know if you got any experts on how Southern accents got started? Specifically, I'm wantin to

149

know why folks in my part of the country, which is the hill country of east Tennessee, learned their way of speakin English so different than folks from elsewhere."

She laughed, not in a mean way. She could hear for herself what I was talkin 'bout. We do have a certain twang.

"That's a very interesting question, Mrs. Perkins. I'll ask around the department and see if I can get a proffessor to call you."

Wasn't more'n a couple of days later, the phone rang. "Mrs. Perkins, my name is Henry Beauvois. I am a history professor at the University of Washington. I was given your name by our department secretary, Mariam Carter. She said you had questions about accents."

My heart started doin a steady thump in my chest. "Well, thank you kindly for callin me back, Professor."

He went right on talkin like he hadn't heard me. "I teach a course here titled, *The United States during the Era of the Civil War and Reconstruction 1840-1870.*"

"My, thet's a real interestin mouthful," I said. "1840 was the very same year my great, great, great grandmother got hitched to my great, great, great grandfather, accordin to the family bible."

There was a pause. Then I heard him say, "Wonderful!" Like I'd jest given him a present. "Would those happen to be the same people who lost seven sons in the Civil War?"

"Yessir," I said, puttin two an' two together. "Seems like you must have been readin the paper or watchin the TV last spring."

"Yes," he said. "In fact, I saved the one article and used it to springboard a discussion on Tennessee's unique position before, during and after the Civil War."

Well, thet puffed me up a little, knowin such a man remembered me. "Professor," I asked, feelin hopeful, "are you aimin to answer my question 'bout why folks from my neck of the woods talk the way we do?"

"Yes, indeed I am. But then I also have somethin to ask you, if you don't mind, Mrs. Perkins."

"Glory be!" I said, "I reckon this is my lucky day. Who gets to go first?"

150

Well, his turn took nearly an hour; me mostly listenin, sayin now an' again, "My, if thet isn't the most interestin thang!"

He said thet the first settlers, my ancestors, kept on usin the language they brought with 'em from the British Isles. Said there were many theories 'bout mountain talk, only he called it a "dialect." He said one popular theory likened it to language spoken in England durin the time of Shakespeare.

"Is thet so?" I said, some amazed.

"Yes. Unfortunately, with improved transportation and communication, we are losing many of our dialects."

"How's thet?" I asked. I could hear real sadness in his voice. Made me like the man without even knowin him.

"It was the isolation that created the Appalachian Mountain dialect, Mrs. Perkins. For example, I notice you don't put an 'a' in front of words like coming and going, but my guess is you know people who do."

Well, thet made me laugh. "You mean do I know folks who say, 'I'm a comin or I'm a goin? Sure I do. Sometimes I fall into it myself when I'm visitin my mammaw an' my pappaw who live in the foothills of Mount Le Conte.

"Straight out of Shakespeare and the King James Bible," he said, like he knew what he was talkin 'bout. "I suspect your grandparent's dialect is much purer than your parent's and clearly, yours is greatly diluted."

I laughed. "You'd not thank so to hear the youngens out here ask why I 'talk funny.' But I know the truth of what you say. My own 'dialect' as you are callin it, has gotten some different since I married a man, Georgia-born an' college educated. An' our youngens talk some different from my husband an' me--'cept when they're up on Mt. LaConte with my kin. Then they got the mountain talk in em, thet's for sure. So, I reckon I'm a good example of what you are talkin 'bout."

We were quiet for a minute. My mind felt like a jigsaw puzzle with some found pieces all settlin into place. I was noddin my head though he couldn't see it. "I reckon you got it right. I know, for years, only new words comin into them mountains, other than Cherokee words, were the ones our men brought back when they come home from doin their fightin for the Union."

151

"Mrs. Perkins," he said then, "If you are satisfied with my answer, I'd now like to ask you a question."

"Professor," I said, "I'm plumb tickled to death with what you told me. Folks ask me now, I aim to tell 'em an earful."

"Fine," he said an' then took a deep breath. "Here's the question: I am in the process of writing a book. This one is to be from journals and letters kept by both soldiers and civilians during the Civil War. Reading about the quilt and your ancestor's involvement in that war made me wonder if your family had such a document in their possession."

I thought a minute. "Well, no, least not thet I ever saw or heard talk 'bout." I laughed. "Truth is, Professor, my kin in them days were best at readin sign."

"Like for tracking animals?" he asked.

"Yessir. I reckon to them, writin mostly meant signin their name with an X."

I could hear disappointment in his voice. "Yes, well, I can understand that there wasn't a lot of time for the more academic pursuits in life. Putting food on the table must have been a primary consideration." He gave a sigh. "I suppose I shouldn't have gotten my hopes up. I confess, I was so impressed by the historical detail in the article, I somehow assumed someone had written it down."

"Well, I sure wish they had," I said. "Like I say, 'cause of thet ol' article you got in front of you, I'm bein asked to give speeches an' folks keep askin questions I can't answer. Of late, I've 'bout ruined my eyes readin up on the Civil War an' the history of the South. Seems like when I don't know an answer, I jest got to find out. I can't tell you how many folks won't believe we fought for the Union in my neck of the woods. They somehow got it in their heads thet anybody south of the Mason-Dixon Line fought for the Confederacy...an' if you didn't, you were some sort of a traitor."

"Why, Mrs. Perkins," he said, "what you say is absolutely true. How perceptive of you. Are you able to correct their misperceptions?"

I smiled into the phone, "Why, I jest tell 'em the truth my pappaw taught me: wars are mostly 'bout money an' property an' thet the hillfolk of Tennessee were plumb shy on both. There weren't no plantations where I come from, Professor. Thang most folks was best at was raisin youngens. So, they generally had more than enough of 'em to hep 'em work their little bit of property; didn't need the colored folks like they did in the cotton fields. Saw 'em as jest another mouth to fill. But they did need to be independent an' they figured ol' Abe had the right notion; to keep the states united, I mean. Keep them folks still loyal to England in their place."

I laughed, enjoyin my own words, "Besides, it was them North Carolina boys thet kept runnin off with my great, great, great granddaddy's mules an' stealin his hens."

It was real quiet for a bit when I finished spoutin. Then the professor sighed. "Those mules and hens cost him seven of his sons. I find myself wondering if it was worth it." I heard the sad in his voice again.

"Now, Professor, you got to understand thet them boys plain loved to fight. Wasn't any way their folks could of kept a hoe in their hands when a rifle was offered."

"Ah!" He said an' then fell to bein quiet again afore finally sayin, "I am puzzled, Mrs. Perkins, how, without journaling, you have such a grasp of your own history?"

"Why, shoot, Professor, it's right simple, it's the women's job in my family line to pass on history through their quiltin. We tell our stories in our quilts an' pass 'em on to our daughters."

I heard him sigh again. "Mrs. Perkins," he said, "I have never talked with anyone who made the Civil War more real. I'm wondering if you would consider speaking to my class. And while you're here, I'll arrange for you to use our library, if that would assist you in your studies."

My ears perked right up. "Why, Professor," I said, "you got yourself a square deal. My friend, Mis' Lucille, the librarian here in Snohomish, has been pesterin me to do jest thet very thang. Said you got some sort of computer to hep folks find jest what they need."

"Yes, indeed we do, Mrs. Perkins."

"Please feel free to call me Marilue," I said.

After we hung up the phone, I got a little weak in the knees thankin 'bout talkin in front of so many educated folks. I

153

shook my head at all the ten-dollar words I'd jest heard an' wondered what I had got myself into.

Tickled George an' the youngens though. I kept the news 'til grace was said an' the food was passed. "I reckon I'm goin to be givin one of my speeches to a class at the University of Washington," I said. "I was talkin to a professor today."

They listened real careful to what Professor Beauvois tol' me an' then George shook his head. "You are really somethin, you know that, Marilue? This time last year anybody had bet me you would up and volunteer to give a speech at a big university, I'd wager money against it."

I laughed, "Shoot, the speakin isn't near as hard as doin the drivin thet'll take to get me there!"

Vikki Ann said, "Well, I liked what the professor said 'bout how we talk comin from learnin to read usin the King James Bible. It gives me somethin to say back to those teasin boys."

Billy grinned at her an' made a muscle. "I keep tellin you, you got anybody bein disrespectful just let your big brother know."

She gave him a look an' then gave a sigh. "We've already been over this, Billy Dean. You keep out of my business. I'm takin care of myself just fine."

"Why, Vikki Ann," I said, "I'm real pleased to hear thet. Sounds like maybe the kids are warmin up a little?"

"There's a few I like all right," she said. "Fact is they got 4-H clubs out here too. I been invited to join one for dog obedience."

"Why, honey, you are just likely to show 'em a thing or two," George said. "You always have had a way with animals."

I looked at my daughter, her face pink with pleasure at her daddy's words. "Shadow is an awful smart dog," she said.

I looked 'round the old dinin room table, thankin how, step by step, the Perkins family was findin its way to solid ground.

"Billy, please pass the snap beans on 'round to your daddy," I said. Then I looked 'round the table again. "You know, what with Thanksgivin comin up, I reckon this family has got a basketful to be thankful for." Meant it too. But there was a little

154

empty spot inside me jest thankin 'bout the ol' dinin room table on Thanksgivin Day, with jest the four of us. It was gonna be hard, an' I knew it. Made me start missin folks back home real bad.

Recollectin them thoughts the next mornin, it seemed like my oldest had been mindreadin. On school days, on count of his after school job, Billy was first up, doin his homework. By six he had the furnace cranked up, an' a fire in the kitchen fireplace if he had the time. Rest of us were still buried under quilts. Even George was sleepin sound, all lumped up, dead to the world.

He was still workin too hard. Still gettin up in the middle of the night. But he'd had a talk with Louis, sittin right at our ol' kitchen table, Louis stuffin hisself with my apple pie. Bein the kinda boss he was, Louis figured out the problem right away.

"You aren't a computer programmer, George," he said. "You don't have to write the code. I don't even want you to waste your time on code. We have two programming experts who will do that. Your job is to specify what you want the computer to do. It's their job to tell you if it can be done." He waved his fork. "You need time to learn to use the team, George. Learn to work smart, not hard."

Now, recollectin thet conversation, I spooned myself against my husband, kissed the back of his head with a sigh an' closed my eyes, knowin it was time to get movin, hatin the very thought of it. Thet's when I heard the phone start to ring.

"Momma," Billy called up the stairs, "come quick. It's Junior and he's in a hurry."

I was out of thet bed an' down them stairs quicker than you can shake a stick at a snake, no robe, no slippers. Lucky I had my flannel nightie on. I went so fast that I plumb forgot we had an upstairs phone. "Son, what's happened? Is everbody okay?" I said as I put the phone to my ear an' got an ax handle hol' on thet receiver.

"Well, course we are, Momma. Mammaw and Pappaw are right here beside me. They're both fit as fiddles and so am I.

155

Calm yourself. Doesn't have to be somethin wrong for us to call." He sounded real cheerful.

I took a big breath an' steadied myself. "You're sure right 'bout thet, son. Telephone carries good news as well as bad," I said, feelin my heart settle.

"Now, the reason we're callin, Momma, is 'cause we had a real good idea. But, since we figured we had to wait to call so as not to wake you, and I have a ten o'clock class, Mammaw gets to tell the whole of it.

"You sound real good, son," I said, picturin him so clear it made me recollect all over again how much I missed him.

He cleared his throat. "I sure miss everybody, Momma. You be sure an' tell Daddy, Billy and Vikki Ann I said that."

"Well, we're missin you too. Not a day goes by but what your name comes up. How's Darlene?" I asked to keep him on the line.

"Real fine. Real fine. You'd be happy how hard she works to keep me marchin straight."

Well, thet made me smile. "Bye, honey, I know you got to go. Thanks for callin. You study hard an' be hepful 'round the place."

"I will, Momma."

"I sure do miss you, Junior. I know you're doin what you need to do, but it's real hard on a hen when her chick flies the coop."

"I figured so, Momma."

Seemed real hard to let him go. "You study hard now."

He laughed. "You already said that, Momma. Now, here's Mammaw. I got to be gettin or I'll be late for class."

"Bye, son. I love you," I said right in my Momma's ear.

"Marilue, honey," she said, not mindin a bit, "you two sure brought up a fine boy."

"Well, I hope so," I said, feelin puffed up an' choked up all at the same time.

"But, honey, we ain't callin jest to gab. You'n's son come up with as special of an idee your daddy an I ever did hear. He come home last night a' talkin 'bout this friend of his'n what's got a motor home he rents out cheap in the winter time. It

156

give us the idee to rent it an' come on out yonder to see you folks, if you'ns ain't a goin to be too busy come Christmas time."

It took a bit for my ears to catch hol' of what she was sayin. Then I couldn't seem to find my breath; felt jest like a catfish in a dry pond.

Momma finally said, "Marilue, you still there?" I nodded thet I was, but I was truly speechless an' thet's not often true of Marilue Gracie Perkins.

"Honey," I could hear her say to Daddy, "seems like we might of got cut off. You thank I should hang up the phone?"

Well, thet cleared my pipes. "Momma," I squeaked, "I'm right here. You jest took my breath away is all. Seemed like you were sayin you an' daddy were comin out for Christmas in a motor home, if I got your drift."

She laughed, "Thet's right. Only, it's not jest us, honey, thet's why we're rentin the motor home. It's Junior's school break so he's a comin an' maybe Paw an' Maw, if'n we can get 'em to say so. We plan to go up to the mountain this very day'n ask em. I know Momma will be a wantin to fetch a look at you'ns, jest to make sure an' certain everbody's pert. Reckon you'n all know how she is. But Paw? Well, your pappaw's such a homebody, I'd not be wagerin a guess.

My brain felt like a half-pulled batch of taffy. "How's thet? You are comin clean across the United States in a rented motor home? Is thet what you said, Momma?"

"Yes'm. That's what I been a sayin 'bout," Momma said, like she was talkin 'bout drivin across town. "It was Junior's idea. He figures on bein the one drivin us. Since he's already done it afore, I reckon we'ns figured, why not?"

Daddy grabbed the phone from Momma. "Hi-dee, honey," he hollered. I quick yanked the listenin end of the receiver back from my ear by 'bout six inches. Daddy always did talk loud on a phone.

"How do you like the little plan we'ns are a cookin up?"

"Daddy," I said, "it's like I can't believe my ears. There's doubt I could even tell how much I've been missin you. Couldn't even call, fraid I'd break down somethin shameful. Sure, we're goin to be here, an' we got plenty of room."

157

Then Momma had the phone again. "Honey, we'uns really don't near have ever detail straight in our mind. Wanted to check with you'ns first, see what you thought."

"Momma," I said, "You jest gotta come. I'm already countin the days." Then I had a thought. "Where's Junior?"

"He's scatted off fer school."

"Momma," I said, "you tell thet boy for me, this is the best idea he ever had in the all of his eighteen years!"

Billy, who had been listenin to ever word gave a whoop an' ran for the stairs to spread the news. I hung up the phone, pure joy runnin through me. I thought 'bout pinchin myself to make double sure I wasn't dreamin. Tears were runnin down my cheeks but there was a smile on my face as big as the moon.

I can tell you, it was one happy breakfast table, ever body teasin' me about runnin past the upstairs phone. George started lookin thoughtful 'bout half way through. "If your folks can come all that way; don't see why mine can't do the same. Bring Harlen and Karlen to do the drivin. You know those two'd shut up the shop and come if I said the fishin was good."

"Why, thet's a fine idea," I said. "They'd rather go fishin than fix cars any ol' day. Jest tell 'em 'bout thet steelhead fish you keep talkin 'bout."

Vikki Ann's eyes were full of purple sparkle. "Maybe they'd bring their fiddles and such, Daddy."

George looked at me an' grinned. "Reckon that old wash tub and broom handle is around here somewhere?"

I nodded, glad to say I could put my hand right on thet ol' gut bucket of his, feelin glad 'bout the excitement in his voice. I looked at him grinnin at Vikki Ann. "I sure could use a session on a gut bucket," he said, gettin up an' standin with his foot on a chair rung, like he was gettin set to start pluckin on the strang.

Billy put his plate on the floor for Shadow to slick up an' said, "Momma, I have an idea you'd better start prayin that the mountain passes don't get all snowed in come Christmas time. It sure isn't the best time to be travelin in a motor home."

George looked at him hard. "Better idea would be for you to get yourself busy and plan them a south-comin route.

158

Only thing you accomplished with those words of yours was to set your momma worryin."

It got real quiet in the kitchen. Billy looked shamefaced, eyes on Shadow like her lickin his plate was the most interestin thang in the room; *But no nervous giggle; not even a snicker. He's takin George's scoldin like a man,* I thought, then looked at the clock an' stood up from the table, puttin my hands on my hips. "Well, I don't reckon I'm in the frame of mind to worry today," I said, an' walked over to give Billy's shoulder a pat. "You youngens got lunch money? Best get in gear. I got lists to make and a mountain of presents to think about buyin."

George an' I sat for a minute after they'd gone. "That sure would be fine to have your folks and mine here for the holidays, wouldn't it, Marilue?"

"Like a dream I didn't dare have thet's come true," I said.

"Well, then, I reckon, this afternoon, I'll give the twins a call. No sense gettin Momma and Daddy excited unless the boys are willin to do the drivin."

"Good thankin," I said an' got up to look at the calendar. "An' I reckon, besides the present buyin, I'd better give my tail a shake an' get this house put together. They'll be here in six weeks, George."

He sighed. "Well, in six weeks, that old robotic arm I'm workin on will either make me a hero or it won't."

I rubbed my cheek against his. "Lord made the world in six days; Perkins family made it practically across the United States in five; I reckon you can get a robot's arm built an' I can get a house ready for company in six weeks." I laughed, "'Specially since the weather has turned against sailin."

When I reached across him to clear the plates, George sat back down an' pulled me into his lap. "It's not a robot, honey," he said. "And, it's not really an arm. It's a thing the computer can direct to lay down wires in a certain path."

I looked at him real serious. "Are you thankin you can do it, George?"

159

He nodded. "Maybe. I'm workin with this little fellow with glasses thicker than mine. Every time I say, 'Can you teach the computer to do this?' He says, 'No problem.'"

George sighed. "Then he says, 'Can you get your machine to do what my computer tells it?' And I say, 'Now THAT'S a problem!' and we both laugh like hell. But, I've built another unit that's doin at least part of what it needs to do."

It was the longest George an' I had ever talked 'bout one of his inventions. Fact was, for some reason, I didn't find it all thet uninterestin.

"George," I said, feelin real proud, as I got off his lap an' picked up our plates, "I do believe I understood most of what you said!"

He got up, lookin thoughtful. "Well," he said, givin me a peck an' takin a swipe at my fanny as he left, "maybe it's because this job is teachin me to explain things better."

He was doin his little whistle when he went out the door. I smiled, thankin how like my man it was to take blame for me not understandin what he did. Truth was prolly the job WAS hepin him explain stuff better. But another truth come to me. "Could be," I said to Shadow, "Or could be too, I'm not so fraid of new ideas anymore."

I slicked up the kitchen in jig time, then called the high school an' asked the secretary to please have Mister Jeff Adams call me when he got a break. Seemed like I was goin to need my crew back if I was gonna be ready for Christmas company.

Made up my mind on the spot, anybody else called for a speaker, I'd tell 'em I was booked 'til January. I'd do what I'd already signed up for includin the University of Washington speech for Henry Beauvois, but then speechifyin was goin onto the back burner. I had company comin!

CHAPTER TWELVE
DECEMBER

Our house was feelin ever one of its seventy years as it shivered in wind so strong thet it made the rain do a jig against the kitchen windows. It was still so dark out not even a speck of moonlight was makin it through the rain clouds. So far, winters in Washington didn't impress me much.

"I reckon the two of you know you will never be able to tease Mis' Caroline an' me 'bout sailin in foul weather again," I said, slidin a fresh stack of my sourdough hotcakes on Bill Johnston's plate. "It sounds terrible out there."

Bill laughed. "Marilue, if George wants to catch a steelhead today, I'd cut a hole in the ice if I had to. At Boeing, we pander to those people who save our butts."

"How's thet?" I asked, not catchin his drift.

Bill grinned. "We give them any damned thing they want!"

George gave a snort but the words pleased him, I could tell. Pride in him ran through me like sunshine. No two ways to cut it, my husband had done hisself proud. Course the way "Solution Quest" worked, only a handful of folks knew it was George's newest invention thet was bein talked 'bout when Boeing called their news conference.

"Our computer-designed 777 is currently being developed in our Everett, Washington plant. We are using 3-D graphics in every facet of design and production problem solving. For example, here's our new robotic computer-aided

161

777 wing wiring arm," they'd said. "It does the wiring 16 times faster than doing it by hand..."

No mention was made of George Everett Perkins formerly of Maryville in the great state of Tennessee. Next day Bill an' a bunch of other bigwigs had their picture square on the front page of the *Seattle Times*. Nobody took George's picture. Course, like I said, thet was the way "Solution Quest" worked an' George didn't seem to mind a bit. Soon as the announcement was done, he locked up shop an' went fishin. Found out real quick, catchin a steelhead on a fly was harder than it looked, even though he had bought the flies Bill told him to an' along with that, had bought hisself a proper rod an' fancy neoprene chest waders for the col' water. I'd told Mis' Caroline an' she'd told Bill. So then, he'd called to say did George want his hep on learnin how an' exactly where to fish? I heard George say on the phone, "Is a blue bird blue?"

"Today's the day, Bill." George tucked his elbow to his side, stiffened his wrist an' did a few pretend casts. "I do believe I'm gettin the hang of what you showed me yesterday." He rubbed his hands together, an' then reached for his wool sweater. "Today I'm goin to land the big one."

I noticed thet his shoulder wasn't givin him a bit of trouble. "Good thang your shoulder's all healed up," I said as I handed him a thermos of hot black coffee an' a poke full of ham sandwiches an' homemade moon pies.

I was havin a heck of a time findin stone-ground or old fashioned grits, but the stuff for my moon pies were in ever grocery store I went to. "You go an' have a wonderful time freezin your butts off."

Meant what I said 'bout havin a wonderful time. It was jest plain good to hear my husband laughin an' foolin 'round. Truth was, it was doin my heart good to see George takin some time for hisself. I knew he wanted to be ready an' able to show his brothers a real good time once they got here...an' I wanted thet too.

He handed Bill the lunch poke an' put his arm 'round me. Said, "Marilue is makin a speech at the University today, Bill. Isn't she somethin?"

162

I wish he hadn't reminded me. "If I hadn't given my word, I wouldn't go," I said. "Don't know what I got to say to interest a bunch of college students anyhow."

George looked at me, knowin I had the butterflies. "It'll come to you," he said, givin me a squeeze, "just like it always does."

I nodded an' sighed. "Reckon you're right."

After they got gone, I looked an' it was near six o'clock. Made it mite near nine in the mornin in the Cumberland Gap country. I dialed the phone. "Howdy, Karlen," I said, knowin it was him, since Harlen couldn't abide talkin on the telephone. Neither of 'em boys had ever married, though they'd come close a time or two. Seemed like havin each other was enough for em.

"Howdy, Marilue, we figured it was you callin. Our baby brother caught onto the party bein for him yet?"

"Not even gettin suspicious, far as I can tell, Karlen. He's jest so plumb tickled you're comin, he mite near can't sleep nights."

Karlen gave a happy chuckle like he sometimes does when things are goin his way. "Well, thet's good then, real good. He caught hisself one of those big steelhead fish yet?"

'Nope, but I jest sent him out the door lookin like a bale of cotton, he has on thet many layers of clothes. He figures today is the day."

"Weather set in out there, has it?"

"Well, folks tell me it's 'bout normal for December, so you boys better brang ever pair of long handles you can find. You're goin to be standin in water so col' there's ice in the shadders an' still places."

Karlen laughed. "You an' George got us so damned excited with y'alls phone callin we already got ourselfs mostly packed up, music instruments, Billy's fine 'trip planner,' his map an' all, Marilue. Daddy's packin his Jew's harp 'round in his shirt pocket, twangin on it when he thinks nobody can hear."

"Why, thet's fine. This is gonna be some celebration!"

Karlen gave a hoot. "Baby girl, you don't know the half of it. Daddy snuck out yesterday an' dug up three jugs of his

163

special sippin whiskey from where it was hid. He said he was goin to pack it away in the motor home so good it cain't be found should we get stopped by the law. Said it ain't ever day we Perkins gets to celebrate havin an 'in-no-va-tive genius' in the family."

His words sounded like they were pokin fun, but I could hear the proud in em.

"We're meetin up with y'all's kin at first light. Harlen's got the Caddy tuned up an' purrin like a kitten--paid full price for two brand new snow tires."

"I'm real glad you're drivin out together, Karlen. Takes a load off my mind, what with this weather," I said.

"Don't you worry 'bout a thing, Marilue. Thet ol' pink Caddy is as sure footed as a goat."

"It's not you two I'm worried 'bout, you're near professionals. It's thet boy of mine drivin a big motor home," I said.

"Well, shoot," he said, "didn't Junior tell you the motor home come with chains?"

Thet news sure lightened my load. We talked a little more an' then hung up. I closed my eyes, wonderin how I was ever goin to wait another ten days.

When Billy come down from upstairs carryin his school books, I was studyin our wall calendar with all its marked off days like I hadn't seen it ever before.

"Jest talked to your Uncle Karlen," I said to him.

"They like the map and the trip plan I sent em?" he asked.

"Yep, said they had it all studied. They're chompin at the bit to get on the road. Goin to see the Cowboy Hall of Fame in Oklahoma City, like you suggested, then head south to Fort Worth, Texas, all the men 'cept Pappaw Joe are tradin off drivin the rigs like you told em to. Seems like they think the whole idea was their own."

Billy grinned, "Ten more days," he said.

I looked back at the calendar. "Yep," I said, "I know. I've been standin here countin, tryin to make it less." I sighed. "Not workin though."

164

After the youngens got gone to school, seemed like I couldn't get mysef settled. It wasn't like I didn't have a heap to do. Jeff an' the boys were mostly done, but I still had curtains an' dust ruffles to make, trim to paint, bakin to do an' a bunch of other piddly thangs thet I could be doin to keep my mind off the speech I was goin to give the history class.

Course I wanted thangs to be near perfect when everbody showed up, but instead of gettin busy, I wandered through the house. Sure made a difference in the livin room to have the walls all painted an' the furniture set back where it belonged.

I'd bought a ten-foot tree from the Boy Scouts. It was sittin, picture purty, at the far end of the livin room, decorated with all our old ornaments, the old glass star leanin jest a touch, at the top. Vikki Ann an' I had gotten some carried away in the present buyin' department and you couldn't hardly see the bottom of the tree for all the presents under it.

On that same round coffe table the boys left their beer bottle rings on was our old nativity set Pappaw had carved for me when I was jest a girl. He'd even made the stable where baby Jesus was borned. Only gettin to see it come Christmas time made it extra double special. Then, Vikki Ann had set ever single one of the animal carvins Pappaw had given us in the fir boughs an' holly I'd put on the mantel in the livin room. Thangs were lookin real festive, if I did say so myself.

I squeezed my eyes tight, picturin the party we were throwin for my husband. Course, George knew we were havin the party, but he was goin to be plumb flabbergasted thet it was in his honor. All of our new friends: Jeff an' the boys, Mis' Lucille an' her family, our neighbors, folks from church an' from "Solution Quest," my family an' his, toastin him. I could practically hear Louis an' Bill givin little braggy speeches, each takin credit for the discoverin of him. I thought, *If they do, Mis' Caroline an' I will be lookin at each other, both knowin it was her thet set the whole thang to goin after the Boeing Company deal fell apart.*

Thankin 'bout Mis' Caroline made me smile. She was plumb beside hersef 'bout gettin to meet Pappaw. She'd already written him a real nice thank you, but she wanted to thank him,

165

face to face, for the carvin he'd given to her. Clear as yesterday, I recollected the givin of it to her.

"Why, Marilue," she'd said, real excited, when I handed her the found packet, "what's this?"

"It's a thank you from my pappaw for bein such a good friend to me right from the beginnin."

"Oh, my God!" she said, feelin its knobs an' bumps through the brown wrappin. "It's one of the carvings he makes, isn't it?"

"Yes'm. He gets premonitions sometimes. You might see somethin of yourself in what he's done. He said for you to 'look close'."

She got it free of the paper an' let out a squeak. "Oh, my!" She held up what first looked to be a half-carved block of pine. One side hadn't been whittled on at all. On the other side though, was the prettiest little banty hen half-hidden under a big catalpa leaf. She had her neck stretched an' her head cocked, like she was listenin careful. Between her feet, its head barely pokin out of her breast feathers, was a baby fluff ball of a chick.

I laughed out loud. "Look at thet! A mother hen!"

Mis' Caroline cradled the little piece in her hands, jest lookin at it. Then she said, real soft, "I guess it's true, though I don't have children of my own, that I am. But how in the world could he know?"

"Likely, he figured only a banty hen could fit the whole Perkins family under her wing like you done."

After I cleaned up the dishes an' freshened my sourdough crock, I took to wanderin 'round our house again, straightenin pillows, checkin for dust, thet sort of thang. I knew what I really was doin was avoidin thankin 'bout my speech at the University of Washington. Thet's when Professor Beauvois called. I reckon he must have known how skittish I was feelin.

"Marilue," he said, "how would you like to come in early? I'll buy you lunch, we'll take a tour of the campus, visit the library and get your library card before it's time for your presentation."

"Why, Henry," I said, feelin real grateful, "I'd like thet fine. Seems like I'm havin a time gettin myself settled to get one blessed thang done 'round the house today, anyway."

"Don't forget your map to the Paddleford Parking Garage," he said. "Like I said, from there, everything is within walking distance."

"I sure won't forget it an' I'm much obliged for you sendin it, Professor. I already got it studied six ways to Sunday. Seems like I should find it without much trouble."

"Call me just before you leave the house and I'll be waiting for you there. But, Marilue, please remember to call me Henry."

"It won't come natural, but I'll sure try to recollect," I said. "Now it's gonna take me a little to get myself together. So, considerin the drivin time, I'd say, don't be lookin' for me before ten."

Drivin over the 520 Bridge, seemed real simple now. I found my way to the University an' then to the parkin garage, thanks to the good map Henry sent me. He was waitin, just like he said he would do.

I don't know what I was expectin him to look like, but what I got was an oldish, smallish man with a headful of white hippie hair. I judged the first look on his face to be one of relief thet I'd showed up.

"Ah! Marilue Perkins," he said, smiling ear to ear. Then he closed in, grabbed my free hand an started pumpin my arm like he was puttin air in a tire, "the picture in the paper didn't nearly do you justice."

"Well, I have dropped a pound or two since then what with the movin an' all," I said. "Right proud to meet you, Henry."

"You have no idea how I have looked forward to this meeting," he said finally droppin my shook hand an' lookin down at the suitcase I was packin. "Is that the quilt?"

"Yessir. An' your students are the last to see it up close. I'm settin it on loan to the Snohomish County Library soon as the case thet has a special filterin glass to protect it from the sun is finished. A copy of General Grant's letter is goin in there too."

167

"Astonishing!" he said, lookin at me real hard. I had no idea what he meant, but after an eye blink or two he said real soft, "Lending the quilt must have been a big decision for you to make."

I nodded. "Yessir. Reckon it was at thet. Been in my family's care for way over a hundred years."

He shook his head. "You're quite a person, Mrs. Perkins. I don't know that I could be so magnanimous with such a treasure."

Whatever he said I was, I hoped it was good. "If I'm callin you Henry, you gotta remember to call me Marilue," I said.

He smiled. "Thank you. I will. Now, how about the grand tour, Marilue? Then we'll have lunch at the student union."

"Why are you so quiet, Marilue?" Henry asked, as we walked back from the student union to Smith Hall so I could give my speech.

I stopped an' looked at him. "I got small call to be givin speeches to folks, Henry," I said, feelin flat as a penny on a railroad track. "I can't thank now why I thought I should be. I been ponderin if I'm gettin above my raisin."

He laughed like he didn't take me serious. "This campus is a bit grandiose, isn't it?"

I started walkin, my chin tucked, lookin at the sidewalk. "It isn't the grandness of this place; it's how much I don't know…how much I haven't read. Sure, I been readin what I can find in the history books, but what I been sayin to folks mostly isn't book learnin, it's jest family stories. I don't even know half the ten-dollar words you folks here use."

Henry stopped me with a touch to my arm. I looked to see him shakin his head like maybe I'd let him down. "Clearly, you don't yet appreciate your gift, Marilue. You are already very knowledgeable an' it seems to me that you have a great capacity to share that knowledge in an absolutely captivating fashion. In addition to that, despite what you say, it sounds as though you are becoming very well read in your areas of interest."

168

He looked at me, real thoughtful like. "It seems to me that you might even decide to take your degree some day."

I looked him square in the eye to see if he was pokin fun, but he wasn't. I could tell. It made me feel funny on my insides. I laughed. "All I was aimin for, when I called you folks was to answer the youngens thet asked why I talked so funny. Now you're sayin maybe I should thank 'bout goin to college?"

He nodded, real serious like. "Yes, I am. The question you wanted answered regarding the Appalachian dialect is an interesting one. It has been explored, but for every theory, someone develops a counter theory. It seems to me you are in a unique position, due to your heritage, to explore it from a new angle, having grown up hearing it spoken. In fact, I'm wondering if you can replicate what you have heard."

I gave a little snort an' said, "Fiddlesticks! You'n hain't been a monkeyed with less'n you been acrost this h'yar country an' come up again hit." I used the best twang I could muster.

He looked at me smilin and givin a happy little sigh. "That was exceptional! Please, Marilue, at least take some classes," he said.

I shook my head, plumb flabbergasted. What he said was mite near too much to take in, what with havin to stand up an' give a speech in jest the shake of a lamb's tail.

"Well, I sure can't thank 'bout it now, Henry, I got to get my head together," I said, feelin plumb riled up.

He walked beside me keepin quiet. Finally, I sighed an' said, "You'd best take me some place where I can sit a spell an' get myself thankin straight an' then we'll see what 'em students of yours thank of my stories, Henry."

Thet's what I did too. Sittin in Henry's office, it come to me thet the whole place, from the bigness of the library to the fast way folks talked, cowed me. I decided I purely didn't like the feelin, *but it prolly wasn't anythin compared to the way my kin felt when they landed, tryin to talk their Shakespeare talk to them Cherokee Indians,* I thought.

Henry come in lookin a little worried. "It's time," he said. "Ready?"

169

I got up an' took a deep breath, nodded my head an' said, "Yessir. Let's get 'er done." I picked up my suitcase an' followed him.

He walked me down the hall an' into a classroom filled with students, all sittin an' watchin us. On each desk was a copy of the clippin from *The Seattle Times* 'bout me capturin the muggers.

When we got to the front of the room, Henry said some right nice thangs. Then afore I knew it, I was standin behind this little podium all by myself sayin, "Howdy. Only reason I'm here talkin to you is thet my kin happened to take a heap of pride in passin along family stories, an' I reckon the Good Lord set me with the kinda mind thet recollects what I've heard."

I took a big breath an' looked 'round. Everbody was lookin relaxed an' friendly. My stomach stopped flippin an' threatin to give up my lunch. Thangs were feelin better all the way 'round.

I even managed to smile a little at them then I said, "My Mammaw Ada has a big hump-back chest in her attic thet's plumb full of thangs thet have been kept over the years to hep us with our recollectin."

I shook my head an' smiled. "Makes folks like Dr. Beauvois here plumb nervous to thank on thangs like a hand-written letter from President Grant sayin how proud the family should be for the givin up seven sons for the sake of preservin the Union, jest sittin 'round in an ol' wood chest in a mountain cabin. I don't have thet letter with me, but I do have a copy she let me make. An' I have, in this here suitcase I'm totin, the quilt the womenfolks made 158 years ago to honor an' recollect them kilt sons."

When it came to the question and answer time, I was plumb relieved when the hands around the room jumped up. Seemed like those students were some interested. I snuck a peek at Henry who was leaning against a window sill in the back. He was lookin at me like I was pick of ol' Charlotte's litter. He smiled and said, "You have nearly fifteen minutes to answer their questions, Mrs. Perkins."

Time picked up a little 'round our house with the youngens out of school for their Christmas vacation. Billy was workin more hours, hopin to get time off when everbody showed up. Even at thet, he was home more, bein hepful when he could. An' it seemed like Vikki Ann was always at my elbow, askin what she could do to hep too. Reckon she'd figured out keepin busy made time pass, jest like I had.

I first put her to wrappin presents. Then next I showed her how to machine-baste a double row of thread an' had her take over makin the flounce on her bed skirt. She did so well, we picked out more material so she could do a dust ruffle for a little round table we'd got for her down at Star Antiques.

Then, right after she finished, she brought a couple of girls home to meet Shadow an' to show off her room. Did my heart good to hear all them girl giggles driftin down the stairs.

George surprised us. After he'd solved thet work problem by buildin thet robotic arm, he went truck shoppin an' brought home an almost new, tan-colored, Jeep Grand Wagoneer. "Pickup's too old for me to be puttin that many miles on it," he'd said. But, I knew he'd also bought hisself a fishin rig to haul the menfolks when they wanted to go fishin for steelhead together. I gave him a hug. "Makes real good sense to me, honey," I said.

Once they got on the road, our families, mostly Junior an' Karlen, took turns callin in collect, to give us progress reports.

"How's everbody settlin in?" I asked Karlen when he called from jest outside Little Rock, Arkansas.

"Real fine...the ol' folks are swappin back an' forth between ridin in the Caddy an' the motor home. Your great granddaddy an' our daddy are ridin with us now."

I laughed. "Thet sounds 'bout right."

"Momma," Junior said from Oklahoma City, "you'd be tickled how everybody liked the Cowboy Hall of Fame. We could hardly get Pappaw Joe out of there."

I tried hard not to mind thet their sightseein was keepin 'em on the road stead of dustin a path straight on to our doorway, but I kept thet to mysef. "You jest let him look his fill, honey, he prolly won't be doin this again," I said.

171

"We're on our way now, Momma. Me, Uncle Karlen and Granddaddy John are swapin off drivin the motor home. From now on, we figure to take turns sleepin; maybe even make over nine hundred miles a day. Uncle Harlen is lettin Uncle Karlen spell him in the Caddy when he needs it."

Well, thet cheered me some. "I'm sure on pins an' needles 'til you get here son," I said.

I only got to talk to Momma once. "Honey, I got it figured why they call this here place in California, 'Needles'. There ain't a real tree in sight an' practically ever plant you see is plumb covered with spines. They shoulda named it 'Spiney,' you ask me."

"Momma, we got lots of real purty trees an' great big mountains to go with em," I said, "Jest hurry 'em menfolk along as best you can. I cain't hardly wait to see you."

"I recollected to brang you a couple of pokes of stone-ground grits, jest like you asked for, Marilue, honey," she said.

"You are a wonderful woman, Mildred Cable," I said as I hung up the phone.

When they were a tad less than two days out, Karlen called from Redding, California. "Marilue," he said, "there's a storm a comin south out of the Gulf of Alaska."

"You thank I don't know thet," I said, "I been walkin a worry circle on Momma's good rag rug. It's snowin in our mountains right now."

"Thing is, Marilue, it ain't hit here yet. Wind's picked up a little is all. We can see that big ol' Shasta Mountain clear as a bell under the clouds. So, instead of stoppin here, like Billy's plan calls for, we figure to drive straight on through. We get them Siskiyou Mountains behind us, we'll find us a place to stop."

"Karlen," I said, "I want you here so bad I got the taste in my mouth. But, you got to be thankin foolish to tackle them mountains at night when you got no idea how unfriendly they might be."

He laughed. "Now, Marilue, it ain't like you to be a worry wart. We ain't stupid. It gets bad, we'll pull over an' hole up in the motor home. It's got its own heat an' lights you know."

172

Well, thet made me feel some better, but not much. You can bet we were some shy on chit chat in the Perkins house thet night. Mostly we sat 'round the kitchen table, our eyes goin from the clock to the phone. The clock kept on tickin, but the phone didn't ring. At ten o'clock George called the Oregon State Police's number an' found out they'd closed the pass down over the Siskiyou Mountains an hour earlier.

"What's thet mean, George?" I asked.

He shook his head. "Don't reckon I know. I do know they said that other than the two semi-trucks that jackknifed up there and caused the pass to close, no other accidents have been reported."

"Was it snowin, Daddy?" Billy asked.

George nodded. "Hard...since 'bout 8:00 PM, accordin to the law."

"Well," Billy said, "If they happened to get over that pass before those trucks spilled, we'll be hearin pretty soon. If they got turned 'round we won't hear until they get themselves back down out of the snow. If they got caught between the two trucks, they got a long night ahead. Like Uncle Karlen said, it's lucky they've got the motor home."

His words heped a little to calm the mind pictures I was makin of the motor home tipin face first over some canyon edge. I mean, it prolly bein blacker than the inside of an outhouse hole, snowin hard, an' them bein from a different kind of country, it could happen without their even bein seen. Thet thought gave me the all overs.

"Are you cold, Momma?"

I looked at Vikki Ann an' could see she was tryin to read my face to decide how worried to be.

"Honey, I am a little chilled," I fibbed. "Be a good girl an' fetch my sweater from the bed post."

After she left, I looked at my men. "No sense me passin on my mind boogers to my daughter," I said.

They both nodded. I looked hard at my son, recollectin what he'd said 'bout snow in the mountain passes back in November, wonderin if he was takin after Pappaw in his premonitions. Knew it wasn't my business to ask.

173

"I reckon we owe you an apology, son," I said instead. "You sure tried to warn us 'bout the mountain passes."

"Aw, Momma, reckon I wanted them here just as bad as any of us. Don't know what made me say what I did. I keep thinkin, if I hadn't suggested they stop at the Cowboy Hall of Fame, they might have made it over the pass just fine."

Vikki Ann come back an' draped my sweater 'round my shoulders. "Thank you, honey," I said an' pulled her onto my lap to rock her, feelin some comforted by her head on my shoulder.

A little later, George whispered, "Your daughter has gone to sleep on you, Marilue. I believe it's time for all of us to at least try to do the same. Can't do any good for anybody if we're all woozy from a lack of sleep."

Real gentle, he pulled Vikki Ann's arms free of me an' scooped her up. Thet's when the phone rang. It was jest a little after eleven o'clock. I have no recollection of snatchin it out of Billy's hand when he was right in the middle of acceptin the call, like they said I did. But I sure recollect hearin Junior's words comin over the line, calm an' cheerful.

"Howdy, Momma, hope you don't mind us callin so late. Figured you'd want to know we're down out of the mountains safe and sound."

"They're all safe," I said to my family. I covered my other ear so I wouldn't miss a word.

"Where are you now?" I had to holler a little to be heard over the whoop-te-do George an' the youngens were makin.

"In a little motel in a town named Ashland, Oregon. The old folks are really tired from the excitement and havin all of us jammed into the motor home."

Well, thet caught my attention. "How's thet? What are you sayin, son? Why were you in the motor home? Where's the Caddy?"

George was at my side then, slidin the phone away from my ear a little so he could hear too.

"The Caddy bent a wheel and had to be towed, but we all came on in the motor home."

George pulled the receiver from me then. "Howdy, son," he said, an' I swear there was a twinkle in his eye. "My brother have a little trouble with snow drivin?"

174

He put one shoulder to the wall, listenin hard. Then he laughed an' said, "Now that might peeve a body some."

Then he said, "Bet they weren't a bit sleepy after that little joy ride."

"What? What?" I kept askin, 'til George told me to hush. He wrote down two numbers on the blackboard an' hung up the phone.

"What?" I said then.

"They nearly made it, but comin down the mountain, ol' Harlen got to showin off his new snow tires; only the Caddy got ideas of its own. Junior said they watched the whole of it from the motor home, those big fins were flashin red light all over both lanes. Then it turned itself in to a spinnin top. Lucky for Harlen, he didn't hit anythin but a snowbank."

"Black ice?" Billy asked.

George shook his head. "Nope. It was only a couple of inches of heavy slush. Junior said Karlen and your daddy were ridin with Harlen, both sound asleep when it happened."

"Where's the Caddy now?" I asked.

George hunched his shoulders. "I reckon it's wherever it got towed to in Ashland."

He pointed to the first number on the blackboard. "I'm supposed to call that number for Harlen tomorrow and try to get his parts ordered from some place in downtown Seattle. The tow truck driver gave it to him." He smiled at me. "The other number's the hotel, 'in case you want to call and reassure yourself' Junior said."

He looked 'round at us. "Right now, it sounds like the best thing for everybody down there is to get some rest." He looked at me. "Your oldest son's carryin a pretty big load."

"George," I said, "do you figure they'll wait for the Caddy or all try come on up in the motor home?"

George smiled. "Harlen's already rented himself a front-wheel dolly from the fellow who towed him on in. Junior said the fellow was mighty taken with the Caddy. Said he'd never seen a '59 totally restored like the twins had done. He couldn't get over those fins and the twin tail lights."

He looked at me hard, thankin, an' then shook his head. "I don't believe Harlen could have made himself leave the fixin

175

of his baby to some stranger's hands...and Karlen wouldn't have left him on his own. It was awful nice of that man to trust a stranger from out of state with his tow-dolly. It's a lesson to us that there are good people everywhere."

Billy said, "Tomorrow, they'll have to drive real slow. So I reckon it'll be takin them at least ten hours. This rain sure isn't goin to let up anytime soon."

My whole insides felt like a lump of lead. I was tryin to thank only of how glad I was thet they were all safe, but I kept seein George's party an' our whole Christmas fall flat on its face.

"I reckon if they can get emselves up an' out real early come mornin, I'm not goin to have to call up folks an' cancel the party," I said, tryin for a hopeful tone. "Your daddy is right. Best we go up an' try for sleep."

Vikki Ann, smiled. "You and I have a big day in the kitchen tomorrow, don't we, Momma?"

"Yep. Thet we do, honey. They get here, this is liable to be some party."

They did get here an' it was some party! Family hit the driveway, honkin an' whoopin 'bout five o'clock. Junior was the first one up the steps. "Howdy, Momma," was all he said afore he had me grabbed 'round the waist an' was swingin me 'round on the porch like I didn't weigh more'n a feather. He plumb knocked the combs out of my hair.

Then, there was so much huggin an' laughin an' back slappin goin on I couldn't keep track. "Come on in. Come on in out of this weather." I finally hollered, recollectin my manners.

Now, I don't know thet you recall how George an' the youngens acted the first time they saw the house, what with gettin real quiet an' then tellin me I'd bought a mansion when it wasn't even fixed up yet. I'd had some private worries thet my kin might thank the same an' thet we'd gotten above ourselves. Don't know why I wasted time lettin thoughts like thet into my head.

Truth was, everbody come in the front door talkin all at once, jest plain excited to be there safe an' sound, ready to party! Course, they all wanted a house tour an' George an' I took some razzin 'bout havin a fireplace all to our ownsefs in the bedroom.

176

Harlen was so tickled, both to have his big pink baby safe in our garage an' seein what a good shop George had, he set thangs goin. I mean he was laughin, teasin Vikki Ann, tellin stories on hisself an' coaxin his daddy to dig out a jug, afore we ever even got the motor home unloaded.

"Wh-o-o w-e-e-e, I am in the mood to do some fiddlin tonight!" he hollered, grabbin Vikki Ann, throwin her over his shoulder, packin her 'round the front yard an' over to his twin in the rain, like she was a sack of feed, plumb ignorin her protest an' her little fists thumpin on his back. "Ain't you, Karlen?"

I smiled an' thought, *thet man has always loved teasin my daughter.* "Well, boys," I said, tryin to slow thangs up a mite, "company's not set to even get here for a couple of hours yet."

"Hells Bells, Marilue," Karlen said, "couple of hours, me an' my brother'll just be gettin our whistles properly oiled for the shindig!"

I looked at George, then at his daddy. They all had thet blue Perkins sparkle in their eyes. An', lookin at my own daddy an' my pappaw didn't put a plaster on my misgivins one bit. It come to me then thet maybe George's party was gonna be more'n I'd bargained for. I gave a sigh they could hear back in Maryville an' said, givin in, "Oh fiddlesticks! Might as well go ahead an' dig out your jug, Daddy Perkins. Rest of you men get the rugs rolled an' the furniture set an' the bags packed in afore you even thank of takin one sip," I said soundin jest like Momma. "We ladies'll be in the kitchen."

I'd like to be able to tell you ever little detail of thet party, but I can't. Truth is, thangs were movin too fast, an' I was too busy seein to ever little detail. I do recollect Junior comin into the kitchen to fetch me to hear the speeches Bill an' Louis were makin on George.

Ever time they said a nice thang, Harlen an' Karlen would egg 'em on by givin a whoop an' makin their fiddles squeal like a hog caught in a fence. George's face was redder than Santa's suit. Everbody was laughin an' clappin an' sayin, "Way to go George!" 'til George's daddy got feelin so proud of his youngest solvin thet problem for Boeing, he started handin 'round what was left of his jug, right there in my livin room.

177

Once the menfolk had a taste, they kept slippin out the glass doors off the dinin room where Jeff an' the boys had built my new veranda. Seemed like they were comin back in, happier an' happier. So, I figured I knew where the other two jugs were stashed.

Later on, Junior come in, snitched a piece of the ham I was carvin an' said, soundin more surprised than disgusted, "Momma, you know those boys that Vikki Ann wouldn't even talk to when we were unpackin? Well, she's in there teachin every last one of 'em how to square dance."

"How's she doin?" I asked.

"Fine, I reckon."

I handed him the carvin knife. "This I got to see, honey. Who's doin the callin?"

"Guess."

I looked at him an' grinned. "Pappaw Joe?"

He nodded. "And from the looks of things, he's feelin no pain. Every once and awhile he stops callin and he and Granddaddy Perkins wail away on their Jew's harps."

I heard Mammaw Ada give a snort from where she was stirrin gravy at the stove. "Thet ol' fool a mine's been sippin from the jug an' he hain't goin to thank hisself come tomorrah."

I heard Granny Perkins an' my momma laugh. Momma said, "Well, Marilue, least your Pappaw's not aimin to go a fishin like them other menfolk are talkin on a 'doin."

I looked over at Mis' Caroline with her hands deep in suds. She'd come right in, took off her coat, rolled up her sleeves an' started hepin. All my Tennessee kin were taken with her, I could tell. I said, "Come on, Mis' Caroline, take a break. Let's go have a look at our favorite wood carver afore he wears hisself plumb out."

It was hot in the kitchen, what with all the cookin, but it was even hotter in the livin room. Harlen an' Karlen were red-faced an' sweatin. "Lordie! Open the windows, Billy. Let some of this heat out, else your uncles are goin to turn toes up on us," I hollered, fannin myself an' thankin the good Lord I'd had Jeff an' the boys break the windows free from bein painted shut.

I stopped an' got a cup of Christmas punch to cool myself while I watched everbody dancin to Pappaw's callin.

178

Figured out with the first sip thet there was more than frozen strawberries, seven-up an' ice cream in the fancy cut glass punch bowl that Betty Jean had given us for a weddin present.

I looked over to where Mis' Caroline was standin tappin her foot an' grinnin at Pappaw in the fondest way an' decided even though I don't generally drink, thet this was special—an' thet I'd take her a cup too.

I smiled at my husband who was thumpin his heart out on the gut bucket. He caught my eye an' we both looked at our daughter. She was somethin! Reminded me of an angel in her new green velveteen dress with the matchin hair ribbon in her long blonde hair. But she sounded more like a school teacher, showin them glassy-eyed boys how to promenade an' do-si-do.

"Well, now ye all jine hands an' then circle the rang, stop where ye air an' give yo'uns partner a swang…" Pappaw warbled. Mis' Caroline was lookin like she was watchin Ernest Tubbs, for sure.

I left her watchin an' went back to the kitchen to relieve Junior of the carvin knife. "Somebody doctored my punch a mite," I said. His face was already so red I couldn't tell if he blushed or not. "Might explain your sister's behavior. Best go keep an eye on her."

"It's not much doctored, honest, Momma," he said, "just a little."

I couldn't hep but smile at him, bein he was the one that got the whole ball rollin. "I reckon it's okay, jest this oncet, but you gotta promise me we'll find time to sit down an' have us a talk about your schoolin' an' such when thangs calm themsefs a mite."

"Sure I will," Momma he said. "Other than missin y'all, seems like things are going like they should."

It was sure a good thang to hear.

Sometime later Junior come to get me again. "Momma, there's folks at the front door. Said they could hear the music from the street. They wanted to know if they could stand on the porch out of the rain and listen."

179

I laughed an' threw up my hands. "Best you go make 'em welcome, son. Least they won't be callin the law down on us."

He grinned. "This IS some party, Momma. I'd say it's right up there with our family reunions."

I said, "You go tell them fiddlin fools to slow their pace a mite or they'll never last. See if you can't coax your Uncle Karlen to do a few slow songs on the guitar."

When Karlen settled down on his ol' Gibson guitar, he sounded a whole bunch like Merle Haggard. I reckon, had he worked at it, he could of gone professional.

'Round one o'clock in the mornin, our guests started thinnin out. Pappaw Joe an' Mammaw Ada had long since gone upstairs to Billy's room an' both George's momma an' daddy an' my momma an' daddy made their goodbyes an' headed for the motor home. But a few couldn't seem to quit us. Mostly, they'd nap in their chairs from time to time, then wander out to the table for another piece of my pineapple upside down cake, banana puddin or some other piece of baked goods. The ham, black-eyed peas, beans, Jell-O salad an' such bein jest scraps on the buffet table. I also kept the water pitcher full. After they'd got what they wanted, they'd go back to listen to the music.

The twins were finally sittin on chairs. Karlen was playin his guitar an' they were singin ballads together, harmonizin like they could do. Ever once an' awhile, Harlen would pick up his fiddle or his banjo an' come fillin in jest at the perfect time, addin the right notes to make the song sadder or gladder, whatever was called for.

Karlen always played whatever come to his mind, which is a special talent of his. I could tell they'd sobered some an' were gettin ready to quit.

'Bout two o'clock, George come in to where Mis' Caroline an' I were washin up the last of the dishes. He put his arms 'round both us. "Time to take off your aprons, girls, the boys say they have only one more song in them, and Bill and I have a real hankerin to dance with our women.

He gave the twins a nod when we walked in an' Bill come right away to claim his bride. I put my head against George's shoulder. Karlen played a few chords on his guitar an'

180

started singin, "I was waltzin with my darlin to the Tennessee Waltz..."

I heard Harlen join in, then George, then my youngens. Purty soon all us folks from Tennessee, an' any others who knew it, were singin along. We'ns weren't Tennessee Ernie Ford, but we sounded purty good an' it was a fittin end to George's party.

Next day was real quiet at the house. Lucky the weather had turned some nicer an' the wind had died down, since George an' the twins had gone fishin; all three of 'em packin achin heads. Other folks 'round the house were nappin, visitin, or watchin the T.V. Pappaw Joe an' Mammaw Ada didn't even show emselves 'til nearly noon, they were thet tuckered.

I was feelin purty tuckered myself. But, when my mind finally got to workin again, I started feelin bad thet I hadn't invited the professor to the party. I knew he was a bachelor man, so to make it up to him; I called his home number an' asked him, would he like to come to Christmas Eve supper.

"It'll be mostly leftovers, Henry, but I thought you might get a kick out of meetin my kin an' we only got 'em three more days."

"Why, I would enjoy that very much, Marilue, but I know how precious family time is for you. I wouldn't want to intrude."

"In this house, we don't open presents 'til Christmas mornin. They don't even go under the tree 'til then. Santa has got to make his rounds is the way George an' I figure it. So, you won't be interferin a bit. It will jest be us sittin 'round visitin. Besides," I said, "I want you to see the house, Henry. We've got the prettiest fir tree all decorated up an' everthang looks so nice, 'specially with Pappaw's carvins among the holly an' boughs on the mantel. It's real cozy."

For some reason, all the sudden, I really wanted him to come. "It'd mean a lot to me if you could," I said.

He paused for a minute an' then asked, "Would it be presumptuous of me to bring a tape recorder for interviewing?"

I laughed. "I reckon Mammaw Ada would be happy to share her stories, but you better brang a big bottle of whiskey for

181

Pappaw if'n you're after his." I said. "He's not over fond of machines."

Thet's what Henry did too, brought a half gallon of Jack Daniels. Besides thet, he brought me a catalog from the University of Washington. *University of Washington General Catalog*, it said.

"What's thet thang for?" I asked, like I didn't know.

He gave me a little smile an' then patted my arm. "Just think 'bout it when you have some time, Marilue."

I tucked it away in a drawer real quick so nobody could see. But I knew it was there an' couldn't hep but thank on it some. Made them butterflies march 'round in my midsection some more.

Men come off the river braggin 'bout gettin strikes, but without landin a single steelhead. Said tomorrow would be better, beins as how they'd gotten some wiser on how to go 'bout it. I wasn't a bit surprised thet all of em, after swearin they'd never drink another drop the night afore they planned on goin fishin, got right after the whiskey Henry brought, sayin they needed to warm their insides some.

I imagine they did. When they'd come in, Harlen snuck a hand to the back of Vikki Ann's neck an' she gave a holler thet brought Momma out of the kitchen at a run, jest in time to see her granddaughter a tryin to wallop her uncle. Couldn't hurt him much, he was still all padded up.

I drawled, "Harlen, your niece's awful good at pay back. Thet might have been a mistake."

He chuckled an' said to her. "Shoot, honey, I jest wanted me a little sympathy for freezin my butt off all day, tryin to get this family some groceries to eat. Thet dang river was colder than a witch's breath. An' tomorrow, I gotta fix the Caddy so I won't be goin," like it was the saddest thang in the world.

Pruty soon fish stories an' family stories were flyin faster than bats over a swamp. I reckon Henry was in hog heaven. He'd had himself quite an afternoon listenin not only to my kin, but to George's momma and daddy. Now, ol' Harlen and Karlen were addin their two cents.

182

I took Vikki Ann upstairs to rid up. "Momma," she said, while we were shakin up the quilts an' makin beds, "folks come a real long way to just stay five days."

"Honey," I said, "don't be lookin a gift horse in the mouth. We only had 'em for one day, I would be plumb grateful."

"Aren't you feelin sad with their leavin time comin so close?"

I straightened up an' gave her a look. "Thet I am, but I got to fight it. Otherwise, I'll be wastin what time I got. Now how foolish would thet be?" She hung her head so I couldn't see the sadness in her face.

"Tell you what," I said, "we'll wave thet motor home and Caddy out of the drive with big ol' smiles, an' then we'll come back in an' have us a five-hankie cry, jest us. No men allowed. Then afterwards, we'll get real busy, doin somethang fun."

It was only then, bein so busy and everthang else, that I remembered what Mis' Caroline had said the night of the party. I put a smile on my face and said, "Fact is, I reckoned Mis' Caroline and Bill had it all figured. They knew we'd take it hard when the family left an' they wondered would we want to go sailin should the weather cooperate. What do you thank about thet?"

"I guess," she said real low. "Right now, it's real hard to think about though."

I nodded. "Keep that thought in you back pocket, honey. I got to tell you, there's nothin like the cut of rain, wind an' spray to wash the sadness away."

She smiled a little. "You made a little rhyme, Momma," she said.

Christmas mornin was real special. We'd gotten everbody up once Billy had lit the fire in the fireplace an' I'd gotten the coffee made. Then we sat 'round, still in our house coats an' such, openin presents, everone sayin, "Thank you." "Really, you shouldn't have." "I can sure use this." an' "My, how thoughtful!" Course, with all the wrappin paper an' ribbon that come from the unwrapping of presents for thirteen people and one dog, we made a real mess of the livin room.

183

Then, when we were all done an' sittin 'round, Billy got up an' made a little speech. "Momma," he said, "You might think I haven't, but I've been payin close attention to how you women have been preservin your family history an' it got me thinkin what would happen if we didn't have a baby girl born for a generation or two." He pulled a wrapped package from behind his back an' handed it to me. "So, I made us a little history book of our trip. It might not be a quilt, but I believe it will last," he said.

I looked at him an' his eyes were shinin. The tops of his ears were pink, I thank from nerves. "Why, Billy Dean Perkins, aren't you jest full of surprises," I said and looked 'round the room to see if I could spot who else was in on the secret. Seemed like we were all in the dark. Everone was lookin as puzzled as I felt. Seemed our Billy had done his work in secret.

Well, I had to open it quick, afore my curiousity kilt me. An' there, lyin in my lap was a little three ring binder. The cover read in nice big letters:

"The Travel Adventures of the Perkins Family"
August 25, to September 1, 1980
by Billy Dean Perkins
(Wagon Master)

I knew right then what I was goin to find inside. An' I did! Thet boy had preserved our whole, entire trip of movin across the U. S. of A. On the first page it had all our names listed along with the picture he'd asked the nice lady at the El Rancho Motel in Spokane to take of us. The next couple of pages had his trip plannin notes, scribbles, cross-outs an' all. Then come his silly pictures of us with somethin cute written under ever one. He'd done a fine job.

When, I was done turnin pages, I said, lookin up to he was standin. "Why, son, you've done a real fine thang. This is truly special. Now, no matter how many years go by, we'll never forget a thang. You've made us a memory." I'll admit my voice wobbled a little an' I had tears in my eyes. I was thet proud of him.

184

I handed George the book an' got up an' gave our son a big hug. He put his arms 'round me an' hugged me back real good. "Billy Dean, I couldn't like thet book more if I tried," I whispered into his ear. "It's my favorite present."

While everbody had a turn at the book, I got busy makin up hotcake batter an' fryin both bacon an' some of the grits Momma had brought me. Pruty soon, Momma come in an' started flippin hotcakes. Between all us women, took no time to have breakfast on the table.

Then we all sat 'round thet ol' dinin room table with all its boards in, hol'in hands an' listenin to Pappaw Joe say grace. While we were eatin, we, one at a time, went 'round the table sayin what we were grateful for, somethin we always do on special occasions. All thirteen of us mentioned bein grateful for our family bein together as one of their thangs, even my youngens. It sure touched my heart.

Course, Harlen had to go on at some length talkin 'bout the real nice man who rented him the tow-dolly, an' thankin George for lettin him an' the Caddy have the garage 'til its axle was fixed.

When it was Karlen's turn he finished by winkin at Vikki Ann an' sayin, "Best I not thank the Lord for lettin me catch thet steelhead. Seems like it wouldn't suit to 'cause folks to feel some jealous instead of feelin the full glory with this here celebratin the first day of Baby Jesus' life."

Even with my brave words, seemed like we'd no more opened our presents an' gone to church than time ran out afore I was ready. I could hardly stand to look at Junior without bustin into bawlin. Seemed like Momma, Mammaw Ada, Momma Perkins an' I hadn't even scratched through the top soil of all we had to talk on. An' Pappaw! I found him in the livin room, my ol' cane rocker pulled up to the fire, a throw over his knees, head thrown back in sleep, an' it come to me what the trip had taken out of him. I went to find Mammaw Ada.

"Pappaw feelin all right?" I asked her.

"Course he is, honey girl. He's jest oldish an' not yet learnt to take hit easy."

185

"Thet's good to hear," I said. But I went back in an' looked at him sleepin for the longest time without knowin why. I still couldn't believe he'd left his home, his mountains an' his hounds an' come all the way across the country to see thet his kin were doin okay.

Mammaw Ada grabbed me real close when she hugged me goodbye. "You'ns made a real home here, Marilue. I'm sure glad to see hit. I'm right proud an' thet's a fact."

Then when Momma hugged me, she said 'bout the same thang, only she added, "Only thang I wisht is thet you'ns weren't so damned far away." An' my momma hardly ever swears. Jest shows how much she was missin us already.

"I'll be comin back home, usin George's frequent flyer miles, you jest wait an' see if I don't," I said. We were cryin a little an' tryin hard not to.

Then they were gone with the same hootin an' horn blowin they come in with. An' the whole world seemed empty an' dry. Too dry for tears even. Seemed like I couldn't even bear to go back into the house. Billy was at work, but George an' Vikki Ann felt the same, I could tell. Even Shadow was givin funny little whines an' lookin 'round. She'd done real well with all the commotion, even took up a little with Pappaw, which tickled him.

I looked at George. "Mis' Caroline and Mister Bill invited us to go for a sail on the *Tarpon,* knowin' we'd be feelin' flat what with everbody leavin. Want to come, or would you rather go fishin?"

George gave a snort. "If Karlen hadn't finally landed that one big steelhead, they would have claimed I was lyin 'bout there bein fish in the river, so I'd be out there tryin to catch one just to prove them wrong. But he did. So I don't have to go. Beside, now that the rain has let up, and the weather is some improved, I don't believe they would be bitin today anyway. I reckon you recollect what Bill and Jeff said 'bout that." He smiled. "If I've got a choice, I'll spend time with my women any ol' time."

I looked at Vikki Ann. She was standin tucked under her daddy's arm. "I expect we got time for our cry," I said to her.

She looked up at him an' then at me. "No, thank you, Momma. I reckon I can make do with a sail an' save those five hankies for another day."

We smiled at each other. I said, "Me too. Now, let's go in an' make thet lunch I promised Mis' Caroline I'd brang."

New Year's Eve the youngens went off to parties, but George an' I decided what we wanted to do was to stay at home to do a little celebratin of our own, if you know what I mean.

So after watchin the ball fall in New York at the Times Square, George said, "Reckon you can find that black Frederick's rig, Marilue?"

I nodded. Believe or not, I'd taken them panties out of the shoe box where I'd kept 'em with the top for the trip, an' put 'em back between the box springs an' the mattress of our bed, leavin the top where it belonged in in my shoe box. "You go up an' start thet little fire you laid in our fireplace an' I'll come up an' start fillin the the tub with some of thet Herbal Essence you gave me for Christmas, soon as I let Shadow back in, honey."

He walked over an' gave me a kiss thet had my insides quiverin like I hadn't ever been bedded. "Don't be long," he whispered, grazin my ear with his lips.

Afterwards, lyin all spooned up, I said, "You know, George, I been thankin 'bout Loretta Lynn, least I thank it was Loretta Lynn.

"How's that?" he asked, soundin more sleepy than interested.

"Well, I heard one time thet right afore she got married she bought hersef a bus ticket home. Tucked it in her purse, jest to have in case she was ever broke an' wanted to leave her husband. Thet ticket was her guarantee she could always get back home to her kin in Butcher Holler, Kentucky."

"She ever use it?"

He didn't sound near as sleepy. I smiled against his arm then turned an' gave his shoulder a little kiss afore proppin

187

myself up an' lookin down on him. "Nope. But seems like thet's what I kinda did too, in my mind, I mean."

He lay there for a minute, jest lookin at me. His eyes were real serious. "What do you mean, exactly, Marilue?"

"Well, what I mean is, clean 'til the folks come, a part of me was still pretendin we were only stayin here 'til you got bein an inventor out of your system an' thet one day, you'd look at me an' say, 'Honey, what would you thank 'bout us all movin back to Tennesee?' I'd even picture me givin a squeal an' jumpin into your arms. Then jest lately, I got to recollectin somethin Billy said at supper, after I gave my speech at the University an' was tellin you 'bout why we talk a little different. He said he didn't thank we should be tryin to be somethin we aren't. It come to me jest when the motor home was pullin out thet the truth was jest the opposite. We aren't pretendin to be different, We ARE different now George, an' it's takin us awhile, leastwise it is me, to get comfortable with it. I'm not sayin we can't go back home, should we want to. I'm sayin when I thank 'bout you askin me thet question 'bout movin back, the part where I squeal an' jump at you jest isn't there any more."

He reached up an' brushed my hair back over my shoulder. "My, my! You sure are good at keepin secrets, Marilue. To me, it seemed like you took to this new life like a duck to water. I guess I was so wrapped up in this job, I didn't stop to consider that you weren't happy here, what with this house, your new friends and all."

I sighed. "You had plenty on your plate, honey. But, what I'm really tryin to say here is thet even if we were to go back, none of us would fit like we used to. Seems like we left a time in our lives an' not a place."

George jest looked at me for the longest time. Then he put his hand to the side of my face, his eyes real blue. He nodded, an' craned his neck up to give my forehead a gentle kiss. "It seems a little strange now...how hard we used to try to make life stay wrapped in a nice knot-tight package, isn't it, Marilue?"

He said "we," but I knew he was really talkin 'bout me. I grinned down at him. "George, I got somethin surprisin to tell you."

188

He gave a chuckle. "Nothin new there! To me you are a surprise every minute, Marilue Gracie Perkins. So, what have you got up your sleeve this time?"

"Well, I reckon you better be the first to know thet I'm givin some real serious consideration on goin to the University of Washington come spring term," I said, plumb enjoyin the look of amazement thet come to his face.

Acknowledgements:

In 1993, Barbara Wortley and Susan Fick kindly edited the first iteration of *Grits to Granola*. Now, twenty years later, the book has matured and I now have a new set of editors: Bob Ferraro, Marilyn Swanson, Sally Brown and Joanie Dellefield. There is no way to thank them enough for their excellent critiques and eagle eye for errors.

Also, I want to thank Terry Haver, Gary Allen and Roy Butler, Tennessee friends who corrected and refined both the dialect and grammar of those characters raised in the Great Smokey Mountains of East Tennessee.

Don and Julie James and Bob and Sally Telzrow were a great help in refining details about sailing on Lake Washington.

As always, I thank my husband, Tony Bâby, both for his creative ideas and execution of the cover art and for his constructive criticism.

www.ingramcontent.com/pod-product-compliance
Lightning Source LLC
Chambersburg PA
CBHW071233130626
46556CB00003B/994